First Place Gold Medal
One Paper Heart
By Donan Berg
Feathered Quill 2016 Romance Award

What readers and critics say:

A Body To Bones

"A winning plot . . . ."

Kirkus Discoveries

"The author has crafted an intriguing and suspenseful mystery novel. The tension builds slowly and keeps the reader engrossed throughout. When least expected, the narrative takes unexpected twists and turns. The well-drawn characters are an interesting group as are their roles in the story. I found this to be a well written and engrossing novel. Highly recommended."

E. Harris, reader

"I found myself quickly drawn into this book…Author Donan Berg (creates) interesting mix of mystery, suspense, hidden secrets, sin, deception and intrigue to weave a book that is well worth the price and in fact is a book which I so readily recommend, that I would strongly suggest purchasing it for gifting."

S.P., national online reviewer

Donan Berg

"Donan Berg writes a nice, clear, consistently readable prose, and he manages to create a winning character in Sarah Hamilton."

Writers' Digest judge

"Excellent. Greatly enjoyable book, well written and filled with intrigue, suspense and drama. Five Stars."

L.C., national online reviewer

Alexa's Gold

"Alexa's Gold by Donan Berg sure keeps the reader gripped. Our heroine Alexa is such a damaged character and she confronts enough challenges that part of the thrill and mystery is how she will persevere through the gauntlet of tragedies that confront her. Berg weaves a compelling tale here."

M. Hartnett, author

"Lost a lot of sleep on this book as, after a busy day, I would read far into the early morning hours twice, to keep following the suspense until the book ended. Whew, I thoroughly enjoyed it.
Great family drama."

G. Bixler, reviewer

The Bones Dance Foxtrot

"Five Stars. If you enjoy a good mystery with twists, turns, false leads, a little gambling, betrayal, clues left in the unlikeliest of places and a hidden stash of bank loot, then pick up a copy of The Bones Dance Foxtrot."

Featheredquill Book Review

"Clues eventually fit together in clever and significant ways … dramatic tension builds around which woman Jake will pursue."

National reviewer

Into the Dark

"From the exciting opening, Donan Berg's *Into the Dark* relentlessly builds a thrilling mystery centering around election tampering, a stack of money, a counterfeiting operation, and a dead body. In order to reveal the truth, Sheriff Jonas McHugh finds himself compulsively returning to a rustic cabin with hidden compartments and trap doors and to a cave that is the source of more than its share of secrets and disturbing activity. Berg's skillful sorting out Jonas's complicated thoughts as he reaches disturbing conclusions makes *Into the Dark* a smart, engaging novel.

M. Hartnett, author

Dedicated to:

Each and every caring person who, in this worldwide pandemic era, steps forth with compassion to aid, assist and/or to care for those in need of food, shelter, medicine or kind words, be they family, friends, neighbors and/or strangers.

Aria's Bayou Child

A Thriller

Donan Berg

DOTDON Books
Moline, IL

DOTDON Books are published by

DOTDON Personalized Services
514 17th Street
PO Box 1302
Moline, IL 61266-1302

Questions: books.dotdon@yahoo.com
Author Email: Bergdonan@gmail.com

LCCN: classification pending

ISBN 13: 978-1-941244-19-7 (E-book)
ISBN 10:   1-94124419X   (E-book)
ISBN 13: 978-1-941244-20-3 (Paper)
ISBN 10:   1-941244203   (Paper)

Cover design by James, goonwrite.com
Copyright © 2020 Donan B. McAuley

This is a work of fiction. The places, characters, establishments and events portrayed in this novel exist only in the author's mind or are used fictitiously. Any resemblance to any entity or person, living or deceased, is unintentional and purely coincidental.

Printed in United States of America
First U.S. Trade Paper Edition 2020
15 14 13 12 11   1 2 3 4 5

Aria's

Bayou

Child

Women's Prison, Louisiana
Forty-eight months ago

Light, slivered into fuzzy spokes, radiated through the six-inch windowpane thirty-six inches above Aria Gleason's infirmary bed. No yellowish or brilliant sunlight flattered her exposed thigh flesh before two soft hands tightened the blindfold.

Aria's battered mind grasped no escape thread. This solidified when two distinctive baritone voices augmented the soft matron hands that washed her bare legs and applied a compress to her forehead.

The unexpected pain of a needle jab to her groin dulled or blocked her sensory feeling between pelvis and toes. She believed the blindfold hid her ghastly reaction. Her scream-inducing abdominal pain begged for a second injection.

After the thwack of a skin-on-skin slap, a newborn's high-pitched wail dominated her surroundings. The infant's cry added reassuring comfort. A whimper resonated within her heavy grief-stricken heart.

Aria's unblocked ears recorded metal-clinking instruments until the harsh reality of her confined predicament was amplified by an unsuspected terror. A male voice heard twice that morning broke through the surrounding din: "Get the guard's money-making hot pocket washed."

Aria swallowed her gasp when an unseen, never heard before, Cajun-speaker barked: "We don't need to falsify a bloody corpse report."

Trembles traversed her shoulders.

Her deep inhale fought off recurring shakes.

Her soul nursed a weak budding hope that sanity would creep in and expel her gnawing loneliness.

Chapter One

Standing motionless, her right palm hard against cotton blouse fabric that concealed concaved abs, Aria Gleason silently continued her day count.

The locking mechanism of the Louisiana Women's Prison gate clanked. Aria added one vertical pencil stroke to the prior 1,460 that, row after row, graced the margins of her Gideon Bible. She stowed the Bible in her brown tweed satchel. Neither her diligence in marking off her days of desperation, nor their accumulation, guaranteed salvation, promised her a painless life resurrection or reconnected her with a heartbeat she helped create.

Why should God today answer her prayer? He'd ignored her since the first day she'd been forced to exchange civilian clothes for white tops, blue slacks and slippers.

She sighed; guilt pangs challenged her exaggeration. *Well, true all eighteen years since age nine.* Until age eight she'd not begged for, nor been starved of, either nutritious food or loving affection.

Aria couldn't recall her commission of any intentional five-year-old act contrary to man or society worthy of her punishment. Why had God allowed false evidence and a lazy public defender to stuff her into prison after her inability to hire a competent attorney? If she believed detention cell gossip, all out-of-state defendants such as herself faced cultural prejudice not alleviated by a crowded court docket.

Convicted and hidden from society's sight and compassion, why had God let her mind be goaded to insanity's doorstep by the cacophonic thrumming of critters thriving in a Louisiana bayou with a name she couldn't pronounce? No ready explanation cracked a fissure into her suffocated mind nor enlivened Aria's comatose faith.

Spawned by a rapid heartbeat, adrenaline pulsed into her veins. As she stood invisibly scorned by parish inhabitants as an ex-con, perspiration dripped into her eyes and stained the armpits of her blouse.

Except for mealtime gumbo, the strictures of her four year incarceration easily confused with her volunteer service to a Sudan refugee camp and a Botswana malaria clinic.

Contrite and demure behind bars, Aria today flipped off the highfalutin words of the prison's exit counselor, a gruff Cajun woman with threatening voodoo allusions. She'd stuffed her parole release letter into a black clutch purse, next to her prized GED graduation certificate.

Aria stretched her proud chin skyward; her neck muscles ached as when a guard had pinched a leather restraint collar one notch past comfortable.

A mid-morning cloud momentarily draped her in shadow.

"Stand clear. You better be fixin' to leave."

Relieved the arriving guard's baritone voice didn't command her to assume an awkward or painful physical position, Aria, nevertheless, telegraphed her disdain with a long silent stare. She raised her palms, not to acknowledge his authority, but to protect herself should his musclebound chest ping one of his uniform's golden buttons at her.

What rule had her pause to savor a whiff of freedom broken? A freshening south breeze from St. Gabriel stroked her hair. Life's contradictions evident when the same breeze gagged her with its pungent manure aroma. She captured her left thumb beneath her hand's fingers and squeezed. Her nostrils breathed in the bayou's familiar decayed-tree odor, a summer irritant Aria wouldn't miss even if wacky naturalists praised it as perfume.

"Move along now." The strident words circled her stationary head from behind. "You heard me."

Aria flinched at the touch of a firm hand on her left shoulder. Her released satchel thudded on the sidewalk's concrete. Even if her ears hadn't detected a guard's footfalls, how could she have missed the scent of a man closing in?

How dulled had her senses become? How long would it take after four years of involuntary confinement with women who shunned her for being both a northern "Yankee" and a lighter-skin woman?"

After a half-pivot, guard or no guard, her right hand cocked her clutch purse into a raised clubbing position. Her head and torso jerked sideways.

"Don't touch me," Aria shrieked. No family awaited to witness her release or to protect her.

One of her Havington-styled brunette curls limited her peripheral vision and blurred what she could see. She fixated her hazel-eyed gaze on sculptured features with blue eyes submerged in sockets surrounded by gold-toned tanned skin.

"Keep your filthy hand off me," Aria barked. She summoned the reproach last uttered to a court bailiff after a jury convicted her of stabbing a kitchen butcher knife into her husband while at their rented honeymoon cabin.

In sync with her purse squeeze, Aria began, then stopped, a mumbled plea, "I beg you. . . ."

At her trial she couldn't deny three days cabin residence, her non-bloody fingerprint on a kitchen steak knife, nor the letters "A R I" scribbled in Brad's blood atop wall blood splatter twelve inches above the floor.

But she cursed her public defender's refusal to locate a cabin passerby who a local turkey hunter said heard Brad shouting at someone minutes before Aria returned from a Calhoon convenience store.

The guard's right hand slid off her shoulder.

Still wary he'd grab her with force and drag her behind the bars she'd just escaped, Aria retreated two steps.

The guard's sneer disappeared as his lips relaxed. "I've seen you scared." His eyes narrowed as his lips oozed into a smirk. "For your return, I'll promise to keep your mattress warm."

Aria shuddered. She balanced her weight on the balls of her white sneaker-clad feet. Her frantic gaze halted by a multi-colored RTA sign across the street. Not seeing rails, she assumed a bus stopped in front of the unpopulated wooden bench.

Aria grabbed two satchel handles and backpedaled. When the guard didn't advance, her parted lips released an elongated exhale. Without a complete shoulder blade turn to the prison gate, she quickstepped across the street. Resting on the transit bench, she compressed her right ear lobe between her forefinger and thumb, a childhood habit unbroken.

After repeated mental commands to remain calm, she breathed easier when no second person joined her. Her total infrequent outside world contact had been holiday and birthday letters from her wheelchair-bound Aunt Maggie in Chicago, a twenty-two-hour Amtrak trip north. The last arrived Mother's Day week.

Her aunt's handwritten note said she required a relative to sign her out of Harmony Square nursing home and, from the inserted Bible-page family tree, Aria reckoned she alone comprised her aunt's surviving kin.

Aria's left hand tried and failed to smooth the Goodwill blouse wrinkles. In her satchel a second blouse and skirt plus chemise, panties and a bra, all also not ironed.

She shrugged off the prison's last attempt to belittle her crushed self-esteem.

A bus brake squeak alerted her to be ready to board. Through the open bus door, she asked the driver: "Will this bus take me to the train station?"

A broad smile encouraged Aria to step up.

"One transfer, but I'll make sure you don't miss it."

Aria handed him a pre-paid voucher and accepted the tendered transfer ticket. At the first open seat, Aria shoved her satchel to the window and sat. Rural fields merged into residential streets before the bus driver waved at her.

As she thanked him, he said, "Wait here the Union Station bus. Saturday's a reduced schedule so don't wander."

Aria joined a diverse crowd lined along the street curb. Not until a bandana-clad woman angled her walker, did Aria find a gap to lean forward to read the arriving bus's electronic destination indicator. Relieved to see "Union Station" displayed on the second bus, Aria trudged forward and up to hand the driver her transfer ticket.

Bus lurches stiffened her left hand grip on the seat in front of her. With her satchel tight against her abdomen, she protected it through several stops until a massive gray stone building swallowed a line of approaching buses.

Alighting last, Aria scurried past forlorn faces, piled suitcases and corralled kids to enter the Amtrak lobby. The only working ticket window agent recounted Aria's change before he handed her a boarding pass. She paced the waiting room until a booming speaker announced the one p.m. departure of her north-bound Pullman.

Onboard and settled, Aria rested her curls on a brown headrest. Her half-hearted tries to doze thwarted when her ears channeled hours and hours of steel track clickety-clack into her brain.

When the horizon ingested the evening sun, star clusters welcomed an ascending quarter moon. Passing light streaks and infrequent train sways and pitches stymied Aria's struggle for restful sleep.

Dawn ignited a glint on the nearest window. The reflected warmth caused Aria's raised hand to rub her right cheek. Her fingertips smeared the night's accumulated gloom while she traipsed to the dining car. A stale breakfast muffin washed down by creamed and sugared coffee failed to alleviate her chronic fatigue.

Aria cherished her first glimpse of Chicago's distant skyscrapers. Her hope for renewal boosted. As her eyes feasted on adjacent fields green with crops, cud-chewing Holsteins and then zero-lot wall-to-wall houses, the skyscrapers remained an ever present beacon of freedom, a realized goal soon to flourish.

Unlike the movie *Silver Streak*, the Amtrak locomotive didn't crash into Chicago's Union Station. Elbowed by a man in a rush, she waited beneath a portico for her brown-tweed satchel, sorry she agreed to have it checked. In hand, she carried it into the vaulted-ceiling station lobby hubbub flooded by the brilliance of a high noon sun.

A woman waving her arms shouted, "Aria, Aria."

Exhilaration exploded within Aria's brain. *Can't be.* The woman appeared not as emaciated as Aria remembered, but a cherry-apple-red scarf meant but one person.

Aria dropped her satchel and hugged Tillie, her protector of years gone by. "How'd you know?"

"Your aunt. My African years after you left bearable until the abductions. A year ago, civil riots chartered me a flight home. Started at the nursing home January first."

Aria squeezed Tillie tight before she released her. "Aunt Maggie didn't tell me."

The glint of a twinkle animated Tillie's eyes. "Bribed her. Convinced her you needed a surprise."

"Baby Ruth?"

"Cost me three bars, and not those little fun-sized ones."

Aria laughed, a genuine five-year first. Within seconds her intuition alerted her to be on guard. A lanky man in black trousers and a blue shirt open at the collar jostled others as he strode direct to where she and Tillie stood.

"Tillie, incoming, behind you," Aria whispered as she bent forward to grab her satchel.

Fingers bent, thumbs tucked, Tillie pivoted. Her raised right elbow and shoulder diverted the oncoming man without slowing his advance or lessening Aria's original alarm.

With a two sidesteps the man stepped past Tillie and his outstretched right hand reached for Aria's thigh-high satchel. "I'll take that."

Aria pulled back. "No, no. I've got it."

Beneath his hooligan-style flat hat, she glimpsed a miniature chin scar that evoked fragile memories. She dismissed the scar as common to pugilists and jailed inmates.

"Let him take it," Tillie said. "Sorry. I should introduce LeRoy. He's a friend of Robert, who's the half-brother of my current boyfriend."

The explanation befuddled Aria. Her right hand one of two hands that tugged at her satchel's leather straps.

Tillie raised both hands to her cheeks, hiding the beginnings of a blush. "Okay, it'll be, you know, easier to explain after dinner. I'm assuming you've got no place to crash, so you're coming home with me. It'll be crowded." Tillie stopped short. "Sorry, didn't want to make it sound like you'd be back in prison."

Aria released her satchel grasp. While she cringed at the word "prison" or any synonym, she chided herself for her sensitivity. "Sounded like a sleepover."

"Right," Tillie replied. "A girl's slumber party."

LeRoy lifted his chin and the exuberance of expected joy danced in his eyes. "That'll be great."

Tillie whirled toward LeRoy. "You're not invited."

"Why look at me?" Aria said to LeRoy. "Not my house."

She thought of Roscoe, the black terrier she'd loved and gave up. Maybe the neighbor girl who unofficially adopted Roscoe still lived along Cicero Avenue and Aria could again scratch a docile Roscoe behind the ears. No. She wouldn't tempt fate's disappointment by expressing aloud what would be a sweet reunion. A male voice broke through the stupor Aria had lost herself within.

"Boy, this bag is light. Bikini, I'd guess." LeRoy flashed a grin at Tillie, then Aria.

Tillie wedged herself between LeRoy and Aria. "Forget him and follow me. He drove only because I didn't want to mess with the CTA's Red Line to get us to Wrigleyville."

Aria fought to regain her depleted energy to savor the once enjoyed bustle of downtown Chicago exemplified by the commuters who shared Union Station as both an Amtrak station and a metropolitan transit terminal.

She relished a second morning of not being forced to wear an inmate's blue slacks, flip-flops and an over-starched white T-shirt. Tired arteries circulated the inhaled oxygen of freedom into her toes and longed for them to lead her to Macy's on State Street with a fantasized unexpired debit card with no credit or cash withdrawal limit.

When Tillie stopped at a double-parked sedan, Aria's forced smile acknowledged LeRoy gallant bow when he opened for her his car's rear passenger door. She ducked in before a blast of smelly exhaust from a metro bus wafted across the Buick's roof.

From her rear seat vantage point, LeRoy displayed an intriguing profile, a rounded chin beneath a fighter's nose. His palm brushed away wavy brown hair. When he commandeered the rearview mirror to launch a flirtatious wink, Aria's protective shyness rotated her gaze beyond Lake Shore Drive's S curve to Lake Michigan's sparkling blue water and a beach crowded with July sun worshippers.

The perceived chill of the lake's breakwater spray rekindled in Aria the early morning shivers of an unheated eight-by-ten-foot prison cell.

By the time LeRoy exited at Belmont, Aria's heart, filled with God's nurtured love, struggled to fend off the growing rancor of a promising marriage stolen by a knife-wielding intruder. Her grief enhanced by the slow drawl of a New Orleans prosecutor as he preyed upon the safety fears of six senior citizen jurors to notch a guilty verdict that ignored the crucial evidence her bloody fingerprints weren't on the deadly knife.

LeRoy spoke to the windshield, "I'll stop in the street to let you out and then try to find a parking spot."

When neither woman responded, he rotated his face right to direct his words to Tillie who sat buckled into the front passenger seat. "I'm allowed to hang for a little while, ain't I?"

"If you behave." Tillie twisted to gaze at Aria before she flashed a coy smile.

Aria refused to allow Tillie to carry her satchel into the Sheffield Avenue brownstone. The expansive living room with a wood-burning fireplace awed Aria.

"Got three bedrooms and four roommates. Sofa okay?"

Aria nodded and refused to enter for fear her one-size-too-large white sneakers would scuff the hardwood oaken floor buffed to a reflective shine.

The gray sectional to Aria's right appeared larger than the cell Aria had occupied with a roommate two nights before.

Chapter Two

LeRoy lay stretched across Tillie's gray sectional when Aria returned from rejuvenating her skin with a freshness scrub.

"Wow," he exclaimed. "What you say we blow this place and grab dinner."

Aria scanned Tillie's living room unable to find support for her courageous "maybe another time" refusal or, if not, to unwind her spool of unease into a web to block all comers.

"Well?" LeRoy swung his feet to the floor.

Aria's right foot crossed her left to angle her next four steps toward the fireplace. Its poker and a mantel vase, accessible weapons to protect herself.

An eerie silence heightened her monophobia.

Hadn't the prosecutor against her prattled on and on to pound into the jury the fact that defendants commonly relied on a claim of domestic violence as justification for murder. A home, he claimed, deadlier than a darkened alley.

LeRoy bounced to his feet.

Aria trembled. Shielded by her left hip, her fingers traced the swirled knob of the wrought-iron fireplace poker. An indefinable moment gripped Aria's psyche. Had the ticking seconds convinced LeRoy not to approach?

No. After one stride he pounded his right fist into his left palm. "C'mon, I've asked you nice." He opened his fist to fish car keys from his front trouser pocket. "You can tell me you're waiting for another dude."

"Won't." Aria focused her gaze on LeRoy's shoes.

"Play hard to get. Cool with me. Tells me a hellcat lives inside you, ready to come, ready to be stroked."

"Doesn't," Aria mumbled. "Maybe you should leave."

"Why? We can enjoy ourselves." LeRoy halved the distance between them. "You can't imagine how much I offer."

Aria tightened her fingers around the poker grip. Shallow breaths interspersed her thoughts. Is it swung like a knife? Chopped like an axe?

The poker jangled against the ash shovel.

LeRoy's eyes widened. The outside door burst open.

"Pizza, pizza," Tillie shouted. Her sneaker heels squeaked in her abrupt stop. "You're both here. Great. There's enough for a party."

Aria released her poker grip.

"I'll go wash my hands," LeRoy said.

When he left, Tillie asked, "You two getting along?"

"Fine," Aria replied, her tone sharp.

"That's good. LeRoy's okay once he understands where you're coming from, what you'll put up with."

How had Tillie learned that? Aria hadn't prepped combative psychology to be safe. "Good to know."

"He's offered to drive you to your aunt tomorrow a.m."

"Wouldn't wish to impose. Better I reacquaint myself with the CTA."

"Suit yourself."

LeRoy sauntered into the living room.

With Tillie gathering plates and silverware in the kitchen, he winked at Aria before he shouted in Tillie's direction. "Got pepperoni?"

Chapter Three

Tillie's luxury organic sheets cooled Aria's body but didn't suppress LeRoy's scent radiating from the sectional's interstitial fabric spaces.

Without a strong effort to wish it away, Aria recalled her fiancé's, then her husband's, gallant efforts not to hog their bed. If only she could remember his aftershave. A chuckle overwhelmed her. Old Spice, a constant tease, it wasn't. If only she could replicate the sweet clover that engulfed their first embrace. *If only . . . . If only . . . .*

Her double sigh recognized their mutual joy forever lost. "You up?"

Aria recognized Tillie's voice. "Yes, yes."

"Join me in the kitchen. Coffee's perking."

"Give me a sec."

Aria scrambled to slip her legs into borrowed blue jeans and her torso into a baby-blue cotton pullover. Her sneakers laced, she folded and stacked two sheets on the pillow.

"Scrambled?" Tillie peeked around a left doorjamb. "Or, eggs sunny-side up?"

Aria strode toward Tillie. "Either." She couldn't remember the last time she'd eaten eggs. She struggled to identify the acrid scent that irritated her nostrils. A head twist left identified the culprit to be a daisy bouquet left on a chair cushion. The caffeine aroma tugged Aria into the kitchen to face a stone-like counter set for two.

Aria hesitated to allow Tillie to direct her where she should sit. After her friend's left hand pointed, Aria asked, "Your lover leave the bouquet."

"Hell, no!" Tillie's brusqueness startled Aria. "Sorry, delivery person left at the rear door with Linda's name."

"Linda?"

"One of my roommates. She and Tanya return tonight." Tillie filled Aria's coffee cup and slid creamer and sugar packets in Aria's direction. "Perhaps you wanted LeRoy to leave them for you?"

"Hell, no!" Aria clasped her right hand to her mouth before her thumb and forefinger cupped her chin to join Tillie's laugh.

"Okay, enough LeRoy. I've got errands, but you're free to lounge here all day."

"Plan to visit Aunt Maggie, if that's all right?"

"Of course. And don't leave before I give you my burner phone. You'll be okay, but prudent to be careful."

Aria stopped her cup halfway to her lips. Had Chicago changed? Was violence now any everyday occurrence? Without an answer, she sipped her cooled coffee. Better she focuses on her reunion with Aunt Maggie.

"I'll help with the dishes before I find the CTA."

"No worry," Tillie replied. "Dishwasher is a savior. Stay here while I find that phone I mentioned."

Aria rose and waited in the living room. Handed the three-by-two inch cell phone, she pocketed it and hugged Tillie. With a last good-bye, Aria exited the brownstone through the same door she'd entered. No deliberation nor expansive thought once outside guided her right hand to the clammy iron handrail.

Two opposite-direction passersby on the sun-dappled sidewalk raised no alarm bell for Aria. A half-block later, she stepped over a discarded Cubs scorecard near the ascending two-stair flight to the CTA platform.

At the top, not finding a ticket window with a human seller confused her until she watched a youthful man feed cash into an ATM-like machine and extract a magnetic swipe card. He inserted it into a turnstile slot. She did likewise to board a Chicago Loop-bound train.

Aria calculated she'd arrive near her aunt's nursing home by half past ten if she encountered no Red Line to Orange Line transfer delay at Roosevelt Avenue.

A nun in a habit asked Aria if the seat next to her was free. Aria nodded. They sat in silence, Aria not in prayer, until both exited the train and proceeded up the escalator into the Orange Line terminal across from Midway Airport.

When the crowd pushed her toward the airport skywalk, Aria pressed her body against a glass wall to steady herself until the surge subsided and a path existed to exit to the street-level commuter parking lot.

With the CTA terminal behind her, train tracks and unfamiliar street names slowed her walk until she gambled that, if she continued east, she'd eventually meet Cicero Avenue. The street name revived memories of Roscoe, but North Cicero Avenue, where Aria last hugged her dog, miles from her South Cicero location. Multi-stepped stoops and trimmed grass front yards convinced her she'd complete a successful journey.

The cell phone in her pocket vibrated. *Who knows where I am?* When it stilled, she realized Tillie did.

Aria stopped beneath a fully-leafed sycamore. She read the unsigned text: "Till, honey, get the daisies? If your visitor's there don't say nothing about her son."

The text sucked life-supporting breath from Aria's lungs. She could be Tillie's visitor and she'd suffered blurry and pain-infused nightmares her baby had been a boy before she had been told the fetus delivered stillborn.

Aria's left hand thumb and forefinger squeezed her left ear lobe; every abdominal muscle twitched with the anxiety to telephone Tillie. How could she? Her right hand clasped the phone connected to the Tillie number she'd memorized. Even jogging to borrow Aunt Maggie's telephone unnerved her.

Aria pocketed Tillie's cell phone and, without a local resident to give directions, she doubled her pace.

One block, then two and a huge four-story high principal building flanked by two wings filled Aria with joy. A symmetrical red brick facade laid in Flemish bond met the Harmony Square brochure picture and description Aunt Maggie had forwarded.

Aria pushed the front door bell. *Quaint.*

"It's open; just push," said an elderly gentleman at rest in a brown Adirondack chair to Aria's right.

While the gentleman appeared ready to encourage a lengthy conversation, Aria turned away after a quick "Thanks" and a successful stiff left-arm jab aimed at the unbolted six-panel wooden door.

A row of six persons, Aria gauged to have celebrated seventy trips around the sun, greeted her lobby entrance. She smiled and accepted the mixed-gender head-to-toe scrutiny. Her raised glance noticed a manned reception desk.

"May I help you?" The woman's demeanor pleasant.

"Maggie Tinsman. I'm her niece."

"Aren't you late? She expected you yesterday."

Aria stammered to articulate a plausible answer. *How can I explain not rushing to see Aunt Maggie when first arriving?* Tillie had been her friend; they battled overseas charity hardship together. Aria then thought of LeRoy. She didn't want to give him any idea where Aunt Maggie lived. Also best Aria had a safe location unbeknownst to LeRoy.

"Delayed train," Aria lied.

The gray-uniformed woman smiled. "Doesn't it just happen all the time? Wait until winter. Everything's late."

Aria nodded.

"Clip on this visitor badge and take the elevator to your left. Third floor. Room 312. I'll buzz so you're expected. Thank you and enjoy your visit to Harmony Square."

Aria pivoted. The prominent elevator sign directed her to an efficient car to whisk her to the third floor where an arrow above numbers 301 to 325 pointed left. While she expected carpet, vinyl tile didn't impede her stride. On a smooth chocolate-brown door, she tapped on the painted number twelve. Beneath her knuckles, the fake woodgrain vibrated like steel.

When no human sound filtered into the hallway, Aria fisted her right hand for a vigorous rap. Before her biceps propelled her hand, she heard a vigorous voice.

"I'm decent. Come in."

Aria twisted the knob and entered. Across the room Aunt Maggie sat in her wheelchair near the room's one window.

"Good Lord, child. Don't you eat?"

Aria flinched. Unwilling to allow an open door to spread gossip, she stifled her response until her push engaged the door's latch. "Absolutely I do auntie."

"You following one of those crazy TV diets."

Pressed lips prevented Aria from reminding her aunt no prison chef blended chopped vegetables into smoothies. The energetic window light, insufficient to halo her aunt's gray hair or accented the lines beneath her eyes, didn't hide Aunt Maggie's age spots liberally sprinkled across pale skin stretched so thin the dermis nerve network visible.

"You look well."

"How nice of you to say. Rest your bones in my self-described lonesome-me armchair. It's cushioned, a definite plus. Harmony's garish-floral covering hurts my eyes. If it weren't for Tillie's occasional drop-ins, I'd ask housekeeping to store it far from my view."

Aria perched herself on the chair's front edge. "That you heard my first knock says your hearing's good."

"Strong hearing my salvation. You can't believe the whispers and backbiting that goes on here. Eat a second brownie cut in half and you're a glutton starving a third-world hungry child and/or his family."

"Oh, come now, auntie."

"Trust me. It's so."

How could Aria argue? Better to change the subject. "Tillie said you told her of my arrival."

Aunt Maggie's gaze swiveled from her bed to the adjacent nightstand. "She pried it out of me."

"Not surprised." Aria remembered the Baby Ruth candy bars. None in sight.

"You've got to believe. I've lived my life wasting little or nothing. This place will gobble up all of my savings unless you can help me."

Aria waited as her aunt's hands rocked the wheelchair by its hand rims. When convinced the conversation fell upon her, she asked, "Why leave here? Room's bright, appears clean. And I can ask Tillie if there's a hidden danger."

"It's not just for me. Can't you see?"

Within the room's environment, Aria tried to eschew fantasy and stay grounded in reality. What had Aunt Maggie desired she see? The neatly cornered bed coverlet with its equidistant stitches a manufactured loom product not seamstress designed. The fixtures reproducible at a DIY store. Then, the chair she sat on, although comfortable, not a star attraction if offered at a local auction. If Aunt Maggie ventured forth in her motorized wheelchair, she commanded the most expensive jewel the room contained.

What did Aria miss? "What can't I see? You've stowed hidden treasure under your mattress?"

"Don't be silly. Can't you see my leaving here is best for you as well as me?"

"What's for me?"

"To find your son."

Aria gulped, bounced her shoulder blades into her chair's curved back. If she inhaled, perhaps she could breathe, reinvigorate her inhales and exhales.

Tears welled behind her eyes; embarrassment saved when they didn't flood her cheeks. *Her son.* The two words unleashed sharp-edged memories to burrow new heartaches.

Old cranial scars scabbed over a stillborn delivered in a prison room unfit of any hospital birthing room designation. With her ankles in metal stirrups, a clipboard with two sheets of paper pressed to her face as a guard's guiding hand forced her fingers to grip a pen and scribble her name. If there'd been a burial, it had happened outside Aria's knowledge.

Wooden white crosses outside the prison walls kindled the horror she'd one day find her chosen grandfather's name etched on the grave they marked.

Streaming afternoon brightness blurred Aunt Maggie's facial outline. In subdued tones, Aria asked, "What proof?"

"Vi."

"Who?" Aria asked.

"Your mother."

This second jolt softer than Aria's first. "How can that be? My mother died three years ago." Stated matter-of-factly, her words de-emphasized the loss. "Before that she barely had the clearness of mind to fight a brain tumor yet alone have compassion for my circumstances."

"You underestimate your mother. If she could've, she'd have moved heaven and earth for your freedom."

"Don't disbelieve you." From a forgotten deep loneliness, Aria's maternal grief unraveled inside her. Incarceration scars hadn't entombed family strife or intentional hurts. "Just hard to reconcile."

Aunt Maggie released a hand brake to glide closer. "Your mother hired a private investigator. He claimed babies didn't die, but an adoption ring spirited them away to be sold."

The floating filmy mental image of her never visiting mother flashed and disintegrated. Aria attributed her vision to the vignette photograph Aunt Maggie displayed on a side table next to a ragged-edged Bible. Her shoulders slumped. "My baby, my baby."

"Can't be sure."

"But you said . . . ."

Aunt Maggie clasped Aria's right hand. "We can finish what your mother started."

Aria shook her head. "'Fraid it takes money I don't have. In fact, unless I find a job . . . ." Her aunt's hand pat prompted Aria not to blabber on about her problems.

"We can bolster each other, pool our efforts. You and I can be an everyday family. I'd like that; wouldn't you?"

A hard swallow slowed Aria's response. "Yes, definitely a yes. I'll promise to visit regular. And, Tillie can keep me up to date. You see her here, don't you?"

"She leads weekly sings." Aunt Maggie dropped Aria's hand. "Once in the dining hall, last week on the patio."

"See, it'll be great."

With her aunt's hand push, the wheelchair rolled backward a half wheel turn. Aunt Maggie's bland expression, halfway to a frown, siphoned off the enthusiasm her face had displayed minutes ago. She mumbled, "Where did I go wrong?"

Aria rose to lean forward to hug her aunt's shoulders. She whispered into an ear, "You didn't. I know you don't wish to be here, but there are worse places."

"Not if you're imprisoned."

Aria jerked erect.

"Sorry, awful word choice. You know what I meant."

Aria refused to equate her real-life debasement with her aunt's fresh sheets, nutritious meals and generous privacy, especially when eliminating body waste. "It's fine. Maybe time will offer the answer?"

"One can't be too sure. A wheelchair can compensate for my withered legs. One's heart beats original."

"Aw, auntie." Rational instinct said Aunt Maggie exaggerated. And Aria suspected she required time to heal her weariness. "Your heart's as strong as your hearing. But, no matter what, I'll be here for you."

"I know dear." The plaintive voice signaled a disappointment not conveyed in words.

Aria couldn't bolt. She again embraced her aunt's shoulders. "Tomorrow we'll explore."

Chapter Four

While Aria's burdened heart dreaded to fulfill her promise to return the next day, she hid her angst and smiled when she turned in her Harmony Square visitor badge.

Purposeful strides and jaywalking inspired by impatience halved Aria's return time to the CTA's Orange Line. A throng's transit platform jostling unrelieved by an overcrowded Bombardier car until her Roosevelt Road Red Line transfer. Two-dozen people decked out in Cubs jerseys and t-shirts and bright with excitement confirmed her destination. Joyful banter distracted Aria from loneliness.

Aria extended her elbows, once scraped in childhood soccer falls, but since healed, as she zigzagged through the Sheffield Avenue crowd. The diversion of look-alike turn-of-the-century brownstones and the mid-afternoon bustle resulted in Aria's two-house walk past Tillie's doorstep. A higher house number alerted her to retrace her steps.

A smiling Tillie answered her knock. "Bet Aunt Maggie exuberant to see you."

"Yes." Her white lie better than a long explanation.

"Oh, come in." Before she slammed the front door closed, Tillie stepped aside to allow Aria's entrance. "Have you eaten?"

Aria scanned the room. No LeRoy. Had she anticipated his presence? No. That she even thought to think about him chilled her. "Grabbed a bagel."

"Sit down. Tell me everything."

Aria sidestepped the sectional. Words swirled in her head. She slid into an armed chair. "Nothing earthshattering. She looked so pale . . . so frail."

Tillie paced, a ringmaster in control without a whip. "Your aunt doesn't desire to stay at Harmony. She tell you?"

"Not directly. Said we could go away."

"A vacation? Where?"

Aria gazed at her toes. *What's believable?* To distill five difficult years into words a daunting, if not impossible, task. She lifted her gaze to Tillie. "No vacation. Long story."

"If you don't want to talk about it, that's fine."

"No, no. It's hard. And, you don't want to have a blubbering soul spoiling this fancy carpet."

Tillie leaned against the mantel. "Take your time. Rest. I'll busy myself to stack ham and cheese on rye. Would you want a salad, too?"

Aria shook her head.

Tillie bowed before she wiped an actor's sheepish grin from her expression and shuffled backward toward the kitchen. Within the room's silence Aria's gaze bounced left and right on a haphazard journey without a destination. When the front door hinge creaked, a subtle sound any conversation would've sponged, she jerked her head left.

"You're back. Lucky me." LeRoy grinned ear to ear.

Aria popped erect. "Temporary." She refused to admit, even to herself, she encouraged LeRoy's attention.

Tillie appeared, a towel clutched in her hands. She nodded toward the both of them and withdrew.

A long beat of silence acknowledged the unease that gripped Aria's ability to breathe. She swallowed hard to maintain her stability while she fixed her attention on LeRoy's closeness with frequent glimpses toward not losing an escape route to the kitchen.

LeRoy's retracted lip stretch eased his grin. "Temporary, you say. With neighborhood rents at two to three grand a month, I can see why you'd want to skip town."

"Please don't prejudge." If she screamed it to the rooftops would it be more believable? This wasn't prison, but the encircling tension escalated by Aunt Maggie's soft-sell saddled her soul. Years of pain endured in prison steeled her psyche, if not her body. Within her brain cells one three-year-old overheard conversation memory forever etched. A shadowy figure whispered to a hulking phantom as Aria's lower abdomen ached, "If not pregnant, what good is she?"

Aria's muscles relaxed when LeRoy didn't veer toward her as he swaggered toward the kitchen door.

Whew! At first she embraced her emotional release that LeRoy hadn't tried to force himself upon her. Then her conscience registered a greater reality. Regardless of metaphor, she couldn't bury related family if heartbeats still pulsed genetic DNA into her veins. She couldn't divulge any of this to LeRoy. Tillie presented a different proposition.

Aria tiptoed to the kitchen. Would there be madness revealed if she spilled her gut? If a risk existed, it would be hers. She couldn't endanger Aunt Maggie.

At the doorjamb, Aria stopped. No voices filled her ears. *Wouldn't Tillie and LeRoy speak? Silence. Strange.* Two raps against the doorjamb preceded Aria's entrance.

Tillie faced her with a plate in each hand. "Sandwich?"

"Where's LeRoy?"

"Claimed a last-minute meeting. You shut him down?"

"Keep your thought should I ever weaken."

Tillie stifled a chuckle. "Sit down. Let's eat in the kitchen, if that's okay by you?"

Aria pulled a wooden chair to the light-colored round dining table with a dark base to indicate agreement. "Earlier, you were kind not to inquire. Really gracious."

Water wobbled inside the filled water glass Tillie placed next to the sandwich she served Aria. "Most of us have pasts we'd like to forget, rather than wake dripping wet in the middle of the night. If I were an essayist, I'd argue that compassion is a learned art, not inherited."

Aria enjoyed her first sandwich bite as Tillie continued.

"Figured, when we met in Africa, you, as many of us, ran away from adversity. Activate your left brain. I did. To find us crossing paths gives credence to the old adage that coincidences are but fate in disguise."

"Or, you can't keep strong women down."

"Touché." Tillie added a second chuckle. "Prefer a drink stronger than water?"

"Not today. Have to ask: do you think Aunt Maggie comprehends reality?"

"On a continual basis?"

"Absolutely."

"She's definitely lucid, not counting the occasional lapses we all have. You know, we all forget to turn off a lamp or fail to bring home a needed pantry staple. I'd not worry. I'd venture ninety-nine times out of one hundred she's capable of rational thought."

"She tell you . . . ?" On her plate. Aria pushed together two uneaten bread crust pieces. "She tell you my mother hired a private investigator?"

A seated Tillie shook her head. "Haven't I mentioned I've only worked at Harmony Square six months? During half that didn't even realize your Aunt Maggie lived there."

"Then that's a no?"

"Duh."

Aria's shoulders slumped. Prison's sluggish gloom still infused her pores. Without question the burden to proceed fell on her. Move. Go back. Her option to flip a coin she dismissed as an act of cowardice.

With a last water sip, Aria asked, "If you're working tomorrow, perhaps you can join me with Aunt Maggie?"

"Don't see why not, but first we need to finish here, hop the EL and find the Macy's outfit to impress your aunt."

The misty nostalgia of childhood birthday dresses decorated with rose petals or sunflowers mentally edged out the stark image of the utilitarian uniform she wore while distributing rice, beans and water to Libyan refugees.

"Shouldn't." Aria's soft-toned denial in tune with her lack of a strong conviction to waste money.

"What else you doing?"

Boxed in, Aria grasped for an answer to evade the truth. She'd always sided with those who recycled and protested waste. Fashions for the sake of glamour may have filled the manufacturer's coffers without the ignition of an iota of excitement with Aria. Expressed to Tillie, such an answer unsatisfactory. Her failsafe became the truth. "In my predicament there's scant money for personal frills."

"Oh c'mon."

Aria rose. "What's that to mean?"

"Don't be goody-goody, all self-righteous. Remember I was there in Africa. We promised each other that sooner or later, meaning when stateside, we'd pamper ourselves."

Faint dish clinks trailed Tillie to the sink.

Her friend's goodness dulled the darts that pricked Aria's skin. "There's an alternative."

Tillie pivoted. Soap suds dripped from her fingers. "Target? Hopefully not a Walmart."

"Neither. Was thinking of a thrift store."

Tillie's left hand cupped her right. With the tinge of defeat, she asked, "You're kidding, right?"

"Absolutely not."

"I'll have to think. Don't regularly visit."

Aria stepped forward. "Can't you google?"

"Let me grab a towel. Sure we can." Tillie pointed Aria to the living room. "Go sit. I'll be there in a sec."

While Aria sauntered to and fro, she greeted the fireplace mantel with drummed right fingertips on each pass. Her tensed twisted innards foretold the terror the forthcoming morning harbored and the catastrophe she'd so far dodged.

"Ready to go?" Tillie's voice upbeat.

"Not Macy's."

"The Blindfolded Raccoon."

"What?"

"It's a thrift shop we can walk a few blocks to. Isn't that what you wanted?"

* * *

Blue vertical corrugated steel panels, the center one cut for a frosted glass door, encouraged passersby to keep moving.

Tillie slowed.

Aria imagined stacked wooden crates on a dusty floor in the darkness behind the panels before she saw the thrift store open sign.

"We're here," Tillie announced.

Aria swiveled her head. No one who passed her reached for the three-foot long door handle. Signs in four rectangular windows two feet above her head touted two-for-one, BOGO and fifty percent off clothing specials. The twelve-foot-long banner with the words: "Blindfolded Raccoon Windy City Discount Store" accented the point Aria hadn't arrived at a suburban Macy's.

"You sure it's open?"

"Do I have to drag you?"

Aria's right hand clasped the door handle, gave it a tug and bowed to encourage Tillie to lead the way.

Inside, metallic racks decked out with vibrant colors framed football-field-length aisles. "There's no way I'll find anything here," Aria said.

"Forget the summer shorts and halters. Follow me."

Tillie marched straight ahead. Aria's left hand swiped at multi-colored sleeves until a sign said "men's". At the second cross aisle, Aria slipped on the gray linoleum as she tried to match Tillie's abrupt veer to the right. In a dozen steps, Aria caught up.

"Didn't expect this. Wow!"

Aria couldn't see what excited Tillie until two sidesteps to the right. A decked out mannequin's hip-flared navy blue jacket paired with an A-line skirt transported Aria to high school history class photographs of 1940.

"Wouldn't Aunt Maggie think you're the cat's meow?"

"Doubt it. Mother wore dresses, not suits. Bet Aunt Maggie did, too."

"What then?"

"To clear my name I need to return to Louisiana sooner or later. Out-dated clothes will make me stand out as a Yankee. Won't help."

"Chill. I'll spend ten bucks as a welcome home gift." Tillie smiled at Aria. "Now find a couple tops and black slacks so we can get out of here."

In the women's section, Aria grabbed six tops, two pairs of slacks, one black and the second blue, and strode to the fitting room. Its large size with a return table surprised her as did the bagginess of Aria's former size. Three plain small-sized, minimally decorated, tops fit her tastes.

Satisfied with the slacks, she searched for Tillie. With a hand wave, they met at the checkout counter.

Purchases completed, Tillie motioned Aria outside. They agreed Tillie would visit Aunt Maggie and Aria on her first work break the next day.

Chapter Five

Aunt Maggie yelled, "Come in."

Aria's first Harmony Square front door encounter imprinted on her to be assertive, not bashful, push the door, don't ring the bell. On today's late afternoon visit to sync with Tillie's shift, she grabbed a visitor badge from an unmanned receptionist desk. By not signing the register, she'd endure all negative consequences, if caught. With confident strides, Aria rode the elevator and entered the resident hallway with no staffer challenge.

When the latch clicked, Aria entered Room 312 with an upbeat, "Hi, Aunt Maggie." When she saw her aunt in bed, bundled with sheets and an unlined coverlet within an inch of a chokehold to her throat, Aria tried to dispel every illness concern. Her gaze left detected an abandoned wheelchair.

"You look nice," Aunt Maggie said.

Aria, taken aback, offered no immediate reply to the unexpected compliment to her new Blindfolded Raccoon top and slacks ensemble. She recovered to mutter, "Thanks."

"I told everyone you'd come."

"Can never forget you letters." Aria wished to be more specific, but the uncertainty of why her aunt lay in bed disquieted her. She switched subjects. "You said mother hired an investigator. Is there a report?"

"Only telephone calls to your mother."

"Oh."

"But we can still contact him."

Aria's fierce desire to believe her aunt ricocheted against the reality Aunt Maggie hid her mother's death until six weeks after her burial when Aunt Maggie let it slip in a letter. Now thirty-six months later her mother's investigation, like cream, rises. Aria questioned the circumstances. "After three years?"

Aunt Maggie tried to raise her head and succumbed to gravity's invisible force. "He hasn't given up on trying to collect the last three hundred dollars promised him."

"That might as well be three million."

"It's a pittance."

"No it's not."

"Don't cast doubt. Where's your faith? When a door closes, a window opens. You believe that, don't you?"

"Sorta." Aria heard a door slam, multiple metal tinkles. She rotated her head with Tillie's knock expected. Silence.

"Aria, honey, if you sign me outa here, money's no problem."

"I should earn my own, not take yours."

"Don't be silly. Not mine; yours."

Aria's throat tightened. *No.* Her knees quivered. Nothing near the room's center within Aria's grasp to steady herself.

"You all right, honey?"

Aria nodded once, sat in the room's chair. Her struggle for words so feeble. "Can't . . . can't lose you, too."

Two knuckle raps on the door vibrated in Aria's ears.

Without hesitation, Aunt Maggie shouted, "Come in."

Adorned in a blue smock, Tillie flashed a broad smile. "Didn't see you signed in."

"You the warden?" Aria teased.

Aunt Maggie grimaced as she pressed her elbows into the mattress. If an attempt to rise, she floundered.

Aria hurried to her aunt's side. "You okay?" Aria couldn't apologize for her unguarded verbal backslide for to highlight it would compound her accusation's implications.

Aunt Maggie mumbled, "Fine." The single word tumbled from her lips.

"Sorry, Mrs. Tinsman," Tillie said. "No exercise today."

Aunt Maggie collapsed into her prior prone position.

Tillie pointed Aria to the room's chair. "I'll stand." She gazed at Aunt Maggie. "Didn't wish to be a bother, but Aria said she'd be visiting you."

Aria nodded, her hands clasped in her lap.

Aunt Maggie twisted her face a second time toward Tillie. "There's a secret I must tell Aria."

"You wish me to leave?"

"No. This room doesn't keep secrets. Can you wheel me to the patio?"

"We'll help you get dressed."

Aunt Maggie folded the coverlet off her shoulders. "No need. Just help me up and into that doggone chair."

Aria leaped to her feet. No spectacle of Aunt Maggie in male pajamas slowed Aria's rush to her aunt's bedside. Her aunt, exposed to her waist, wore what she'd refer to as her "going-to-church" dress. When Aria assisted with the bedclothes, Tillie swung Aunt Maggie to Tillie's side of the bed and Aria heard shoe heels click on the floor.

With a push to unlock the brake, Aria guided the wheelchair to where Tillie's armpit hold raised and steadied Aunt Maggie.

"Let me grab that chair arm," Aunt Maggie said.

A wheelchair pivot and Tillie's guiding support let Aunt Maggie plop into her wheelchair.

Tillie glanced at Aria. "I'll lead the way."

The threesome started their patio journey with an uneventful hallway-to-elevator troop. After crowding into the elevator car, they rode to the main floor and Aria bowed her head as Tillie waved to the manned reception desk.

The late afternoon sun created long shadows unruffled by the manufactured breeze of two industrial-sized box fans. Aunt Maggie gestured toward the middle of three unoccupied tables. A candy-striper hustled to them.

"Three waters, please," Aunt Maggie said.

"Yes, madam."

"Wait," Tillie said, "only two." She angled toward Aria. "I've no time to stay. My break ends in a minute."

Aunt Maggie fixed her gaze on Tillie as if to ferret out a chink in her armor. "You'll return for me?"

"If I can." Tillie, her right hand hidden from Aunt Maggie's view, flashed a thumb up to Aria. "See ya."

"C'mon Aunt Maggie, let's enjoy the fresh air." Aria lied with the last two words. Warm and muggy abler descriptors. When the fan breeze ruffled her slacks, she stepped left.

Aria, aware of the fleeting hope clear in her aunt's eyes, pulled a wood-slat chair away from the table and sat, straightening her spine to its full length as if nothing weighed on her shoulders.

"Guess you're right." The courtesy frosting transparent in Aunt Maggie's words offered no concealment of her deep internal disappointment.

Aria appreciated the candy-stripper's return with iced water for two reasons: one, its refreshment; and two, the time given to regroup mentally.

"Thank you," Aria said. Her words echoed by her aunt.

With a glance left and right, Aria squelched a haughty urge to utter a snide remark about the pudgy middle-aged woman in a midnight-blue silk tunic, tight black pants and gold sandals. If she couldn't make fun of a stranger, she'd no right to challenge Aunt Maggie's lying in bed fully clothed.

"We should make plans," Aunt Maggie said.

Aria let her elbows rest on the table. She didn't need fantasy to fill her mind with the scheme galloping through Aunt Maggie's brain cells. The what is an easy deduction; the where posed the mystery. She braced herself. "What plans?"

"To finish what your mother, my sister, started."

"Don't you remember?"

"Honey, I'm not senile. I remember." Aunt Maggie sipped from her glass. "You're fixated on the money. Don't blame you, but it's no problem."

"You win the lottery?"

"Better. No taxes. Your mother squirreled away a secret insurance policy naming you beneficiary."

"And, you hid it from mother's probate?"

Aunt Maggie squinted toward the sun. "Lovely blue tunic over there, don't you think?"

Aria deflected the diversion. "Yes, but still waiting to have you explain why mother hid this money?"

"Don't let me rouse your suspicions." Without warning, Aunt Maggie directed her sincere gaze at Aria, "What harm? No one's touched your money."

"That's not quite an answer."

Aunt Maggie waved the candy-stripper away before she flashed an inviting grin. "Then come with me." A twinge of doubt twined her seriousness.

"Huh?"

"Money's in a Calhoon bank box. The investigator will surely find the address if I mention it to him. I'm ready to leave today." When Aria didn't respond, her aunt added, "Would you help if I told you how much money?"

With an instinct not to dilly-dally and play twenty questions in a semi-public area, Aria tossed hesitation aside. "Five figures?"

"Definitely." Aunt Maggie counted her right hand fingers. "Not six, mind you, but a high five."

Aria's gaze lingered on her aunt's expectant expression. "There's a greater need than money."

"Are you trying to create roadblocks so I can't blame you for saying no?"

"Just listen. We'll need a car in Louisiana even if we ride Amtrak's Spirit of New Orleans. I've lost my driver's license and that wheelchair says you can't chauffer me."

"Can't hide a thing from your nimble mind." Aunt Maggie chuckled. "However, we're covered."

"There's an admirer I haven't met?"

A gentle sheepish smile confused Aria. Had Aunt Maggie's family bible page been a crafty, but honest, hoodwink light on the full truth?

This question paled compared to a greater one. Had her aunt succumbed to a senior with an unexpired driver's license, a romantic seduction? Her Harmony Square room, though seen only twice by Aria, displayed no picture, romantic candies or flowers.

"No dear. Tillie promised me she has a friend with a car."

"Oh, no," Aria muttered, ostensibly to herself.

"You know Tillie's driver friend?"

Aria bowed her head. "Hopefully she has more than one."

Chapter Six

LeRoy, bathed in sunlight, stood next to his car's front bumper. To Aria, his broad grin compounded her anxiety. Aunt Maggie's gleefully clutched her traveling bag as Tillie pushed her wheelchair away from Harmony Square toward LeRoy's open sedan door.

With her shoulder blades to LeRoy, Aria offered her last caution. "Auntie, this Louisiana trip threatens your health."

"Nonsense." She lifted her bag from her lap.

Aria grabbed it before Tillie. The chance Aria possessed to tote her aunt's bag to Room 312 slimmer than not hearing the summer katydid in a Louisiana swamp.

"Miss Maggie," Tillie said, "I'll help you get steady on your legs. Easy now."

LeRoy steadied the wheelchair with his right hand. "Let me help. I'll crawl into the rear seat from the other side."

"No need," Aunt Maggie said. "Let me clear my head and in a minute we'll be off."

"Yes, but it'll not be easy. There's 900 miles."

Aunt Maggie rubbed her forehead. "We're stopping for the night halfway and its interstate driving, no dark twisty roads. Right, LeRoy?"

"Yes, madam."

Aria whispered to Tillie, "Experienced similar distance twenty-two hours by train and you say fifteen hours driving. LeRoy fill his car with jet fuel?"

"Wish it were possible. Or, I stay south with you."

"You must return. I'd be crushed if you lost your job. Besides, Aunt Maggie hasn't given up her room, rent's paid a month in advance."

"You tell her that?"

"Heavens, no. If my baby lives, it won't be near the prison. Could be anywhere, even overseas. Aunt Maggie's in no condition to be Indiana Jones."

Aunt Maggie shouted out the open car window. "We going to leave before they light the torches?"

"Right away," Aria said. "LeRoy's making sure the spare has air." Perhaps a white lie, but Aunt Maggie was in no position to rotate her gaze to the taillights.

Aria climbed into the front passenger seat. Tillie next to Aunt Maggie. Aria now faced the brunt of LeRoy's glances rather than the occasion peek into the rearview mirror. She'd endure for her aunt's sake.

LeRoy smiled. "Buckle up and wagon ho."

Caught off-guard, Aria bounced into her seat. Expected to offer no driving directions or scenic bypass routes, she anticipated reliving her train ride in reverse.

From the rear seat, Tillie said, "Illinois road signs never seem to end."

"That's Route 66 and Interstate 55," Aunt Maggie interjected. "My sweetie and I twice drove to St. Louis."

Aria twisted her neck toward the rear seat. "Your husband? Never knew you were married. Is that a secret?"

"Sweetie was a cocker spaniel. Oh, how I miss her."

Aria silently lamented she hadn't taken an afternoon of the four spent in Chicago to track down Roscoe. "I'm ready to cuddle another dog."

"I like dogs," LeRoy said.

A silent Aria jettisoned all canine thoughts. She'd given LeRoy an opening, and he'd barged in. This trip difficult enough with caring for Aunt Maggie and the promised hurt.

"What breed of dog, LeRoy?" Tillie asked.

Shut up, Tillie.

"How about a hot dog?" Aunt Maggie asked.

"Guess we could all use a comfort break," Tillie said.

LeRoy exited the interstate at the next sign for a truck stop. Aria listened carefully to Tillie's explanation on how her aunt's wheelchair collapsed and was re-assembled. Another half dozen stops and she'd be a certified pro.

None of the four wished to dilly-dally. Tillie offered to drive, but LeRoy refused to surrender the keys. Aria graciously swapped seat locations with Tillie.

While LeRoy passed slower drivers and blended into traffic, Aunt Maggie napped. Aria, as she'd done on the train trip, counted cows and grouped Holstein, Angus and Jersey into separate totals.

Aunt Maggie rubbed her eyes. "Where are we stopping?"

"To eat or sleep?" Tillie asked.

"Sleep."

"Jonesboro, Arkansas. Reservation made at Campbell's Inn. And, before you ask, two rooms with twin beds." She swiveled her gaze toward Aria, a sly sparkle in her left eye. "How we split up still undetermined."

Aria's mind measured the rear seat's length with the assumption Aunt Maggie slept inside one motel room. *Works with a pillow and blanket.* Inn housekeeping none the wiser if bedding returned before checkout.

Aria embraced her fallback plan, ready to argue a guard needed to protect their sole means of transportation.

LeRoy thwarted her plan. After Tillie paid for the two adjoining rooms, he grabbed a pillow and promised to sleep in his car if allowed bathroom access to shower. Aunt Maggie shushed everyone.

"Here's what we will do. LeRoy will occupy one room. As the driver, he deserves an uninterrupted good night's sleep. We women will share the second. There's two beds and a sleeper sofa. That's mine. No objections."

Aria pinched her expression. Tillie shrank back. If anyone doubted whose quest ruled, Aunt Maggie had answered the question.

"Whatever you say works for me," Tillie said. The confident Harmony activities leader reduced to a servant.

Once inside the adjoining rooms, Aunt Maggie locked the connector door. If this had been an adolescent boy-girl sleepover, Aria expected no less.

She answered the front-door knock.

"You up to pizza?" LeRoy asked.

Aria spoke over her right shoulder. "LeRoy offers pizza, that okay?" Aunt Maggie and Tillie nodded.

"Nothing exotic, but yes," Aria said.

"Be back."

Aria closed the door. Aunt Maggie, TV remote in hand, surfed for the TV news: riots, floods, nothing extraordinary. When the news anchor announced a special program on illegal adoptions, Aunt Maggie clicked to Celebrity Feud.

"What was that?" Aria asked.

"Rerun," Aunt Maggie stated.

"Not Steve Harvey, that other."

"Rerun. Do I have to repeat myself a third time?"

Aria knew when to leave enough alone. "You sure you want that sleeper sofa? I'll take it."

"Better than Harmony Square."

"You're kidding," Tillie interjected. "They use the highest quality mattresses, high-end bedding."

"Let's not argue," Aunt Maggie said. "If either of you wish to ask LeRoy for his extra bed, there'll be no objection from me nor any mention tomorrow or the next day."

Aria gazed at Tillie. Neither volunteered a response.

"Okay then, you two decide on which bed you want and then help me with this sofa bed. Did I ever mention I loved hammocks as an adolescent girl and service trips to Appalachia with my church?"

Both Aria and Tillie shook their heads. Aria pointed to the twin closest to her and Tillie nodded. Aunt Maggie had either persuaded or terrorized them into acting like monks.

When LeRoy arrived pizza box in hand, none of the three objected to his joining them to eat. No objection surfaced to the two-liter lemonade or the beer six-pack, of which LeRoy chugged four.

"What's tomorrow's plan?" LeRoy asked, the last slice of pizza chosen.

"We visit the investigator," Aunt Maggie said.

"Then I'm free," Tillie asked.

"Not so quick," Aria said. "We don't know what the investigator will say. We might be all driving back together."

"Long way to drive for gumbo," LeRoy interjected. His downcast expression visible for all to see. He turned to Tillie. "You promised me an adventure, excitement, dancing girls. And I don't see either you or Aria strutting. Sorry, Miss Maggie, a guy's gotta dream."

"Don't be disappointed, LeRoy. All will work out." Aunt Maggie gazed at Aria. "You'll help LeRoy, won't you?"

Pinned in, Aria groped for a response. Her nod subject to interpretation. "Thank you for the pizza, LeRoy. I'll promise to splurge for lunch tomorrow."

LeRoy stood. "That's a splendid start." He winked at Aria as he exited through the outside, not the interconnecting door.

She felt her cheeks warm. If Tillie or Aunt Maggie perceived her reaction, she'd be embarrassed and dared not ask either.

"Then we're ready for morning?" Aunt Maggie asked.

Aria interpreted the question to mark the evening's end.

Tillie pushed Aunt Maggie into the bathroom and shut the door. Aria collected a sheet and blanket from the bottom dresser drawer to prepare the sofa bed and waited her turn to splash her face and extract the AC dust from her pores.

When Aunt Maggie emerged, Aria and Tillie hoisted her onto one of the two twin beds.

After Tillie disappeared into the bathroom, Aunt Maggie spoke of the day to come above the shower spray squeal. "Don't take everything B.J. Breaux says tomorrow at face value. He's akin to a politician, although don't know he's ever been elected dog catcher."

Aria leaned close. "Why did mother trust him?"

"She told me she loved his accent."

"That all?"

"Honey, don't we all do things because at the time it's easy? Once you meet this B.J. you'll understand he's not successful because he's good looking." Aunt Maggie chuckled. "He blends into the woodwork, a Cajun wallflower. That's what earns him jobs."

"Perhaps he won't want to help me?"

"Don't you think that. We'll settle your mother's account, promise him more and, shallow or deep, he'll dive in head first, no safety vest required."

Weary of standing, Aria dragged a wobbly desk chair to her aunt's bedside. "I'm scared."

"Because of what he's found?"

"That and because it's been two or three years and what was true in the past doesn't necessarily exist today. You remember those convent graves unearthed in Ireland?"

"That's not the same. Unique countries."

"Yes, but not religion's apart."

"Oh." Aunt Maggie ran her tongue across her upper lip.

Aria, who had never seen her aunt do that, disregarded it as she would have an eye tic.

Aunt Maggie regained control of her tongue. "From what I read, those babies in Ireland conceived contrary to God's law, a Christian virtue perversion. Damned in the womb."

Aria cringed.

"Now don't you worry, honey. You were officially married. Not long, but married. Nobody's counting months or cycles. Your arrest to conviction lasted six months, at least."

Aria bowed her head, her gaze welded to the floor.

Tillie bounded into the room. "Did I miss a prayer?"

"No," Aunt Maggie replied. "We're all safe and that's God's bounty. He's given us one fine day. We can trust that tomorrow we'll encounter challenges no harder that what we can bear."

Tillie bowed her head. "Sounds like a prayer to me."

"Amen," Aria said. "Now maybe you've left enough hot water for me."

"If not, blame LeRoy. I'd swear when we see him in the morning he'll be a prune."

"Go on you two," Aunt Maggie said. "If anyone needs sleep, it's me. And I need to start soon."

Aria closed the bathroom door, showered and returned to a darkened room. She extended her right hand to avoid obstacles. The crack of light escaping the curtain's edge aided navigation to the sofa bed. She placed her toiletries on the floor atop a damp towel, confident she'd not trip on them in the morning.

Aunt Maggie whispered, "Good night, honey."

Chapter Seven

Gone, done and gone. Aria lay prone and bemoaned her predicament. Half-past six a.m. She swung her legs to the floor. The bathroom hers if she desired.

She sat still on the sofa bed edge. Reality subdued her. Since siding with Aunt Maggie, Aria now too beholden and too poor to bribe LeRoy to turn back. Jonesboro epitomized the lifeblood of Arkansas. Soon they'd be in Louisiana. If she opened the Campbell Inn door, an internal fear predicted she'd cower anew to the bayou critter chorus.

"Can you help me?" Aunt Maggie contorted her shoulders.

"We both will," Tillie said.

"You're dears, blessed dears. Swear to God I will outfit my new home with at least two lift chairs, one comfortable enough to sleep in."

Quick to her feet, Aria and Tillie maneuvered Aunt Maggie into the bathroom. Aria's embarrassment faded when Tillie assisted Aunt Maggie with her catheter. This secret explained why rest stops limited to meals.

With LeRoy's aid, they shuttled bags and Aunt Maggie into his sedan.

"We buckled?" he asked. After three yeses, he announced, "Breakfast next stop, then gumbo."

Aria conjured no reason for LeRoy to be so chipper. Perhaps the lengthy shower, but no prune ridges adorned him as Tillie had so explicitly suggested the evening before.

Aria rode in front next to LeRoy. Her choice. While LeRoy smiled and drove his reach insufficient to endanger her, especially if she nestled herself against the door.

"I could live in a house like that," Aunt Maggie said.

Aria refused to glance right. Or, had her aunt gazed left past Tillie? No matter.

"Decision time ladies," LeRoy announced. "No Red Hen, that was Illinois, might I suggest Popeye's?"

"Can we do takeout?" Tillie asked. "Didn't think my butt would be this sore, but after yesterday."

"Amen," Aunt Maggie said. "The sooner we get to north Louisiana the better I'll be."

LeRoy glanced at Aria. "And you?"

"Take out. Po'boy, mild."

"Make that two," Tillie interjected.

"Miss Maggie?"

"If they add biscuits, chicken tenders, mild."

LeRoy exited the interstate and, within a quarter mile, spotted a Popeye's. "Stay here. Be quicker if I run in."

"Let me use the bathroom," Tillie said. "You okay, Miss Maggie?"

Aria heard no response, so she assumed Aunt Maggie waved Tillie away. Within minutes, LeRoy and Tillie delivered food and bottled water. Aria drank cautiously and held her bottle to allow LeRoy full cup holder access.

"Where exactly we going in Calhoon," LeRoy asked.

"Hold on," Aunt Maggie said. "We're three hours away. And we're not stopping in Calhoon exactly."

"Auntie, you said."

"Honey, Calhoon ain't a Chicago suburb. Picture it as a stand-alone store with a half-dozen houses nearby."

Aria twisted but couldn't face her aunt. "But the address Brad and I rented said Calhoon."

"Don't fret. We can both be right. Doesn't matter."

The hum of Leroy's sedan wheels and the time required to reach their destination gave Aria a reason to munch on fried chicken. Next time she'd order tenders and avoid the slippery chicken bones.

Except for uncut kudzu, the unrelenting southern pines and pastures outside her car window never changed.

"LeRoy," Aunt Maggie shouted. "We missed our exit."

Startled, Aria caught her head bob.

"Don't worry, Miss Maggie," LeRoy replied. "Around Shreveport there are several. This next one will do."

"Sorry," Aunt Maggie murmured. "Please stop when I tell you. Aria will call B.J. Breaux to coordinate our visit."

Aria swayed left, then right, appalled each steering wheel jerk thought to be necessary. Apprehension peaked when quick swerves and brake squeals ended in a ranch home's driveway.

"This it?" LeRoy asked, his smirk ready to be a smile.

"Splendid job, LeRoy," Aunt Maggie said.

Aria paced her exit to rely on LeRoy's repeat of yesterday's wheelchair and luggage handling. After two days, her aunt's judgment in their grand scheme still ruled. LeRoy behaved as a gentleman.

The ranch home sported a for sale sign. "Auntie, we at the right place?"

"Let me see. Yes. Committed to a week-to-week. Go ahead. Lock box code 5432 should give us a key."

Aria impressed at the ramp-equipped porch. The lock box yielded a front door key. Inside, a parlor and a short hallway led to what Aria assumed to be bedrooms and a bathroom. A spacious eat-in kitchen began two paces right.

Tillie dropped a bag behind Aria. "Cute. Are there beds?"

"Haven't checked, but trust Aunt Maggie."

"You talking about me?" Aunt Maggie sat in her wheelchair, LeRoy behind her.

"You ladies make yourself comfortable. I'll locate pizza. One must be open since it's after four."

"You need money?" Aunt Maggie asked.

"We'll settle on my return."

Aunt Maggie turned to Aria. "My wallet's under my seat. It has Mr. Breaux's number. Find it and give him a ring."

Aria unfolded the white note paper she extracted from Aunt Maggie's wallet and punched the numbers into her, well Tillie's, burner phone.

She left a message after unanswered rings. With Tillie, the two of them found pillows, sheets and unmatched pillowcases. Together they assigned Aunt Maggie the master bedroom and LeRoy the bedroom with a single twin. They dropped their suitcases in the third bedroom, a kid's room with a wall-painted unicorn opposite a sturdy wood bunkbed.

Aria surveyed the kitchen. A Formica table with four serviceable chairs adequate. Plastic glasses and a stack of paper plates enough to share pizza.

Two window air conditioners, one broken, judged unlikely to chill the house. To create a sultry air cross breeze, Aria opened the kitchen's back door and switched on the rackety ceiling fan. When that proved insufficient, she swung the front door wide while locking the screen door.

Tillie entered the kitchen with a smile. "Toilet flushes. Is this heaven or what?"

Aunt Maggie wheeled herself to the kitchen sink. Her extended arms not long enough to reach the faucets. "I'm sweating like visitors here should sport horns."

"Makes you long for Harmony Square, doesn't it?"

Aunt Maggie frowned.

Tillie opened an upper cabinet and reached in for a cup. "Like some water, Miss Maggie?"

"Please."

A loud front door knock surprised Aria. *Can't be LeRoy. He'd shout.* "We expecting anyone?" Aria's question less inquisitive than rhetorical.

A baritone voice inquired, "Anyone home?"

Aunt Maggie responded. "Mr. Breaux, that you?"

"Yes, ma'am. At your service."

Tillie pushed Aunt Maggie into the parlor while Aria unlatched the front door screen.

Into the parlor strode a man in a blue dress shirt and black slacks with a loosely knotted Colonel Sanders bowtie. Short salt and pepper hair unable to prevent the whitish dandruff already fallen on both shoulders. His muddy eyes framed by lined bifocals.

Aria concluded he exemplified an everyman, neither too short nor too tall nor neither too fat nor too slim. Perfect to blend into a crowd, as private investigators often must.

"I was in Frost Valley when you tried to reach me. Thought it best to drop by. Hope that's all right?"

Aria and Tillie sat on the sofa. Their guest filled the one cushioned armchair.

A squeak confirmed Aunt Maggie set her wheelchair brake. "Quite neighborly," she gushed.

Aria watched his gaze dart around the room. "Didn't see a car. Folks around here find it scary to be miles apart from neighbor's homes without transportation."

Aunt Maggie offered a proud smile. "Kind of you to worry about us. But don't be. My driver should be here any second. He phoned he's on his way back with dinner."

"That's good."

"You must know about these things. Does he need to register his gun with local authorities?"

A hard swallow blocked Aria's throat. Tillie's shoulders straightened.

The puzzlement on Mr. Breaux's face evaporated. "Wouldn't worry if your driver has a federal license. That's all I have and I rarely carry. Karate often a better defense."

"Nice to know." Aunt Maggie twisted her gaze to the sofa with a return to their guest. "You have time tomorrow to visit my sister's keepsake? You know, the one mentioned in my letter last month."

"Definitely. Perhaps you stop by my office first and I'll telephone to smooth out the arrangements. Don't reckon the paperwork will be too complicated."

Aunt Maggie cleared her throat. "We can settle up then."

An unexpected glimmer skimmed across Mr. Breaux's muddy eyes.

Aria heard plank creaks on the front porch.

Their guest stood. "That'll be right kind of you."

She anticipated LeRoy. Tillie slid her butt to the sofa edge. That Aria hadn't heard vehicle tires troubled her momentarily until she realized no sound preceded the investigator. She blamed the kitchen fan's racket.

LeRoy, three pizza boxes clutched to his chest, burst in, stopped. Wary, he backpedaled to the kitchen.

"If you'll excuse me, it's been a pleasure. Shall we say ten a.m. tomorrow, my office, it's not moved?"

"That'll be fine."

Mr. Breaux bowed. "Enjoy dinner."

Tillie yelled at LeRoy. "You lock the sedan?"

"Always. Chicago habits hard to break."

Aunt Maggie unlocked her brake and the three females gathered around the kitchen table. LeRoy excused himself and returned with sodas and a beer six-pack.

Tillie flipped the lid on the second pizza box. "There's a ton of pizza, LeRoy."

His smirk widened. "Breakfast, silly. Saves gas not to make two trips."

Aria bit into a four-cheese slice, swallowed. "Our visitor seemed edgy." She stared at her aunt. "We right to put all our trust in him?"

Aunt Maggie wiped her chin. "Not much choice." She scribbled words on a napkin and handed it to Aria. She read it and passed the napkin on to Tillie and LeRoy.

Held tight between his forefingers and thumbs, he raised the napkin in front of his face. Aunt Maggie nodded.

LeRoy ripped the napkin to shreds. The words floated to the floor and lay there ready for sweeping.

Be careful what you say. Walls can have ears.

Chapter Eight

Aria stomped her right foot sneaker on the top porch step.

One less six-legged critter, good riddance.

She didn't regret her impulsiveness. At her feet lay one critter who'd tried to make its way alone. When would her invisible monster act to crush her hopes and drive her loneliness, kicking and screaming, into perpetuity?

The silent house had presented no hindrance to her slipping out of her lower bunk to capture the dawn's last rays. White intricately crossed splotches of spider-web mesh suspended dew drops above far-flung grass tuffs. Vapor trails ringed distant mountains as ground fog crept up ridges until dissipated by the mid-morning warmth.

Aria slowed her inhales. Webs spun across grass blades, fog and a dead critter didn't intimidate. Yet, she'd learned a lack of self-esteem still haunted her.

On this cool morning she stood two hours north of a prison threshold she promised herself never to cross. Her promise generated nervous hyperventilation.

If last night proved one thing, Aunt Maggie had shaded the truth. Aria theorized her aunt conned anyone she could to escape Harmony Square.

But why drag her niece here? What's being gained?

Would Aria be paranoid at Aunt Maggie's age? *Yes, and more so, if her future happiness and money to survive depended on a creepy private investigator's whims.*

"Didn't know you smoked?"

Aria shivered. Only one male last night had slept sheltered by the house behind her. She steeled her nerves against the accusation before she pivoted. "Don't."

Behind the screen door mesh stood the upper anatomy outline of a naked male chest. She dared not lower her gaze.

"Then those strewn butts I saw last night while bringing in the pizza are not yours."

Her lips trembled at the edges. "Definitely not."

"Whatever. There's still pizza if you haven't eaten."

"I'll let others enjoy. Thank you."

LeRoy pushed the screen door against the house exterior. "Beautiful, just beautiful."

In the light, Aria saw a barefoot male who wore trousers without a belt, nothing else. LeRoy's verbal ambiguity, in her mind, left his comment ungrounded. Aria fought to defuse LeRoy's advance with a reference to the nature before them. "Everything's peaceful. Nature's glory."

The invisible energy between them stretched so tight Aria feared an explosion. No crawling insect prickled her skin. She attributed her growing warmth to dispel the prior chill to the ascending sunrays.

"Thought I heard voices," Tillie said. She stepped onto the porch. "You doing laundry, LeRoy?"

"Yeah?" He snorted a laugh before his sly smirk radiated past Tillie and landed on Aria.

She shrugged and waited for Tillie's retort.

"Thought so. No shirt. No socks. What else accounts for a lack of clothing in a female's presence on a chilly morn?"

Aria mumbled, "A cleansing pond dip?"

Tillie gazed at Aria. "That's not LeRoy, believe me. And if one looks here about there's no water, not even a birdbath. I'd be happy if he found a washer; I'd like to take it for a spin, too." LeRoy's laugh interrupted her. "Serious, don't want to lug dirty clothes onto the train."

After two steps, LeRoy grimaced, lifted his left foot and hopped to the doorjamb. "Stupid splinter." He rubbed his fatty protective foot pad, stepped away from the door and gazed toward Tillie. "There's no basement. No washer."

"No hiding place. That's good," thought Aria.

Tillie smiled, "Then there's pizza, right?"

"My guess, box and a half," LeRoy replied.

"Breakfast it is. Coming Aria?"

Aunt Maggie emerged on the front door's periphery. Her torso unsteady, knees wobbly, and her two hands splayed tight against the doorjamb.

Tillie slowed, then stopped. "Oh Lordy, Don't move, Miss Maggie. Let me help."

Aria dashed to find the wheelchair two feet behind her aunt. With Tillie's powerful arms assisting, Aria lowered Aunt Maggie into her wheelchair. She pulled the wheelchair into the parlor's center.

Tillie asked, "There's cold pizza, care to join us?"

Aunt Maggie smiled. "If I can have tea, lead on. We can't dilly all day."

"If it's seeing that guy from last night, no need for me to tag along if LeRoy drops me at the train depot tonight."

Aunt Maggie looked around. "Where did LeRoy run off to? He must've been swimming before I saw him. Brings back summer memories. Oh, to be young again."

Aria shook her head. "Think he's in his room getting properly dressed." She added, "Suggest we not bother him."

Tillie arrayed pizza slices on fresh paper plates. "You must visit a grocery after your business."

"We'll do that," Aunt Maggie said. "Is that water boiled yet? Should've asked that agent for a microwave."

"Your new home will have one."

Aunt Maggie beamed. With her tea bag steeped, she wrapped its string around the bag while nestled in a spoon.

LeRoy, fully dressed in a short-sleeved blue polo, black slacks and shoes with socks, leaned against the kitchen doorframe. "Any pepperoni left?"

"Don't you have a suit jacket?" Aunt Maggie asked.

"You kidding?"

"No. Appearances LeRoy. Mr. Breaux expects me to have a driver and you're it."

"Explain to him I'm on vacation."

"When are you not?" Tillie teased.

Aria slid out a chair. "Its okay, Aunt Maggie. Once we settle mother's debt, I'd venture Mr. Breaux will forget LeRoy's lack of a proper uniform and embrace your modern lifestyle." Seated, she gazed up at LeRoy. "You look spiffy."

LeRoy bowed. "If I'm to be so important. I'll need more pizza and a beer. Know they weren't all drunk last night."

"Pizza's fine, LeRoy. My driver doesn't drink on duty."

Tillie whispered to Aria, "And in Africa you thought I was tough."

"Never." Aria's left eye wink tempered her word.

"Eat up. We've a bumpy ride ahead of us." Aunt Maggie set her tea mug on the table. "I'm expecting we'll hear great news today. Feel it in my bones. Don't you, Aria? Will make your mother's spirit proud."

Aunt Maggie's optimism plagued Aria. The growing strife between unearthing the truth and living with the grief roiled her insides. Easy to placate Aunt Maggie by signing her out of Harmony Square.

Until the one brief encounter yesterday, Aria had never met Investigator B. J. Breaux. Whatever her mother had gleamed from Mr. Breaux, neither she nor he divulged it. That, and her mother's speculations and directives, remained buried with her mother's body and forever lost to Aria.

She tried to stretch her mind to incorporate hope, be it slim. God, she must be insane to risk future happiness on a private investigator who trolled back alleys, waded in bayous, peeked into dimly lit windows and/or dug holes to uncover buried secrets.

She resisted the gloom engendered by the realization she lacked the training and a sleuth's ability to decipher lies.

Better she bites the bullet. "Can we leave?"

"From what I figure," Aunt Maggie interjected, "we'll need thirty and up to forty-five minutes."

"Car's ready at 9:30," LeRoy said.

Tillie rescued a salad bowl from an upper cabinet and filled it at the sink. "Bathroom should be Grand Central. I'll use this." She gazed at Aunt Maggie. "You need help?"

"Yes."

Aria stayed seated. "You two go on. I'll flip a coin with LeRoy for the minutes left."

LeRoy smiled. "Shower?"

Aria shook her head until her neck ached and then grabbed a dish towel from the counter. She gazed at Tillie. "You'll not need that bowl if you go first with Aunt Maggie."

Tillie nodded and handed the bowl to Aria before she rolled Aunt Maggie out of the kitchen.

Aria followed until she turned right for her shared bedroom, now empty with Tillie attending to Aunt Maggie.

Behind the locked door, Aria, stripped to her underwear and intending to hurry, dipped a wash cloth into water.

A rap vibrated her bedroom door.

"Tillie?"

A muffled voice said, "No."

Chapter Nine

"Go away, LeRoy."

The doorknob squeaked. Just when Aria thought she'd scream, an adrenaline rush left her breathless. *He wouldn't! She* reached for her blue slacks.

A second knock, gentler than the first.

Hunched over and unable to reach the door with one leg inserted halfway into her slacks, Aria shouted, "Go away,"

"It's Tillie. Need my stuff."

Slacks at her waist, Aria's right hand switched the doorknob button and retreated. When Tillie entered, Aria asked, "LeRoy still hovering?"

"Didn't see him. Bathroom's yours."

Aria clutched a top to her chest and dashed for the bathroom. Minutes later, she strode onto the porch. LeRoy paced near his car.

"Excuse us," Tillie said. She shepherded Aunt Maggie off the ramp to where the gravel crunched in stereo. Aria assisted Tillie with Aunt Maggie while LeRoy stowed the folded wheelchair in his Buick's trunk and assumed the wheel.

"LeRoy," Aunt Maggie began, "forget Interstate 20 and turn south when we reach Highway 34."

Aria perceived she saw the sign later than LeRoy, so she remained quiet. She practiced this interaction technique in prison daily. The crinkle of paper behind her coordinated with Aunt Maggie's directions to LeRoy. The dash clock numbers flashed in minute intervals. At number thirty-three, Aunt Maggie directed LeRoy to drive into a chain-link fenced area notable for a two-story metal warehouse flanked by a one-story grouping of four plate-glass windowed businesses.

Aunt Maggie instructed LeRoy to park near the end of the smaller building.

Aria exited first. Her left foot tingled. She braced herself with her right hand against the closed car door and twisted her elevated left foot. The tingling slowed, then stopped.

LeRoy retrieved the wheelchair and assumed Aria's job to assist Tillie. She ambled after them to the black curved word "Investigations" painted across a window. A cardboard "open" sign hung haphazard behind the glass entry door.

They met no receptionist. Four unfilled hardwood chairs and a scarred wooden coffee table rested on square gray tile. The floor-to-ceiling partition with a cut-in-door in front of them divided the rectangular room. No wall hangings or potted plants softened the overhead fluorescent glare.

Footsteps approached from behind the partition.

"On time. Appreciate that," B. J. Breaux said. "Have a seat while I grab a file." His half-turn interrupted his departure. "You remember the money."

"Yes," Aunt Maggie replied. She reached into her purse.

B. J. accepted Aunt Maggie's check with a cursory glance. "Thanks. I'll put this into my safe. Be right back. Make yourself comfortable." He retraced his steps.

"So what's now?" Aria asked.

"Wait," Aunt Maggie replied. LeRoy gazed at Tillie and shrugged. His right hand fingered his key ring.

The P.I. re-appeared. An elbow pinned a folder to his left side. His hands carried a folding chair. He stopped to set up shop opposite Aunt Maggie, the coffee table between them.

The flipped open folder flopped onto the coffee table.

"These notes and assorted documents presented to your sister, Violet, at our last meeting."

Aria didn't wish to appear ignorant, but asked, "Who?"

"Your mother," Aunt Maggie interjected. "Right? Mr. Breaux?"

"Right, right." He lifted a bond paper sheet. "We had this contract I was in the middle of. Promised another two thousand dollars, but it's incomplete. You understand that when I learned of Violet's unfortunate death, there wasn't an incentive for me to continue."

"To pay for all this." Aunt Maggie's sarcastic smile deepened as she scanned the room with military precision.

Mr. Breaux slid the paper he held under two-hold punched papers within the folder. "If you have no interest in Violet's grandson, we're done." He rose.

Aria jumped to her feet. "My son, where is he?"

Mr. Breaux frowned. "Don't know exactly."

Aunt Maggie strained to hoist herself from her wheelchair and failed. "Don't con me, Mr. Breaux. My niece told by authorities her child died."

A hint of emotion underlined his reply. "That, I'm afraid, is what all the prison mothers are told."

Aunt Maggie challenged him. "How can you be so sure? Don't bait us with rumors and gossip."

He stared at Aunt Maggie, then Aria. "You think you're been my only client? Well, think again."

Aria's clogged throat reversed her swallow until she coughed. "They had me sign a teared death certificate."

"Forged or legit, no matter. You name your child?"

"Mentioned my grandfather."

"Unnecessary part of the fraud. They rename the child. A fake birth certificate filed after they sell the child."

"Sold! My baby sold!" Aria flopped onto her vacated chair seat. Aunt Maggie patted her shoulder.

"What is this? Africa? Modern day slavery?" Tillie asked.

"Close," Mr. Breaux replied.

Aria struggled to breathe. No prison bars stifled the air, yet an invisible cage restricted her lung's ability to oxygenate her blood. Why hadn't her mother contacted her at least once to inform her she initiated a search for her grandson? Was her mother going to raise the boy without telling Aria? She couldn't dismiss the possibility. Had her mother concluded she failed with a daughter and sought to begin anew with a biological boy, even if not from her womb?

"How close?" Aunt Maggie asked.

"Consider this free information. They couldn't base their activities in St. Gabriel. Too close to the prison. Since a babe's easily transported. Calhoon chosen as safe, yet close, if you get my drift?"

"Guess so."

"And there's the ability to add confusion. Calhoon, while near Interstate 20, is not really a city or county, but a population center of two hundred with no minorities. It's an outpost that draws no attention. And there's a Calhoon County near Anniston, if my memory's sound. If you go by its Calhoon jail name, it's perfect to confuse citizens and visitors in a state with a French heritage."

"You've confused me," Tillie said.

"Me too," Aria added.

"Hear that?" LeRoy asked.

"What?" Aria asked.

"Probably a delivery truck for the warehouse," Mr. Breaux said. "Hear them all the time."

"Not a truck," LeRoy said.

"Not now, LeRoy," Aunt Maggie said. "Mr. Breaux, you've made your position crystal clear as to continued investigation, at least, your participation. Yet not addressed a more important undertaking regarding my sister."

Aria didn't understand her aunt's reference.

"Right, you are," Mr. Breaux replied.

"Then where is my sister's money?"

"You can't accuse me of pilfering it?"

"If it's all there, why worry?"

"Delicate situation."

Aunt Maggie's nostrils flared. "Balderdash."

Mr. Breaux glared. "I've never. My ethical boundaries never violated. It's a point of pride."

"Don't stall, Mr. Breaux."

He coughed.

Aria didn't judge it to be a smoker's cough, but a cough brought about by nervousness. She expected him to barricade himself behind the inner partition, but he remained frozen.

"While I see four, don't know if you're the right two."

"Mr. Breaux, you need to be clearer," Aunt Maggie said.

"Violet's will requires a succession representative and a direct descendent to be present to open her safe deposit box after the IRS has cleared it."

"Well, did they?"

"Yes. And then the bank locked it, but after I saw bundled money with no opportunity to count it."

"You were there?"

"Of course. Violet named me succession representative."

"What's that?" Aria asked.

"To you Yankees, that's an executor."

"Oh," Aria replied.

"Then we're good," Aunt Maggie said.

"What?" Mr. Breaux said.

"You're this whatever and Aria here is a direct descendant. Can't be any closer than a daughter."

"You got proof?"

"What do you mean proof?"

"Birth certificate would be good."

Aria struggled to stop the tears. To obtain her visa to work in Africa had taken four months. She hadn't procured a paper copy of her birth certificate with a named father until she'd bankrupted her saving account with a one thousand dollar payment to a Chicago lawyer. She couldn't swear it was a forgery, but at the time her goal was to protect diseased African babies and she'd overlook anything to reach her goal.

"I don't have one with me."

Mr. Breaux stared at her. "Where were you born?"

"Somewhere near Chicago."

"Cook County?"

"Guess so." Aria wasn't sure. If her Chicago lawyer's deceit uncovered, would she be behind bars? "Is it important? Why do you ask?"

Aria contracted her arms and shoulders into her torso. "We can go online to search public records."

"See," Aunt Maggie said. "That's a solution."

Aria calculated that if she objected, Mr. Breaux could proceed anyway at Aunt Maggie's bequest. What did she have to lose?

"Give me a moment," Mr. Breaux said. He disappeared behind the partition. No conversation or issued instructions seeped from beyond.

Aria leaned toward Aunt Maggie and in hushed tones asked, "Why did mother trust this guy?"

"Can't say. Maybe he promised stuff she couldn't get from another. Who knows? All I can say is she vouched for him in all our conversations."

"Possibly he's a gigolo or a pimp?"

"Wash out your mouth with soap, girl. Your mother was never that kind. Struggled at times as we all do. Never think of your mother as one to toss away values. You hear me?"

"Yes, Aunt Maggie."

LeRoy and Tillie stood. Both paced, but in opposite directions. Neither offered a word.

A slap on wood unnerved them and Aria as well.

Mr. Breaux shouted from behind the petition. "Got it."

A flummoxed Aria stared at Aunt Maggie. "What's that to mean?"

"Quiet. Pray we'll find out shortly."

Mr. Breaux pranced from behind the partition.

Aria braced herself with no expectation of a big hand-clapping revelation or a crushing disappointment.

"Aren't computers great," he exclaimed. "Required magic fingers, but I've confirmed that Ariel is Violet's direct descendent. She and I can satisfy the bank's requirements."

Aria shuddered. Had she interpreted his accent correctly? Her birth name Ariel, not Aria. What should she say? She glanced at Aunt Maggie, who didn't seem concerned.

"Let's go then," Aunt Maggie said.

LeRoy passed Aria to open the outside door for Aunt Maggie, steered and pushed by Tillie.

"I'll meet yawl outside," Mr. Breaux said.

Past Aunt Maggie's shoulder and the open door's leading edge, Aria spotted a black Suburban not present when they'd entered. Her first step into the sunlight caused her to squint.

A car door slammed.

The blurred image of a beefy man dressed in a black shirt and shorts with a holster strapped to his thigh ran toward her.

"Step away; step away," he shouted. His heavy footsteps crunched gravel before they thudded against asphalt.

No one did. They all froze.

His arms pinned Aria's arms to her sides. "You're coming with me." She struggled without result. Her left heel kick missed a shin. Aria grasped for breath as clasped fists dug into her upper abdomen.

LeRoy shuffled his feet with no attempt to attack the tattooed assailant. Tillie wheeled Aunt Maggie to face the attacker.

"Take your hands off my niece," Aunt Maggie shouted.

"She's coming with me. There's a warrant for her arrest."

Chapter Ten

Watery discharges moistened skin pores beneath Aria's eyes; her arms hung limp. Rubbery legs hindered her ability to remain upright.

"Walk or I'll drag you to my vehicle."

In the distance, Aria heard Aunt Maggie. "Where's he taking her?"

A male voice, not LeRoy's said, "Tyler. If it's a PT warrant, there's a county jail there."

On her side across a rear seat, Aria labored to breathe. Hands cuffed behind her back gave her no opportunity to see if an abdomen bruise existed. Her brain said yes.

"Where are we going?" Aria asked.

"You're headed to prison once I drop you off and collect my reward."

Her entire body shuddered. Dread coagulated to force and crowd her brain cells against her skull.

"And, those friends of yours who follow better not interfere. My office tracks this vehicle and they'll know if something funny happens."

To Aria, her abduction surreal. "I've got papers. You're making a mistake, an enormous mistake."

"That's what y'all say. Warrant says different. It's the document I believe, not a fugitive's word. If the prison warden made an error, I'll still get paid for my civic duty."

He laughed, a deep guttural laugh.

Aria's shivers increased. Why hadn't her friends protected her? One reality said they couldn't. Why was it her reality?

In trying to project an air of confidence, not felt, Aria raised her voice. "Didn't you hear me?" The vehicle's swerve caused her head to bang on the seat. "I've got parole papers."

"Until your last breath, you won't change my mind." Her abductor's tone sadistic. "Folks around here decades ago suffered from lawlessness."

The shadow across Aria's face lifted as soon as it clouded her right eye. Had the road dissected a tract of trees? A foreboding detour taken over which she had no control?

If her abductor had continued to chat during her shadow diversion, she hadn't heard a word until . . . .

"Bombs and violence targeted not only freedom riders or burn out merchants. They exploded through the fabric of our society with ripples that still threaten us today. Northern agitators weren't welcome in the so-called civil rights era and time hasn't softened the righteousness of our birthright."

Why did he need to reaffirm she wasn't in a safe place? Her quiet, quaint Louisiana honeymoon destination ablaze with azaleas no longer blossomed in memory or the present.

"If your sole interest is reward money, perhaps there's a way for us to strike a deal?"

"Nice try. I'm no ding-dong. If word got out I'd be no more welcome than a dead skunk."

A second swerve interrupted Aria's grasp of a brilliant thought to waggle her freedom. If that weren't hell, a brief brake screech threatened to run out the clock. Hot humid air rushed across her skin when a nearby door opened.

"Let's go, little lady, payday."

When she squirmed, he dragged her sneakers across the leather seat and propped her seated against the vehicle's side.

She scanned her environs. A two-story red brick building with a Sheriff car parked near an entrance posted as private certainly housed law enforcement. LeRoy's Buick nowhere in sight. She figured it made little sense to worry if her abductor had ditched him by the first or the second swerve.

Brawny hands grabbed her hips. "Up we go."

Blood rushed to Aria's head as she teetered across her abductor's left shoulder.

"Don't you dare kick? Hate to see your pretty face bloodied and scarred by concrete."

Aria sucked in her breath. The not-so-subtle threat she deemed doable and highly likely since he'd get paid for turning her in whether or not her chin bandaged.

They entered the building through a metal door.

After her neck ached, she gave up trying to keep her head focused on the corridor ahead. Greetings and jokes deserved to go two ways, but when she saw a sunburned Sheriff's deputy, the word "redneck" flitted across her mind. She pressed her lips tight lest she utter the common slur.

With a left turn, she lost the comfort of an air conditioned hallway for a stuffy room painted gray and furnished with four steel chairs and a metal table equipped with cuffs.

Her abductor kicked a chair free of the table and plopped her onto it. "Sit still. Don't jiggle while I unhitch you and take my cuffs."

Goosebumps exploded across her skin when he rubbed a thumb up her spine. Her nostrils involuntarily closed, repelled by the stringent disinfectant odor. Alarm, not musty air, activated her sweat glands when she didn't catch her reflection in a large wall-mounted mirror. TV cop shows featured interrogation rooms with one-way glass. The freshly mopped floor hinted at cleaned up prisoner abuse. Aria scrubbed dried blood thoughts from her mind.

Two door knocks and her abductor shouted, "Come in."

A barrel-chested prison-uniformed guard marched in and stood a table distance away from Aria. He stared down at her.

"I know you." He quietly chuckled as if Aria's presence graced him with a joyful exuberance. "Do declare. Small world we live in. You jerked away from me last week as if I'd loosened the leather straps to your wrists and ankles."

This distancing of himself from prison abuse raised in Aria a sliver of hope. A moment's reflection and a Herculean power of will subdued her enthusiasm. The voice before her sounded familiar and the ready-to-pop chest buttons a vivid throwback to last week.

"She's all yours," Aria's abductor said. He pivoted toward the door; his exit completed by a loud clank.

"You're not my friend, are you?" Aria asked.

A sly smirk crossed his lips. "Could be."

Aria rubbed her wrists. While not cuffed, the imaginary skin depressions now hidden by her skin elasticity didn't erase her deeply embedded leather-restraint memories. She debated whether to ask what he meant. Instinct told her to listen further and determine with greater clarification what she faced or what trial was hers to endure.

He straddled the nearest chair. "Confused, aren't you?"

The stuffy air parched her throat. "Why?"

"If you weren't confused you'd have found that train and never again set foot in these parts."

"What's to say I didn't ride north, hire an attorney and returned to sue the whole bunch of you? Bet you signed in today. My lawyer will get your name. You can't hide."

"Don't make me laugh. Not saying that I took part in anything illegal, but all those bleeding liberals who tried that years ago discovered that tar and feathers at least itched."

"You plan to lock me up again, restart the abuse."

"Well, not me personally, you see. I prefer women with a little more bounce. There's an old saying about a roll in the hay. You know that one?"

How could she deny and infuriate him? Still, she feared being complicit. "Yeah," she mumbled. Her fingers pressed a sternum not hidden by fat. "Heard it."

"Well, for me, the hay's not important, but the roll. Years ago my ex-wife had those love handles, the bounce. But nowadays my buddies tell me I should enjoy women both free and emaciated."

His gaze bore into Aria. "What do you say?"

She pressed her lips tight as she watched his fingers flex.

His powerful glare lingered on her breasts.

Tiny sweat beads clung to her top's fibers. When he stood she cowered with her splayed fingers, interlocked palms and forearms protecting her upper modesty until his gaze landed on her blue slack's stitches. Aria sensed the arrogance he wore as an invisible cloak.

She exhaled without relief when his tailbone and muscular thighs again blanketed a chair seat. She'd no "redneck" buddies, but she couldn't admit that. Such an admittance would merely reaffirmed her undeniable Yankee heritage, which he, more likely, guessed.

Aria couldn't rely on her drinking a poisoned potion, not present or expect her prison guard to convulse and die.

He checked his wristwatch and pushed himself erect.

"We leaving?" Aria asked.

"No, got time."

Aria gulped. *For what?* Time, in her head, stopped. If this was a county jail, why wasn't she safe, protected from harm?

Where was Aunt Maggie? An alarm possible if she'd kept Tillie's cell phone and not handed it back.

"Remember my hand on your shoulder?"

"Sorta."

"Trying to connect with you. And what did you do?"

"Ah . . . ."

"Don't want to say it, do you? Treated me as if I was a psycho." He exhaled. "Like I was one of the others."

"Ah . . . ."

"If it was my baby, we'd have raised it. You understand what I'm saying?"

Aria's entire body shuddered. "My baby died and I'll not cuddle another. Your prison doctor guaranteed that."

"Maybe if you treated me nicer, you'd feel different."

Aria cast aside her grief. "Never." She glared at him. Her words resolute and enunciated. "Mark my word: Never!"

"I won't let you throw me aside. Not until . . . ."

The room's door hinges squeaked.

Aria steeled her nerves. With the expected return of her abductor, she foresaw an assault. She prepared to lash out, kick, gouge, until re-affixed cuffs or straps restrained her. She'd nothing to lose.

"Who do we have here?" The gentleman in a blue seersucker suit cast his gaze toward the uniformed male. "Not you. Know who you are. Who's this young lady?"

"Bounty hunter brought her in. There's a warrant."

"Well, well. She ask for a lawyer?"

"Nah. Pretty and smart. Predict she will. Not surprised she traded herself for fake documents to convince the warden to approve her release."

The gentleman cast a wary eye at Aria. "You did this?"

"No, no." An involuntary tear escaped her left eye.

"We'll have no tears. I'm here to assure justice is done. Passed a crowd in the lobby. Any of those here for you?"

"If there's a woman in a wheelchair, yes."

He winked at the prison guard. "Trust you'll keep your paws to yourself?"

Without outward enthusiasm, the guard nodded.

"This woman outside an attorney?"

"She's my aunt. No attorney." Aria wiped sweaty palms on her slacks.

The suited gentleman laid a folder on the table. "Let me introduce myself. Samuel Guidry, Public Defender's Office."

Aria's forehead and nostril muscles tightened. Her stretched lips prevented even the weakest verbal response.

After the prison guard flexed his shoulders, he asked, "What's the big deal here? Saw the warrant. Proper signatures affixed. Don't you mess with the law and try to bar me from driving her to the woman's prison."

"Investigator Breaux outside provides a different, if not interesting perspective."

"So? What y'all gonna do now?"

"You protest keeping the sheriff informed?"

The guard's flummoxed expression raised Aria's internal hope for an abrupt and positive outcome. "Well, no."

"Be civil while I approach the sheriff." He smiled at Aria. "I'll plan to return with him and Mr. Breaux."

With her memories activated, Aria clenched her teeth. Ever since LeRoy's knock on her bedroom door that morning, her day had twirled from her silent "ain't interested," to learning her mother devised money at a bank, to physical threats, to being weird, to locking prison gates.

The prison guard cracked his knuckles. With a visual reluctance, Aria didn't take the bait to admonish, join in, or ask the guard to check his wrist for the time.

When a stoic Mr. Guidry re-entered the windowless room, Aria shivered amid the suspended humidity that oppressed her breathing. *Where was the sheriff, Mr. Breaux?*

"Sheriff will be here shortly." Mr. Guidry stepped to the door where his foot prevented its closure. A white-shirted uniformed man and Mr. Breaux entered. Five persons and four chairs presented an immediate conflict, solved when the prison guard relinquished his chair and stood aside.

Mr. Breaux sat next to Aria, opposite Mr. Guidry and the man Mr. Guidry introduced as Sheriff Fontenot.

"If I may explain," Mr. Breaux began. "This picture here, sheriff, is a duplicate crime scene photo never introduced in Aria's original trial." He pushed it across the table. "I draw your attention to the three letters 'A-R-I' on the wall."

The sheriff tapped his right index finger aside the letters. "Does this ebony color mean they're in blood?"

"Yes."

"Written by who?"

"Not Aria, and I say that with certainty, but give me a moment to backtrack about this trial evidence not released to the public defender."

Sheriff Fontenot frowned. "Don't shackle me with past legalities. What's this mean to me today?"

"The scrawled three letters," Mr. Breaux began, "were written over blood splatter."

Aria interrupted, "I didn't write them."

"I know that, but let me emphasize two major points." Mr. Breaux slanted his gaze to the photo. "Number one, when Brad Gleason was attacked, his blood splattered. It's on the wall. Forensics proved the splatter matched his DNA. Thus, there's no dispute the blood splatter was his."

Aria kept silent as Mr. Breaux visually disengaged his gaze from the photo to survey the attendees. None spoke.

"Trouble is the prosecution speculated to the jury that Brad, with his right-hand index finger, wrote the three letters in his own blood to incriminate his recent bride. No way. And that brings up point number two. His family and friends substantiate, without exception, his left-handedness. Are you still with me? If not, speak up, even if challenging my facts."

He again scanned the three seated men before he lifted his penetrating gaze to the standing prison guard. Silence.

Mr. Breaux reaffirmed no challenge. "Then we can all accept the forensic technician's finding that no blood soiled the victim's left-hand finger pads."

"Not so simple," Sheriff Fontenot interposed. "The victim didn't have to use his dominate left hand if he lay with his right hand nearer the wall?"

A smile exposed Mr. Breaux's upper teeth. "True, except the letters in blood were written over dried splatter, not fresh victim blood. Thus, when enough time had passed to allow the splatter to dry, the victim, i.e. Brad Gleason, would've been dead and unable to write with either hand. If that's double proof, so be it, that's our immutable scientific fact."

Aria squirmed in her chair. This prison guard won't nod or say he believes what her mother's investigator presents. That's how prison worked. Both men and women guards yelled, "Stop lying." They never believed you. Even if you screamed in pain, they never admitted they were hurting you.

"That may be true, but it's the past," Sheriff Fontenot said. "I've got a warrant. That's my reality."

"Let me step in," Mr. Guidry said. "It's a PT warrant."

Sheriff Fontenot blinked in frustration. "We handle these every week. Looks good to me."

The prison guard angled toward the door. "I'll take her."

Aria swallowed hard.

"Isn't," the public defender continued. "It's a PT or prisoner transfer warrant. State paroled Ms. Gleason last week. It's not a bench warrant signed by a judge."

The sheriff jumped to his feet. "Excuse me. If we paid that bounty hunter, he's hoodwinked us."

"Wouldn't worry about that," Mr. Breaux said. "If he wants to keep his license, I'm sure he'll cooperate. Come, Aria. I'm sure it will delight your aunt to see you."

The guard mumbled, "This isn't the end. I'm sure."

Chapter Eleven

Aunt Maggie struggled to clasp Aria's shoulders. Tears glistened her aunt's cheeks. "Fear filled me, Aria. So deep, it truly horrified me I'd sent you to prison."

"I'm here." Aria's shoulders sensed an eased pressure from Aunt Maggie's fingertips.

In a room decorated with law enforcement badges that served as the county jail's visitor reception, Aria tried not to break her aunt's loosened embrace as she cocked her head left and right. While Mr. Breaux braced himself against a reception wall to make a cell phone call, Aria asked, "Where's Tillie?"

Aunt Maggie's right hand released its grip to smear tears across her cheek. "She went with LeRoy to find po'boys since we had no wait time idea. They should be here soon."

Two minutes later, Tillie dashed into reception before LeRoy sauntered in holding two flap-folded paper bags.

Tillie skipped up to Aria and squeezed Aria tight against her shoulders. LeRoy, six feet away, mimicked a wallflower.

Mr. Breaux strode within an arm's length of Aria, Tillie and Aunt Maggie. "Coast looks clear," he said. "Might not be this afternoon if that bounty hunter retraces his steps." A sheepish smile creased his mouth's corners. "Sorry, bad pun. Still, if he doesn't reappear, the woods are still full of skip tracers."

Aria, free of Aunt Maggie's and Tillie's embrace, rubbed her temples. Jumbled expectations and perpetual turmoil vied for dominance with an unfulfilled longing for inner peace. Her plaintive voice eked out a semi-coherent question. "But you said the bounty hunter's warrant wasn't good, and the sheriff believed you."

Mr. Breaux bent close to her right ear. In a hush he said, "Little bluff, but don't you worry none. While I reckon the state didn't strike that PT warrant from the fugitive database, those eager for cash will led astray by your Chicago train ticket. Let's not plant a worry where none lives."

LeRoy's voice overpowered the whisper. "Food's getting cold, ladies." He pointed a right hand toward the parking lot.

Slow to evaporate, perspiration glazed Aria's skin pores. Although internal anxiety slicked her forearms, she refused to lift her top's hem to wipe her dermis skin's sweat glands and its minute hair follicles. Aria longed to escape the jail's compacted air and celebrate an outside fragrance.

She cracked the reception's exit door, sucked in the cool breeze and swung it wide for Aunt Maggie's wheelchair. Her sidestep allowed Tillie to push Aunt Maggie outside.

LeRoy jogged past Aria to station himself at his sedan's rear passenger door.

Aria glanced left to notice Mr. Breaux stride toward a second vehicle. *We can't split up. Where's he going?*

Before Aria said a word, Aunt Maggie yelled, "Who should go with you?"

"Aria can," he replied.

"Go, dear."

LeRoy extended a food bag. "Take this."

Without a quibble, Aria relieved LeRoy of one food bag and slid into Mr. Breaux's front seat. She peeked into the bag, gazed left and asked if he wished a burger.

"Later. We don't have far to go."

Aria fumbled for the exact response as she tried to reassert a semblance of control in what was happening to her. The bounty hunter had thrown her off kilter. She asked her sixty-four dollar question, "Where are we going?"

"Where we should've already been." Mr. Breaux blew out a deep inhale. "It's why your aunt engaged my services. She sought your mother's funds, i.e., her savings account."

"Oh."

As two-lane roads and scrub pine trees blurred into a panorama defined by decrepit shacks and well-to-do homes with irrigated grass interspersed between mobile home clusters landscaped by rock pebbles, flowered pots, tiki torches, wooden decks and/or concrete patios, Aria remained clueless as to their destination.

She dug into the bag LeRoy gave her to clasp a burger. Not her favorite lunch, but it'd satisfy her budding hunger. She ignored the three-sided box with fries.

Mr. Breaux slowed.

"We lose LeRoy?" Aria asked.

"No. Mind distracted. Needed to see a sign."

Aria swiveled her head. She saw no vertical post or billboard. "What sign? If I knew what you sought."

"Mountain bike trail. We'll see a legendry partner from days past: Deputy Cletus."

Aria's mind whizzed past mountain bikes and law enforcement. "He famous."

"Golly, yes. According to legend, best bomb hunting dog this state's ever seen. When he died, they marked his grave alongside a mountain bike trail with a marble headstone."

"Cletus doesn't seem to be a proper name for a dog."

"Never watched 'Dukes of Hazard' have you?"

She diverted her roadside gaze to him. "Huh?"

"Can only relay what the cypress whispers. This canine Cletus picked up the TV-character moniker of a deputy verbally accosted by Sheriff Coltrane. Never abused to my knowledge, but Deputy Cletus descended from a lineage that sniffed out bombs planted for freedom riders."

"Sounds important."

"Decades ago, maybe. Today, just subtle praise when I scratch behind the ears of Jeremiah Prudhomme's dog."

"That's a famous chef, right?"

"No relation. He's a banker."

Aria swallowed her last burger bite. "Then how long until we get there?"

"Five minutes. Town's just ahead."

Her lifted gaze confirmed civilization when Mr. Breaux angled into an unmetered parking stall. Before her, the rectangular four-story State Bank of Henderson. Its non-descript reddish brick with larger sandstone block columns left Aria unimpressed. No citizens lined up outside its single white door entrance. One woman scurried past.

"We need to wait for Miss Maggie," Mr. Breaux said.

"I'll go help Tillie." Aria glanced left. "That okay?"

"Absolutely. We've missed our appointment, but let's assume no one called Mr. Prudhomme away."

Sunrays warmed Aria's back. A self-protective Tillie refused to relinquish her duty to guide Aunt Maggie into the bank.

LeRoy toddled behind. Mr. Breaux pointed him, along with Tillie, to a far lobby window. Without chairs or a bench, both remained standing. LeRoy leaned on a courtesy counter.

Mr. Breaux approached a door to the left of the two teller windows and knocked. A buzzer rang before a woman appeared. She smiled. Aria couldn't see what Mr. Breaux said, but he turned and motioned for her to push Aunt Maggie through the door.

The door's latch clunked when the entrance door behind Aria closed. In opposite corners above her, two surveillance cameras pointed at her head. She assumed their lenses wide enough to monitor Mr. Breaux, Aunt Maggie, her and whoever else entered the room.

A voice boomed, "Mr. Breaux, how pleasant to see you."

Aria's head jerked upward. No speaker box or person visible. Audio waves hadn't carried the baritone voice from the cameras to invade her ears. She assumed the surveillance cameras transmitted their entry to a monitor elsewhere in the bank.

"You, too," Mr. Breaux replied. He twitched his gaze left and right. "Sorry we're late. Unfortunate delay, but we're all here. Let's begin."

A doorknob squeak alerted Aria to the interior door across the room. Aria watched, unable to avert her eyes. Subtle noise detection had been vital to her prison safety.

She squeezed her left ear lobe. Muted and muffled voices beyond the paneled boardroom they entered spooked her nerves. Aunt Maggie compressed Aria's right-hand fingers. Aria believed her aunt's effort to steady the squeamishness both felt.

Aria flicked her gaze to the suited gentleman who entered beyond at the end of a centered mahogany table while he blocked her insight as to what created the low buzz in a wall speaker. He didn't affix his gaze onto her.

"Mr. Breaux, your acquaintance again my pleasure."

Aria detected an ageless steadiness in the man's eyes that contrasted with the shake in his extended right hand. His left elbow clamped a portfolio to his slender torso. "Expected three, including yourself." He retracted his right hand. "There's to be a split?"

"Not necessary," Mr. Breaux replied. He turned to Aria and her aunt and introduced Mr. Jeremiah Prudhomme.

Aria, while exhausted, forced herself to take in the transaction before her. Why her mother crafted her scheme in secret murky to Aria. She listened as memories of the day behind bars when she read of her mother's death flickered deep within her heart.

"There's but one beneficiary . . . daughter Aria Gleason, her married name, although she's a widow."

Aria cringed at the word "widow."

Mr. Breaux waved to Aria. "Step forward."

With one step, she complied with Mr. Breaux's instruction, thankful she wasn't required to shake hands.

"Please be seated. Anywhere fine." Mr. Prudhomme's right hand pulled the portfolio from his left side and seated himself. "I've listed the account assets. There's two accounts. One is a mutual fund, and the second is a cash account." He centered his gaze on Aria. "The share dividends plus any value disbursement are currently blocked."

"What?" Mr. Breaux exclaimed.

Mr. Prudhomme's left hand rubbed his chin. "There's a stated requirement of good moral character and, while I don't wish to be mean, a criminal conviction bars distribution."

"But I didn't do it," Aria blurted out.

"Shush, dear," Aunt Maggie said. "I'm sure Mr. Prudhomme doesn't wish to steal your mother's money."

"This bank has been without blemish and scrupulous in protecting depositor money since my great grandfather."

"Can I or Ms. Gleason contact the investment administrator involved?" Mr. Breaux asked.

"You could. It'd be futile as the account creator imposed the share restrictions."

"I'm confused," Aunt Maggie jumped in. "Why would my sister chose your bank? She's never said she has family or other roots in these parts."

"Hearsay is she became attached to a gentleman from here who traveled to Chicago and Houston to sell his idea to speed the manufacture of oil drilling pipe. Didn't quite happen, I'm told, but he re-engineered his design at Moss Point's chemical complex to devise a safer container and filling method to ship resins and adhesives."

"Explains a hunk of nothing," Aunt Maggie murmured.

Afraid to ask, Aria whispered, "What?"

"No proof, dear. Yet, makes sense that when your mother disappeared for days after her diagnosis it wasn't because she fought depression. She lied that hiking gave her a thrill to live life to its fullest."

"She mention Deputy Cletus?" Aria asked.

A curious expression evaporated the tension in Aunt Maggie's lips. "You know him? Or did your mother mention him to you, too?"

"Never."

"Hush now, child. I need to learn more."

Aunt Maggie waved her left hand to command the room's attention. "Mr. Prudhomme, if I may be so brazen."

Aria cringed a second time. Her aunt's intrusion, even if legitimate and well-meaning, definitely abutted rudeness. Family kindness throttled Aria to hold her tongue.

"Yes, ma'am. Please rest your hand. You have my undivided attention." Mr. Prudhomme closed his portfolio.

"Sir, please return to this fund prohibition based on morals. You saying it's ironclad against a person?"

"Not exactly."

Mr. Breaux leaned forward. "Is that a dodge?"

"My dear sir, no bamboozle or dodge when the written words clear." Mr. Prudhomme opened his portfolio. "Trust me while I read aloud. Paragraph four. 'My daughter shall not inherit any shares if a court shall convict her of crimes against a person or crimes involving moral turpitude.' It then goes on, 'should my daughter give birth to a child, then this child or children shall inherit all shares to which my daughter eligible.' That's the guidance given the bank and what we must follow."

"No conditions on the cash?"

"Correct, Mr. Breaux."

"What if this child died?" Aunt Maggie asked.

Aria dropped to her face to her hands.

"That's not a bank decision, I'd say."

"Why didn't mother tell me?" Aria muttered to herself.

"Dear," Aunt Maggie interjected, "that's not important if we don't have the wherewithal to go ahead." Without removing her hands from her face, Aria nodded. "Mr. Prudhomme, this cash. What we looking at?"

"With accrued interest, $10,321.56."

Aria raised her head. She'd not expected a cent.

"Does Aria need to sign anything?" Mr. Breaux asked.

Mr. Prudhomme nodded. "A receipt, if I see documentation that she's who you say she is."

Mr. Breaux pulled papers from his inner jacket pocket. "Here's a birth certificate and a death certificate proving Mr. Brad Gleason retains no derivative claim. That sufficient?"

"Seems so."

Aunt Maggie leaned forward. "I've a family bible that supports Mr. Breaux's documents."

"Excellent," Mr. Prudhomme replied. "We in this part of the country trust bibles more so than the British."

There was a rap on the door. Mr. Breaux welcomed a frantic Tillie. "That, that black car just raced past. Think it did a donut at the far intersection."

Panic spread from Mr. Breaux's forehead to Aria and Aunt Maggie. "Mr. Prudhomme, will you allow these ladies to stay here undisturbed until LeRoy and I return?"

"Certainly."

Mr. Breaux bent his face to Aria's right ear. "We'll let this car chase LeRoy and I and return in thirty minutes if no longer followed."

Aria didn't wish to be quarantined in unknown quarters. She relented when it fostered Aunt Maggie's safety.

She and Tillie sat on either side of Aunt Maggie's wheelchair. Two doors closed behind them.

When Mr. Prudhomme excused himself, Aria refused to breathe a sigh of relief.

She'd been promised money, although none had been placed in her hand. She'd never known her mother to be financially smart. The words read to Aria could've been contrived. She gazed at Aunt Maggie.

"Did mother ever hint to you she'd stashed a fortune?"

"No dear."

"What about a fellow in Louisiana?"

"No dear."

"Then, aren't you suspicious that the only money personally connected to me is the reward for my capture?"

"You can't think that way, dear."

"Why not?"

"Your mother trusted Mr. Breaux as an honest man. And there's no bonus benefit to him if you get incarcerated."

"Is that what he told you?"

"Dear, don't get emotional. It's what he and I agreed to, and it's in writing." She patted Aria's hand. "I can appreciate your skepticism. In your life you don't trust anyone."

Chapter Twelve

A muffled vehicle backfire drew Aria to the nearest boardroom window. Main Street pedestrians lined the far sidewalk. A military squad raised rifles toward the bank.

Aria pivoted, braced her shoulder blades against the rough brick wall and hugged herself.

"Duck, Tillie," Aria shouted.

Tillie swung Aunt Maggie and her wheelchair right.

Aria's second peek counted four foreboding black vehicles creeping to the right, led by a horse-drawn carriage a half-block ahead.

After the first SUV passed Aria's viewpoint, sparkles glinted off its rear bumper and tinted rear window. While bright sunlight created dark shadows, each vehicle's headlights on high beam illuminated no pavement.

"Turn me, Tillie," Aunt Maggie commanded, her voice strong and demanding. "To the window . . . now!"

Aria's audible gasp didn't stop Tillie. Aria's abs continued to tingle after she compressed them.

Her wheelchair redirected, Aunt Maggie strained to press her nose against the thin window glass. Her face unprotected from the street-projectile threat Aria perceived.

"We should say a prayer," Aunt Maggie said.

A throat lump momentarily gagged Aria. "What?"

"Lit headlights say funeral procession."

"We're safe then?" Tillie asked.

Aunt Maggie nodded.

Aria let her shoulders slump. "Can't believe Mr. Breaux and LeRoy chased cars to a cemetery."

"Maybe he wished to keep you scared," Tillie replied.

Aria, powerless to grasp Tillie's vague inference, twisted from her friend's gaze rather than chastise Tillie for her initial hysterical panic rush. After a heavy sigh, Aria faced Tillie. "We . . . I need to take control."

A frown distorted Tillie's smile. "What?"

"Take control." Aria inhaled. "We can't be overheated horses on too long a gallop. My mother hinted at something." Aria inhaled twice, the second stronger. "Damn."

"What do you mean?" Tillie asked.

"Suspect it's related to Brad," Aunt Maggie interjected.

"Doubt it," Aria said. "Mother didn't fawn over him."

"Seems to me he was a necessary cog to create this grandchild your mother craved or envisioned."

"Yeah. But mother was aware he died before she did."

Tillie breathed deep. "When did your mother create her inheritance? That could be key."

"Don't know. Guess mother didn't trust me."

"Stop it, dear," Aunt Maggie interjected. "She loved you, loved you with all her heart."

Aria pivoted toward her aunt. "If she did, then why this moral behavior clause. She always blabbered to me I didn't have a wicked bone in my body."

"Maybe not her idea. Ever think of that?"

"No."

"Way I look at it. She gave you her money, no strings. As to the mutual fund, she may have been manipulated or under another's thumb. Way I see it, she's the pawn of a controlling Romeo. Speculate he's a Southern Baptist who detests Sodom and Gomorrah."

"Baptist? In Louisiana?"

"Don't you nettle me, dear? I can be sarcastic." Her wayward glance not responded to. "I know Roman Catholic's rule this state, but they're not almighty or invincible. Neither am I oblivious to the world because I'm stuck as I am every waking hour in this rolling metal contraption."

"But you've been my rock. The only person who's expressed a steadfast belief in me."

"Always will, but you don't need me to upend your deep-seated quest."

"You mean mother's money?"

"Money's never been your pivotal point or, say, end-all. I've known you, even if from afar. Your unwavering integrity and your steadfast dedication to what you've desired to be."

"You think what then?"

"Doesn't matter what I think. It's your life. You need to conform life into what you desire."

"Hasn't worked so far."

"Trash every doubt, even little ones."

Aria stared across the street. The car-procession dust settled. If life beyond the window static, next-step doubts filled her cranial voids to freeze her physical movement.

"The world won't wait for you, Aria," Aunt Maggie said.

Mr. Breaux and LeRoy's unexplained absence dampened what little enthusiasm trickled through her veins. The soft squeak of rubber wheels insufficient to break into Aria's lethargy until Aunt Maggie shouted, "Come along, dear."

Tillie's left arm delayed the boardroom door's closing.

Aria, her last sneaker step squeaking, pointed her sneaker toes outside Aunt Maggie's wheelchair perimeter.

Contrary to Aria's wildest, unsubstantiated fear, no evil guys sprayed bullets into the lobby door or stood in the street with revolvers cocked and/or shotguns loaded.

The military honor guard had vanished.

LeRoy, his face glum, hopped out of Mr. Breaux's car.

Elbows pinned to his sides, he gestured with his hands displayed palms up. He hesitated, yet didn't advance to embrace either Tillie or Aria.

"We lost them."

Aria, relieved her fears hadn't parlayed reality, advanced to shoot a glance at Tillie. Neither questioned LeRoy.

The silence interrupted when Aunt Maggie asked the question uppermost in Aria's mind.

"Who?"

Chapter Thirteen

Aria alighted from Mr. Breaux's car and scanned the parking area left and right for black SUVs and tricked-out pickups of any color. The cardboard "closed" sign on his office door frustrated her expected dash to protect safety.

"Wait," Mr. Breaux shouted. With an aggravated vocalized slowness he added a plaintive, "Please."

While her right sneaker pawed gravel, the soft crunch of Mr. Breaux's saunter toward his car's trunk jerked her gaze to a head sliced from a body by his vehicle's roofline. As her gaze followed a rearward trajectory, an uplifted trunk lid edge exposed right hand knuckles before the lid obscured both Mr. Breaux's head and his right hand.

This physical separation forced Aria's mind into parallel universes. The kaleidoscope of horrific in-prison bloodshot corneas, black-eye sockets and weepy red skin rashes. Horrified, she exited to crossover into a hall of mirrors where a distorted, fearful woman bathed in red light collapsed, body and soul, before bleeding into eternity. The latter jumped into fearful reality when a trunk lid slam displayed Mr. Breaux's left hand grasping a zippered, rigid rifle/shotgun case.

Aria stiffened. Her gaze frozen on the case as it swung in cadence with his four steps toward her. No perceived harmony mollified her apprehension, where in her teens Chicago gangs never transported firearms in zippered cases. What bayou country importance did a displayed weapon's case hold for her? She slowed her breathing.

Her try to measure time counted five, then ten seconds before she stumbled at sixty and forsook her effort. As she forced her lung muscles to inhale, Aria's easily scanned the thirty yards of barren gravel behind Mr. Breaux. LeRoy's Buick's skid unleashed a dust cloud that delayed Tillie and Aunt Maggie's exit.

Without fanfare or waiting for his passengers to alight, LeRoy strode toward Mr. Breaux.

"Either of you hunt?" Mr. Breaux asked.

"Never," Aria said.

"No," LeRoy chimed in. "Excuse me." An even smile broadened his lips. "I should rescue my passengers."

Then with a cautious nod, Aria accepted Mr. Breaux's gentlemanly offer for her to follow him to his office door. He keyed the door lock, and she stepped inside.

Two women Aria presumed to be employees scurried through an interior floor-to-ceiling partition door. What did their lush breasts and slim waists add to private investigation? She chided her Tillie-inspired imagination as musty air particles invaded her nostrils. Stifling a cough, Aria grasped the wooden arm of the closest chair to prevent her slipshod collapse.

She stared toward the still open front door. "Still can't understand, Mr. Breaux, why won't you be specific on who threatens me?"

His eyes roamed her face.

In a Victorian defense to his lowered gaze, but not to blunt a physical attack, a seated Aria crossed her arms across her chest. *Can't rival the goddesses he's hired.*

During their motorized trip from the county jail, he'd evaded her repeated questions of who did he believe wished her dead. At the least, she'd suspected he withheld potential assailants to enhance his continued payment by her or Aunt Maggie since Aria hadn't inherited full value. He'd obviously harbored suspicions, founded on what she didn't know. She'd quiz Aunt Maggie.

In front of the coffee table between them, Mr. Breaux hesitated his to and fro pacing before he turned a table corner to be within an arm's length of her.

"How can I?" Mr. Breaux asked. "Any bounty hunter in this state, as has happened once already, could misinterpret that warrant with your name on it."

Distracted by LeRoy's outside shouts he'd get the wheelchair, Aria delayed a seated ninety-degree body twist until after she mumbled, "Know that."

LeRoy burst into the office. His soles squeaked against the gray tile. Without lifting them, he twisted toward the door, grabbed its knob and announced, "Tillie and Aunt Maggie here, safe and sound."

Aria shook her head.

"Don't doubt my driving."

"Wasn't," Aria replied. "You followed?"

He bowed. "With my Chicago smarts? Never."

Aunt Maggie rolled in, pushed by Tillie. The rider's droopy head sent a signal that travel or stress weighed heavy.

Aria spoke first. "We need to make a decision."

Aunt Maggie squared her jaw. "Ain't going back."

"Auntie, don't force me to be contrary." Aria squared her shoulders. Tillie's frown tightened.

"What's this?" Mr. Breaux asked.

"Minor family squabble," Tillie said.

"Not so," Aria shot back. She stared at Mr. Breaux. "I'm on Aunt Maggie's side, but I need to continue on. However, that executor, or whatever his position was . . . wasn't generous, now was he?"

"He's restricted by law and your mother's wishes."

"What about justice, family needs?"

Mr. Breaux shook his head. "Being argumentative won't get you anywhere unless you have documents or recorded conversations with your mother."

A stymied Aria refused to admit or deny her mother had left such mementoes.

"Let's go get the truth," chimed in LeRoy. "I'll drive."

"Hold on, everyone," Aunt Maggie said. "I wasn't referencing the bank guy. I meant Harmony Square."

"Oh." Aria sighed before she collected her wits. "We, or I specifically, need to decide on what to do next." While her spoken words solicited advice, Aria calculated the $10,000 Godsend she now possessed placed a ceiling on her options.

"Get those shares," Aunt Maggie urged. "They're yours."

"She can't steal them," Tillie said.

"Why not?" LeRoy asked.

"She'd be committing a felony," Mr. Breaux interjected.

The room fell silent.

Aria refused to activate her prison memories although, at times, she'd little choice. Aria fidgeted. She needed to grasp reality and dispense with tremors rooted in fear. Her sitting signaled complacency. She stood. *Now what?*

Silence continued to permeate the room. Hapless and misaligned molecules that escaped from the pedestrian furniture siphoned moisture from Aria's throat with each breath. At her feet, the mundane flooring dulled distorted light streaks. At least an opaque partition and door saved LeRoy from distraction by the hourglass office staff.

"Let's go eat," LeRoy suggested.

"Right," Aunt Maggie responded before anyone else spoke. She tried to swivel her chair toward the door, failed.

"Not now," said Aria.

Aunt Maggie's trembling lips steadied into a pout to join Tillie's frown.

Aria's chest tightened. She needed to swallow a chill pill for she'd flounder without allies. "Please, hear me out." Heads nodded. "You've all been great, but there comes a point when I can't burden you."

"Come now, Aria," Aunt Maggie said. "Be specific."

"Those shares. Mother couldn't have known I was pregnant; yet, she built a wall around those shares. Who knows what crazy dream or fanciful advice she succumbed to before she signed on the dotted line."

"How's this going to work?" Tillie asked. "You can't drive. Remember?"

Aunt Maggie nodded.

"I'll stay here with LeRoy. We can drop you and Aunt Maggie at the Amtrak station, catch the City of New Orleans headed north to Chicago."

Aunt Maggie rocked her wheelchair. "Said before, ain't going back. Now that's definite."

"Please, Aunt Maggie. Tillie's been away from work. She deserves to keep her job."

"Tillie?"

"If it's a week, I'll convince my roommates she can stay at my place." She stared at Aria. "Promise. Cross your heart and pray to God."

LeRoy chuckled. "That's stupid."

Tillie glared at him.

"Well, not stupid, maybe . . . just forget I said anything." He smiled at Aria. "You'll be in excellent hands."

"Now we're into commercials," Tillie mumbled. Her right hand partially covered her lips.

Aria shook her head. She wasn't going to answer a rhetorical comment, question or not, nor ignite a fight when the underlying breakup tensions simmered.

She rose and angled her deliberately slow steps to Aunt Maggie, where her aunt's bowed head didn't deter.

"Thank you, Aunt Maggie. A week, no longer. I promise. You'll love Wrigleyville. Tillie's a wonderful hostess."

Aunt Maggie lifted her chin. "Your mother created something I can't explain. She never mentioned this before her untimely death."

"Maybe in a letter? A message or instruction scribbled on the reverse side of a notecard she used for recipes?"

"Dear, even if she did, I can't recall it now."

LeRoy grabbed Aunt Maggie's wheelchair handles. "Then, it's time for pizza. There's an empty rental house that awaits us."

Aria gazed at Mr. Breaux.

"Don't worry about me," he said. "Call me in the morning. We'll meet up. I have an idea better left until tomorrow."

Chapter Fourteen

Tears accented Aria's hugs of Tillie and Aunt Maggie as the three huddled on the Mount Rose train station platform to say good-bye for a week. An hour earlier, Aria had treated them to Waffle House breakfasts.

To her left, LeRoy rolled two suitcases with an overnight bag slung over his shoulder to a waiting baggage cart.

"I fear you'll die in this state," Aunt Maggie whispered into her right ear.

"No, auntie. I'll be at Tillie's in a week with enormous hugs for you and her." Aria turned towards Tillie. "I'll keep you informed and you'll pass it on, wouldn't you?"

"Buy yourself a Top-Up cell phone. They're in marts, other stores. Then call me so I'll have your number."

Like a forlorn whistle blown alongside one's head, an air horn blast jumbled the still morning air. A faint, then louder, train-wheel rumble announced the City of New Orleans. Aria glanced south to watch its advancing cow-catcher pass a side-tracked coal drag, the latter she'd seen on trips to Ford City Mall, near the Southwest Chicago rail yards.

LeRoy offered a shoulder embrace to a reluctant Tillie and a check-to-cheek hug to an accepting Aunt Maggie.

A uniformed conductor shouted, "All Aboard."

Aria folded Aunt Maggie's wheelchair as Tillie's hands on Aunt Maggie's waist empowered feeble legs to ascend one step at a time.

Tillie, with the same right hand, offered her last wave and hoisted the wheelchair into the Pullman car.

"We going?" LeRoy asked.

"In a sec," mumbled Aria. She hadn't fully grasped that Mr. Breaux's brainstorm required her to be alone with LeRoy, in his car no less.

With the train's flashing last car device dim in the distance, Aria suggested LeRoy lead the way to his car. Buckled in, she directed him into the Petrus True Value.

Aria read several mobile phone info cards until LeRoy excused himself to visit the restroom. When he'd cleared the aisle's endcap, she grabbed the cheapest cell phone and a pocket pepper spray canister at the checkout.

"Y'all find everything?" the cashier asked.

"Yes'um." Aria's cheeks warmed. "Meant yes, ma'am."

"Awesome."

Aria, without counting, stashed her change into her front jeans pocket. She decided not to search for LeRoy, it being awkward to stand outside the men's room. Past the automatic exit door, she paced in the parking lot's humid air.

"Nice store," LeRoy said. "You get your phone?"

Aria nodded.

"Better activate it before we drive off."

"Huh?"

"Ain't driving you back if it don't work."

"Sorry." Aria placed the service plan card on her left thigh to fumble with the phone's plastic packaging. After biting a corner, it allowed her to pop out the phone.

"Give me that card." He reached into his front pocket. "I've a nickel to scratch and reveal the pin code."

Aria's left-hand fingers secured the card and extended it to LeRoy. LeRoy scratched. "You ready?"

Aria nodded and, as LeRoy read the sixteen digits, she pressed screen digits into the service authorization box. After

LeRoy said "that's all" her sense of accomplishment rallied when a home screen menu appeared. "I'll call Tillie."

"Doubt you'll get her on the train."

"Voice mail will deliver this phone's number."

LeRoy smiled. "Always knew you to be intelligent."

The flattery, like duct tape, glued itself across her mouth, ready to induce suffocation. Prison flattery carried undercurrents of future abuse. Her soles still sported visible scars, although faded, while the invisible aftermath populated her cranial recesses ready to spume nightmares.

"Okay," LeRoy said. "If I overstepped, my bad."

"No, no," Aria lied. "This phone bell distracted me."

"You've received a message? That's quick."

"Asks me to buy more minutes. Let's go."

"You anxious what Mr. Breaux might say?"

Aria reached for the passenger door handle. "Sorta."

"Hop in and hold on."

When LeRoy clicked his driver's seatbelt, Aria permitted herself an elongated silent exhale. For him to unbuckle provided her a moment to escape. Her exhilaration short-lived when he reminded her to buckle up. She did; her fingers poised to release the belt's engaged steel tongue.

The morning drive to Mount Rose had been less than thirty minutes, add ten to arrive at Mr. Breaux's office and Aria's blood pressure could rebound to normal. She gazed at non-descript buildings and unimpressive fields, uncertain if planted with rice, eggplant or soybean. She sighed. No postcard printed with what she observed.

"Wow," LeRoy exclaimed.

Aria couldn't resist. "What?"

"Eros." LeRoy smiled at her. "Five miles left."

Was the god Greek or Roman? Aria's brain stalled, except to be certain she objected. "Don't care. No turn."

LeRoy's raised cheeks and lowered brows telegraphed he'd taken offense. "We're on a mission. Don't you remember Elwood speeding on Lower Wacker?"

"You may be right about a mission, but Elwood said in the movie he and Jake were on a mission from God. Eros is a mythological Greek god. No comparison."

LeRoy slowed.

Aria pinched her ear lobe.

"If Roman mythology is your preference, Cupid is the Greek god counterpart."

"Maybe another day."

LeRoy smiled. "It'll be my pleasure."

Aria swallowed hard. Why hadn't she offered to rent a car and have LeRoy drive Aunt Maggie to Chicago? She knew why☐to conserve expenses paramount.

Her pragmatic mind whizzed ahead. What did Mr. Breaux think? Why hadn't he spilled it?

The car swerved right.

"What the hell?" Aria rubbed her right shoulder after the stretched harness restraint relaxed.

"Over-reacted. Cardboard box on the roadway. Didn't want to hit it. No time to yell. Sorry."

"Glad you didn't flip a one-eighty and head left." The word "Eros" also unsaid. Nothing untoward had happened this morning and all would be awesome if they arrived at Mr. Breaux's office in due course.

* * *

The "Open" sign on Mr. Breaux's office door radiated an invisible positive karma stream into Aria's heart.

Followed by LeRoy, she didn't knock. Once inside, her "Mr. Breaux" shout vibrated ceiling to office perimeter.

Within seconds, the partition door in front of Aria creaked, and the summoned man strode through the portal to encourage his two visitors: "Please, please be seated."

Aria plopped into a chair among the showroom discards, two removed from LeRoy. She anticipated Mr. Breaux's promise to be a life-changing wonder. Aria focused on his eyes, ready to be enlightened.

"Aria, you remember that muscular man at the jail?"

"Yeah, sorta."

"Well, an overheard hallway quip claimed that this guy filled in as a state prison guard. Stopped me cold. First, didn't believe the state hired bounty hunters. Then asked who he be related to because his job certain to be politically connected. Third, surprised when told he recognized you."

"Possible." She'd never deny her release day's events were exhilarating, yet she never remembered every detail. "Yeah, a prison guard with uniform buttons ready to burst instructed me to move on. He didn't push."

"What about his voice?"

"Who's voice?"

"The prison guard and the jail's hefty guy? Did their voices seem to be the same?"

"Accents close, but so what?"

"We'll call on the guy."

LeRoy stood. "Today?"

Mr. Breaux rolled his eyes. "Yes. My staff ferreted out a hunting lodge he visits."

"He'll be there?" Aria asked.

"That's the word."

"This mean we'll ride in a boat?"

"Heavens, no. He shoots turkeys. Doesn't hunt gators."

Aria choked off a sigh when LeRoy strode toward the door. "Whatcha doing, LeRoy?"

"Getting the car."

"Hold on," Mr. Breaux said. "I'll drive." He cast a glance to the closed partition door. "Wait out front. I'll be around."

Aria didn't race LeRoy to be first. Upright, she rocked, heels to the balls of her feet. Her stress and weight landed on her right foot.

LeRoy twisted his shoulders toward her. "You know this guy?" Without her reply he asked, "We need a gun?"

"This isn't Chicago, LeRoy. We gotta trust Mr. Breaux."

"Well, so far we've trusted him and you got dragged into a jail. Aunt Maggie, in her wheelchair, collapsed."

85

Aria summoned her courage. She hadn't been told of that, but she still needed to trust someone. Who else but Mr. Breaux? Her brain cells offered no alternative.

When Mr. Breaux's car arrived, she grabbed the rear passenger door handle and ignored a request she sit "shotgun." She'd enjoy the back of LeRoy's head rather than his right profile. As the car barreled through unseen territory, her backseat vantage point allowed her views of a left and right outside-the-car vista.

When Mr. Breaux slowed, Aria narrowed her focus to a towering laurel oak Aunt Maggie had pointed out two days earlier. On other days, the two-person "romantic" swing to the tree's right would've plucked her heart strings. "We stopping?" she asked, her voice volume raised.

"He's supposed to be in that house."

Aria swung her gaze left. The white clapboard one-story house that squatted amid rural pasture didn't impress Aria as a hunting lodge. She'd envisioned two-story ante-bellum pillars fronting a porch that led to double width wooden doors framed by dulled red brickwork, or, at the least, mounted deer or elk antlers.

She accepted the reality before her.

LeRoy, silent, didn't burst from their stopped vehicle.

She'd never known him to be skittish or hold-back reflective. What'd spooked him?

"LeRoy."

"Yeah." He lifted his gaze to her. "What?"

"You up to this?"

"Yeah. It's your deal, isn't it?"

Aria nodded. She assumed Mr. Breaux, his back to her, hadn't witnessed LeRoy's hesitation.

Mr. Breaux pivoted. "Aria, you ready?"

"For what?"

"Talking to the prison guard."

"Guess so. You convinced it'll help me?"

"Show no fear and let's see."

Led by Mr. Breaux, the three marched single file into the smoke-filled hunting lodge, its fireplace unlit.

Not one of the four men seated at a room-centered square table glanced their way. Past one plaid-shirted shoulder Aria couldn't count the chips piled on the table. No player, each with a gaze counting seven cards, reached for the pot.

"Wow," LeRoy said, his voice low. "Talk about the good, the bad and the ugly."

"Sshh," Aria whispered. She gazed past the card players toward the lodge's rear exit.

Right of the room's exit sign, the guard Aria had reluctantly obeyed on her prison release day lounged half-prone, his shoulders supported by the brown Naugahyde sofa's arm. As to LeRoy's voiced assessment of the men they encountered, Aria wouldn't challenge his appraisal.

As Aria edged closer, two steps behind Mr. Breaux, the guard's blue eyes receded deep into suntanned flesh. His thuggish resemblance not camouflaged by a light-blue shirt and black trousers that mimicked a police uniform.

"Excuse me," Mr. Breaux said. He stared direct at the occupied brown sofa.

"Do I know you?"

"Perhaps not, but you might recognize this young lady from yesterday or earlier?"

"Who?" The guard rolled toward the cushion edge until he pushed himself into a seated position at the sofa's center.

"Said, this young lady. Her name's Aria."

"Seen busloads of young ladies, if that answers your question. Prison garb blurs remembering specific faces but doesn't hide outstanding virtues, if you know what I mean."

Mr. Breaux nodded.

The guard extended his arms rearward and stretched them across the sofa's crest rail. "Mind you, not that any wished to tout their charms. So, why should I recognize this one? She have a tattoo?"

Aria shuddered. Her skin puckered. What was visible to others her eyes could not see? Had they branded her?

Mr. Breaux interceded. "Don't play games. Citizens have learned what went on inside the prison that everyone now denies. And, it has led me to information you opted to transfer prison sections. Is that why you visit parish jails?"

LeRoy whispered to Aria, "You know about this?"

Aria placed a finger to her lips. "Sshh."

LeRoy's lips quivered; no utterance passed them.

The guard stared at Mr. Breaux. "Why the hassle?"

"I've been up front."

The guard shook his head. "Doubt you have the slightest idea of the crap guards put up with behind prison walls."

Between the start and end of a ten-second smirk, he flicked his gaze at Aria. "Doubt she remembers the rules or what happened around her day-to-day, and she experienced it first-hand. Your knowledge is, at best, second hand."

Aria tensed. "You jerk." Her raised voice added, "Want me to show you scars." She lifted her left elbow.

From behind, LeRoy clamped his hand on her elbow.

As if a chicken wing aflutter, Aria flapped her elbow to free it from LeRoy's grasp. If her involuntary physical reaction upset LeRoy, she didn't care.

Mr. Breaux's calm, but loud, "Wait!" commanded the guard's attention while the poker players swiveled their heads and held their breaths.

The guard swung his arms to his sides, and, aided by his right hand pressed against the cushion, he rose. His muscular chest stretched his shirt.

"Let's take a step outside," Mr. Breaux said.

"Just you. Two strange ears present enough."

"Whatever." Mr. Breaux halted Aria's advance with an upraised hand. "Hangout with LeRoy. This shouldn't take but a few minutes."

The guard smiled at the poker players. "Don't empty their pockets. Use the unmarked deck."

LeRoy clenched his fists. Aria pulled him aside. "We ain't playing nothing. Watch my back and I'll watch yours."

LeRoy shuffled his feet to place Aria's left shoulder between his shoulder blades. He whispered, "We look rather silly this way, don't we?"

Aria nodded.

The exterior door slammed and Mr. Breaux and the guard were no longer in the hunting cabin.

The absence of expected activity like poker banter, the click of shuffled cards, LeRoy's idle chit-chat, and even the soft sound of her own breathing stole Aria's safety illusion.

Wasn't this a hunting lodge? She'd not checked for weapons. Her quick scan exposed no wall-mounted rifle.

LeRoy's elongated gulp enough to have swallowed life-sustaining oxygen.

Aria laughed, a ghoulish penetration of the room's silence. Reminded her of prison cell experiences. Corridors filled with shrieks, moans and taunts strangely silent. The moments preceded by the thrust of a key into a cell lock and the clang of its door. A muffled scream then preceded the hesitant clomp of guard boots straining to carry a heavy load.

From her own experience, Aria knew well the inmate wasn't being summoned for a family-member visit at three a.m., even if half the guards were matrons.

Aria racked her brain to recall if any guard had been as muscular as the one outside. Had he ogled her stripped of her human dignity? Had he himself flicked the punishment cane, or encouraged others? If he lied, how could she refute if he entered after her blindfolding?

"LeRoy, we must go outside. Now."

"Go for it."

LeRoy beat Aria to the door. The poker players acted oblivious to their flight.

"It's locked," LeRoy said.

"Can't be. It's an exit door. What about a fire?"

"Don't you have a key?" shouted the closest poker player. "We do. What you bid? Pants worth double."

A raucous laughter filled the room.

"Ignore the brutes," LeRoy said. He pounded on the door.

Aria collapsed into a sitting position on the floor. "Ain't no use. We've got to trust Mr. Breaux. Aunt Maggie did."

LeRoy kneeled beside her. "If one of these bastards comes near us, I'll break his jaw."

My hero. Aria left her thought unexpressed.

A nearby chair scrape unnerved her. *What now?*

Chapter Fifteen

The hunting lodge door swung inward. Aria missed seeing the guard or any individual framed within or beyond its doorjambs. Had Mr. Breaux departed . . . or been kidnapped?

A queasy upper abdomen distracted her from charging outside to find Mr. Breaux.

She attributed her chilling forehead perspiration to the poker players who'd block her expected retreat route. Her right-hand fingers grabbed and slipped off LeRoy's arm.

He grimaced without an assist to boost her erect.

A conflicted Aria had hoped for civility, but she didn't wish to mislead LeRoy that a positive relationship lay ahead.

When the guard's shadow crossed the doorway threshold, Aria's shoulders sagged.

A baritone voice to her rear asked, "You need help?"

She rotated her right shoulder for a glimpse of the questioner. A burly poker player she'd not heard sneak up behind her extended his callused right hand.

LeRoy, blocked by the player's torso, sidled two tiny steps left. Aria, unable to see LeRoy's facial expression, ignored his body's repositioning and accepted the card player's offered hand. When Aria's leg muscles stabilized her upright stance, she slid her hand free.

The guard, his right hand in his front pocket, ignored everyone in a march parallel to a restroom arrow.

"Aria," LeRoy pleaded. "Let's get out of here."

"Not now."

"Don't be crazy."

"Ain't. You see, Mr. Breaux? He should be here."

"I am." Mr. Breaux stood at the door. "We're done here."

Aria's glimpse toward the restroom found no one. She twisted her gaze to find LeRoy slow-stepping to a hunting lodge exit, which Aria assumed meant Mr. Breaux awaited her outside.

"Darling, where are you going?"

"Huh." Aria stared at the card player who'd offered his courtesy to her. "Got to get my ride."

The player smiled. "I've a tricked-out truck."

"How 'bout next time?"

His frown gave Aria her answer without words.

She scurried toward the door, almost tripping on LeRoy's heels. She steadied herself and swallowed a big gulp of outside air before she sought to locate Mr. Breaux.

He stood next to his vehicle's driver door. "Let's go."

Aria's inner voice told her to resist until she fully understood what Mr. Breaux and the guard discussed.

LeRoy tugged her right arm. "Take the front seat."

Aria complied, her will to argue or fight subdued, but not surrendered, especially if LeRoy's demand or suggestion.

She clicked her seatbelt after a similar sound came from Mr. Breaux's seat. The engine's roar drowned out her weak question to learn what the guard had said.

"Best we return to my office. Any objection?"

"Can we stop for food?" LeRoy asked.

Aria pressed her abdomen. "Fine, but I'm not hungry."

"No, problem. Hang on."

A bounce against her seatback restrained by her seatbelt didn't assuage Aria's stomach discomfort except to test her urge to vomit. Her closed throat choked off even the slightest chin dribble.

A right-hand armrest grip served Aria well. It steadied her budding nausea while the blurred landscape streaked blue and yellow into green. At the restaurant drive-thru, she limited her request to a vanilla milkshake. With infrequent sips she relaxed and projected an outward appearance of preoccupation to offer excellent reason not to take part in the chitchat between LeRoy and Mr. Breaux.

When the latter parked in front of his office, Aria asked, "You ever going to tell me true what the guard said?"

Mr. Breaux shrugged. "Inside."

Aria allowed LeRoy to be a gentleman and open her passenger door. They followed Mr. Breaux into his office's anterior room.

Not wishing to be chippy, Aria sat, lips sealed, her wrists limp on her knees.

LeRoy faked a dive at the seat next to her before he opted for the chair two seats to Aria's left.

"What can you tell me?" Aria asked.

Mr. Breaux strode past LeRoy with his left hand in his dark-colored suit-coat pocket. "Why don't you both slide forward in case my recording doesn't offer the volume it should?" He balanced a Sony recorder in his left palm.

The beginning scratchiness without audible voices deflated Aria's expectations.

"Don't hear nothing," LeRoy said.

Mr. Breaux frowned. "Hold on."

Aria's neck twitched as the guard's gruff voice invaded the room. She tugged her left ear lobe.

"You can't pin misconduct on me," the guard said.

"Not trying to. Just an understanding. Nothing more," replied Mr. Breaux in a hushed voice. "Not jailing you or anyone. They have hired me to learn the truth, that's all."

Static engulfed the recorder's playback. Mr. Breaux smiled. "That's when I took off my suit coat, draped it across my arm. The move to convince the guard he had to neither search nor pat me down."

Words spoken by the earlier gruff voice blared from the recorder's speaker to spark renewed shivers that arced between Aria's spinal vertebras. She steeled herself to listen.

"Turn around."

Aria flinched until calmed by the knowledge she reacted to a recorded conversation which continued with Mr. Breaux's voice.

"If I played games, you'd not speak to me one-on-one."

"Gris-gris."

Aria jumped up. "Stop the recording."

Mr. Breaux's frown didn't delay his finger's successful STOP button jab. "What?"

"What did that guard threaten? Sounds very much the Voodoo a cellblock inmate spoke."

"Could be reference to an amulet or warding off evil. What do you care? It's just what he said. He's no longer a threat. You're not under his control."

Leroy's ugly, twisted facial contortion offered greater expression than his bland request. "Can we get it on?"

Aria nodded.

Mr. Breaux pressed the recorder's START button. Aria shifted her gaze from the revolving tape reels to stave off her being mesmerized.

Her ears perked up when a recorded Mr. Breaux asked, "Tell me sir about the inmate birth recording."

The guard coughed. "All were recorded as stillborn."

"Even if they weren't?"

"Well, if not stillborn, the prison maintained no ward to care for them."

"And, then what?"

"Guard paid to drop child at secret bayou location where child began journey to adoptive parents willing to pay."

"Had to be expensive."

"What I overheard is that wealthy couples shelled out thousands, guessed to be six figures. Explained the rumors a prison matron owned a five-acre Grand Island chalet."

A seated LeRoy squirmed and muttered, "This is boring. Can't we fast forward?"

"No," Aria said. "Be patient." She pointed to the recording device. "Listen."

"If all prison births recorded as stillborn, then the kept records, if we can find them, will be useless?"

"You're smart."

"So, let's say, my client gave birth. How would I determine if her child lived or died?"

A chuckle crackled the recorder's speaker.

"Wasn't trying to be funny. Let me repeat, how do I find out if my client's baby lived or died?"

"Ask her."

"Don't be coy. You know they injected sedatives into the mother's veins to dull her grasp of reality."

"Check the prison graveyard."

"Don't send me on a wild goose chase. I've walked the graveyard's gravel paths. There's no tombstone name except 'Jane Doe' or a Cajun equivalent."

"Guess no one told you the code. The tombstone's death date is but the inmate's last eight ID numerals."

Aria gasped. Mr. Breaux silenced the recording.

"Are we done yet?" LeRoy asked.

"Not quite," Mr. Breaux said.

"What's that mean?" Aria asked. "The tape looks like it's finished. Or is there another?"

"No. Couldn't change reels in front of the guard. So, you must trust me."

"As to what?" Aria asked.

"While the guard said he'd no first-hand knowledge your baby wasn't stillborn, he assumed it lived because of your transfer into a cellblock near, but outside, his primary patrol."

Aria clutched her chest. In her mental agony, she perceived LeRoy watched her pale in obvious distress.

Mr. Breaux grabbed her shoulders. "Steady now, deep breaths, deep breaths, keep at it, steady does it."

Aria clenched her fists, tapped them together. She blinked her watery blurred vision into hazy doubles where, with embedded survival remembrances, she concentrated her visual energy on the larger image of Mr. Breaux's face.

"Aria, you with us?"

"Think so."

Mr. Breaux released Aria's shoulders.

"What did my cell change mean?"

"Guard didn't really say."

Aria tried to remember. Female guards hadn't given her a kind or non-threatening word, except during or after her march to the infirmary. Even then, by infrequent happenstance, her gaze once caught them subduing their pleasurable smirk in her upcoming misfortune.

She never specifically recalled her infirmary needle injection aftermaths except that her eyes, through eyelid slits, recorded matrons' morph into males, or so she thought without ever ruling out a possible hallucination.

Her breast swelling and diarrhea weren't mirages. Since they didn't last into a second week, she never complained for fear of repercussion.

"Aria, you lost again?" Mr. Breaux asked.

"No. no. Trying to think of another question."

LeRoy squirmed. "Sure that's all? Your eyes flashed a get-even glint."

"Huh?"

"Tillie warned me to back off if I spied it."

Aria didn't wish to lie or shade her friend, so she tried to thread a needle. "Tillie always speaks truth, but sometimes I take what Tillie says with a grain of salt."

Mr. Breaux interrupted. "Aria, can you tell me what's important? If your aunt calls, it would be best if I give her an honest idea of what we're to do."

The surreal frightened Aria as never before. She fought her negative thoughts. Now free from prison, she wouldn't freak out if the sinister again grasped her emotions. From deep within her soul, she summoned the quiet courage to say,

"Let's visit this . . . ." She couldn't translate her mind's tomb marker image into an understandable utterance.

LeRoy leaned nearer. "You mean the cemetery?"

Aria's throat tightened. One word successfully escaped her physical constriction and leaked out. "Yeah."

"Then, let's go." He smiled. "I'll battle the goblins."

"Really?" Her question lacked conviction. She watched Mr. Breaux pace and stop before he stared at her.

"I'm ready." Aria gazed at LeRoy. "You're right, but don't let it go to your head." She switched her gaze to Mr. Breaux. "Can we make it by this afternoon?"

He opened the office door without a rearward gander.

Aria hesitated; her sideways gaze didn't locate LeRoy. What had she missed?

Chapter Sixteen

Three sets of soles, two sets ribbed, zig-zagged to and around religious statues and rows of above-ground corner-rounded graves. Each footwear set scurried within defined cemetery sections in search of the name "baby Gleason."

Aria ignored names. She'd unleash her barricaded tears when she found an eight digit identifier targeted within the four-to-six-year period prior to her prison release.

When behind barred prison windows, the descending sun more-often-than-not ramped up Aria's anxiety. Today's sun rays perspired her skin, yet added zip to her quest success. The yellowish-orange streaks between the two lowest clouds forecasted a gray dusk darkening into a night of vulnerability with no moon as a nightlight. With evanescent hope, she shouted at LeRoy, "You find anything?"

"Nah. We should be outta here sipping endless hurricanes. What do you say?" He filled in Aria's hesitation. "You and me, no chaperone."

"How 'bout we recheck the far graves?" Aria pivoted left and quickstepped forward.

Six feet in front of Aria, Mr. Breaux almost tripped. She gasped, uncertain what invisible force propelled him.

He steadied himself and, seemingly unfazed, fixed his gaze upon Aria. "While you finished your physical grave marker survey, I detoured to check the cemetery's burial log. If it's correct, our search here will be futile."

"You're saying?"

"You'll not find answers here."

LeRoy nudged Aria. "Give it up."

"Never," Aria replied. She stared at Mr. Breaux. "What did we miss?" She didn't wish to say "you" or blame Mr. Breaux, although she'd paid him for success.

"Nothing, I'd say."

"Then that guard lied?"

"Possible."

"But I paid you half of what my mother left me."

"Let's not quibble. I've expended extraordinary effort on your behalf. No one else would've exposed that guard."

"But he must've lied."

"If he did, we'll get him."

"How?"

"Can't explain at the moment. But trust me I'll wring the truth out of him if I have to."

"When?"

"Give me until the morning."

Aria waved LeRoy to stand back. "Guess so."

Mr. Breaux reached into a chest pocket. "Let me make a call and meet me at the cemetery entrance."

Aria nodded.

"We sure this was the cemetery?" LeRoy asked. He jumped backward to sit on an aboveground vault.

Her enthusiasm dampened, Aria nodded. She couldn't explain to LeRoy how the nearby prison vibes penetrated the deepest layer of her soul and revitalized invisible past scars into a reality reel. Hadn't society punished her enough? The creeping dusk whispered no answer.

Aria repeated an enhanced nod to LeRoy. "No question. This cemetery offers no truer path then to Hell's gate."

"You're teasing. Unless you claw through mud."

"Hell, no." Aria's right hand slapped her mouth. "Forget I said anything. Let's rid ourselves of this place unless Mr. Breaux comes back with a reason to stay."

LeRoy leaped from the vault and nudged Aria toward the cemetery gate. At the gate he asked, "You thought about supper? Maybe crayfish etouffee?"

"Let's hold off. Here's Mr. Breaux."

"Dead end, I'm afraid."

That wasn't new, thought Aria. Another cut. One of the proverbial thousand. No blood oozed from her pores. If no baby, she could still clear her name, stand tall, conviction expunged. If not in the eyes of the public, she'd know the endured shroud of shame had been ripped from her head and danced on until ripped into shreds.

"I'll take you both to eat," said Mr. Breaux. "Supper is probably what you refer to."

LeRoy flashed a grin. "Etouffee?"

Aria bowed her head. She'd force herself to eat. She quieted the mental echo of a matron who spoon fed one emaciated inmate while she bellowed to others, "There'll be no hunger strike. Y'all hear that. You be eating for more than yourselves."

She let LeRoy ride up front. Mr. Breaux drove a half-mile or so past the house Aunt Maggie had rented to a one-story brick building with "Cajun's Hideaway" painted on an otherwise non-descript glass-framed door.

"We can eat here?" LeRoy asked.

"Undisturbed," Mr. Breaux replied. "Best etouffee."

Aria glanced left and right without noticing a soul. She burrowed deep into Mr. Breaux's eyes. "Can we speak here without the world listening?"

"Unburden your soul; inhale the freedom we enjoy."

Aria hadn't read that on a Hallmark card or in a Bible verse Aunt Maggie inscribed as an infrequent quote.

"Don't be so gloomy," LeRoy said. "Be ready to order your own etouffee for you'll share none of mine."

Aria forced a smile. It reflected plastic in the door's green-tinted glass. The Hideaway's interior could have been a second poker player retreat, although absent the gamblers.

Shown an isolated booth, Aria sat with LeRoy opposite Mr. Breaux. She cut to the chase. "What or who did you investigate for my mother?"

"Not my place to violate client confidentiality."

"If you'll both excuse me," LeRoy started, "I'll clear my head of dead person's names with a short stroll."

"Thanks," Mr. Breaux said.

Aria nodded and waited until LeRoy cleared the restaurant's front door. She gazed at Mr. Breaux. "They must ingrain that confidentiality reply at P.I. school."

"It's on every test." His words somber.

"This search isn't easy for me and I'll respect your withholding your work practices, but my mother had to be, like me, searching for something or an explanation of why."

"To that I can say yes."

"I'm not seeking riches, but to feel alive without insanity. My family's been shattered. If there's a living soul out there related to me, I need to know. Did my mother find what she sought? You can at least answer that."

"She didn't."

Aria sighed. "Did it have anything to do with me?"

"Not exactly."

"C'mon, who? Give me a hint."

Aria stopped as the server appeared. Mr. Breaux took charge and ordered three etouffee specials.

He covered his lips, although the server had gone. "She gave me a newspaper article she said Brad gave her."

"Printed where?" Aria flexed her left hand. "What date?"

"Don't recall." He made the sign of the cross. "And that's the Lord's truth."

"What was it about? Published news can't be sensitive."

"Missing babies."

Aria gasped. "And Brad was incriminated?"

"No, no. Your mother told me you'd made a fabulous choice in Brad. My chore, as related to Brad, only tangential. Of interest to your mother was a man closer to her age."

He peered toward the server station. When Aria saw it vacated, he continued.

"How do I say this? Your mother paid me to follow and snoop on this man to determine if he unzipped his pants in a strange boudoir."

"And this man was rich?"

"Can't answer that."

Aria's facial muscles tightened. "Upper social class?"

"Can only answer it this way: he showered himself with a large dose of self-importance."

"Last question. He from this state?"

"By all impression. Can't confirm. Remember, Aunt Maggie has her own ideas. You must decide what you want. Dump the past or begin anew. Not easy, but your mother exhibited strength and I wouldn't be hesitant to say you've inherited sturdy DNA."

The server's return with a loaded tray prompted Mr. Breaux to switch topics. "I'd better rope in LeRoy before this food cools. Y'all should enjoy the best this state can offer."

As LeRoy zeroed in on the booth, Aria could not help but notice a swelling red mark on his left cheek. "How's the other guy?"

His supercilious air missing, LeRoy rubbed his cheek. "Couldn't duck them all."

"Come on," Mr. Breaux said, "Let's eat."

Before Aria swallowed the last Cajun crayfish stew spoonful, she expected night had descended.

Outside, the hour proved her correct. Dim light streaks escaped from two adjoining and three nearby structures.

LeRoy unexpectedly hugged Aria. "Wasn't that great? Could've told you."

Aria tightened her shoulders and squatted to escape LeRoy's embrace. "You shared the wine. I didn't."

"Come on now, you two," Mr. Breaux said. "I've a wife to attend to and you two need to be fresh for tomorrow."

"For what?" Aria asked.

"Patience, patience."

* * *

Aria stood next to the kitchen table in Aunt Maggie's Calhoon rental. The word "empty" in multiple typefaces spiraled, swirled and tumbled as they cluttered her mind. In reality, Mr. Breaux, without exiting his vehicle, had dropped her and LeRoy. He'd hustled to his prior bedroom with the vague claim fresh clothes awaited.

His kitchen reappearance in a tie-belt ruby robe with no towel or toiletries in his hands threatened to disrupt Aria's peaceful evening expectation. She gawked at him. *Was it naïve to be suspicious?* "Dare I ask?"

He straightened his toes. No tap before he lifted and planted his left sole forward of his right without a terry cloth ripple. "We're both adults."

Pinpricks danced on the back of Aria's left hand. Alone with a man . . . strange house . . . a kitchen knife nearby. Words the prosecutor hammered into the jury. Words that overpowered the single word "empty." She didn't believe in déjà vu nor understand legal double jeopardy. "Seems neither here nor there. Is there a deduction I haven't fathomed?"

LeRoy shook his head.

"Good." She suppressed a chuckle when LeRoy wiggled his left big toe. "Anyway, mutual respect means a lot."

101

"I'd suspect many guys, my age and older, have or would say you're a prize."

Aria's cheeks warmed. She raised both hands to rub the hollow beneath her cheekbones to obscure all visual embarrassment and subdue any radiant heat. She castigated herself for not burying a prison guard's carnival barker's impersonation barked in response to fellow guard catcalls: "Step right up. Take your prize."

Aria shouted at LeRoy, "I'm no prize."

"Whoa." LeRoy quickstepped forward to grab Aria's shoulders. His fingertips compressed cloth deep into her skin. "It was a polite compliment, not a battle cry."

"Please let me go."

LeRoy did.

Aria continued to shudder until her mind reminded her this was a kitchen Aunt Maggie rented, not a honeymoon cottage nor a prison bunkhouse she'd been dragged to where guards drew cards to win a prize.

LeRoy glanced to the kitchen door. "We okay? You have any calamine lotion?"

Aria nodded while she exhaled a shallow breath. With her leg muscles tensed for an attack, she slid her soles two steps to the sink to re-establish her personal safety zone.

"You always this jumpy or is it my imagination?"

"I'll get that lotion and you can take a shower first and drive down the road to that mart for dessert. My treat."

"That include beer?"

Aria averted her eyes from the vertical closed line of his robe. To escape one dicey encounter to agree to a second didn't appeal to her. She weighed whether a friendly bend would forestall a late night ugly fight for survival.

"Non-alcohol best. No chicken wings."

"I can do breasts."

His left eye wink didn't reassure Aria: if anything, it ratcheted up an inner trembling not present during her futile late afternoon effort to find her child's grave marker.

"Get going then."

After LeRoy showered and entered his bedroom, Aria dilly dallied until LeRoy bid good-bye and she heard his sedan depart. She clutched fresh clothes to her chest and entered the bathroom pleased to find LeRoy hadn't shed excess hair onto the tub drain. Her lotion bottle sat on the sink ledge.

Once naked and wet, she scrubbed harder than necessary to remove that day's frustration and perspiration. From three extended showers last week she learned no bearable pressure or soap exfoliated prison from her pores. Still, she metaphorically refused to come clean and express her deepest fears to Mr. Breaux, Tillie or Aunt Maggie. If she wished to keep her dignity, no other course appealed to her.

Dried and clothed, Aria tapped in Tillie's number on her new phone's keypad. Her flip-flop edge caught on the sitting room's worn-out carpet to halt her pacing. It did not surprise Tillie's voicemail message asked her to leave a message.

A spicy tomato smell preceded LeRoy through the front door and drove Aria to silently swear she wouldn't throw the Cajun wings into his face and drown him in beer.

"Your bland jumbo chicken breast order still sealed. I've tested my wings."

"Put mine in the refrigerator for tomorrow."

"Beer's got alcohol. Only choice. Twist-off cap. Hope you're good with that."

Aria shook her head. LeRoy sat opposite her at the kitchen table, his leather-covered toes outside footsie range. He wiped beer foam from his lips. "Can I ask a question?"

"Personal?"

"No."

"Yeah."

"That guard who seemed to know you led us to the cemetery, but it disappointed you. Figured he oozed sinister calculation. Who or what didn't you find?"

"Family member," said Aria, punctuated by a whimper.

"Sure." LeRoy paused. "Now be honest."

Aria squirmed on her chair. "Need to copy my prison records, but don't know how."

"Isn't that what you've paid Mr. Breaux for?"

Aria stood. At the sink she refilled her water glass. To quell her urge to pace, she slid into her chair. "Sorta."

"Didn't you tell Tillie you guessed the guards would've forged your records to hide the truth?"

"Yeah. But I've no proof."

LeRoy bit into his last sauce-dripped chicken wing. "I'd not trust Mr. Breaux."

"Whoa. Where'd that come from?"

"Sensed it. Why'd he interview that slob outside your presence? I say hand signals." He demonstrated with a quick left hand swipe across his neck. "An audio tape wouldn't expose scribbled notes shown or passed."

Aria faulted herself for trusting. "Think that guard's psychotic or a good-ol'-boy not wishing to make waves up the bayou?" She congratulated herself on thinking Cajun.

"Probably the latter, but what's the dif?"

"Let's we have a chat with him tomorrow."

LeRoy's eyes widened. "You sure you want to be Nancy Drew? He might look it, but, if a psycho, they're smart, hide their crimes."

"There's no Prison for Dummies book."

LeRoy let loose a riotous laugh, grabbed the table edge with both hands to prevent his chair's backwards tumble.

"We can get a gun."

Two chair legs thudded against the linoleum as LeRoy sat upright. "Forget Nancy Drew. Annie Oakley here we come."

"Knock it off. What'd you spike that beer with?"

"Nothing, but should have." He winked. "And maybe sprinkled it on your breasts."

Aria's cheeks warmed.

"I meant the chicken ones. Hell, if you don't buy your Saturday-night special, I'll volunteer to be shotgun, sorry, bad pun, to your seducing the truth out of that slob."

Without explanation, a heat splash blossomed and lingered across Aria's cheeks; she turned her head quick and left toward the door to avoid LeRoy's judgmental gaze. Her cheeks itched as if flying fire ants had bit her, not LeRoy.

She completed her obfuscation by swinging both legs right for them to clear the table leg. With her feet positioned, she rose. After six quick steps to the kitchen door, a facially cooled Aria turned to LeRoy.

"What?" he asked. His disdain clear.

"Let's ride at eight."

Chapter Seventeen

Ambiguity often vaulted to be a saving grace within her prison walls. Now released, Aria capitalized on ambiguity to be a reality weapon for post-prison survival.

She didn't expect a rap on her bedroom door at eight p.m.

"Yes."

"I'm here."

Aria didn't have to ask who. It could only be LeRoy. She'd left him at the kitchen table. Why would he knock? No smoke or its smell seeped into her bedroom.

Standing at the closed door, Aria asked, "Why?"

"You said we ride at eight."

"I meant we leave at eight a.m."

"Oh."

"We're good then?"

A low volume, disappointed voice replied, "Guess so."

Aria pressed her cheek to the door. "Good night." She guessed LeRoy frowned, but her past warned her not to unlock the door. Perhaps she'd mentally tortured LeRoy by not throwing the door wide, but how many times had her locked cell door been breached by guards after eight o'clock to visit horrors upon her person?

Aria listened. No second knock. She tiptoed to the bed and hid her body beneath the blue blanket. Clutched in her right hand, her cell phone. On impulse, she punched in Tillie's phone digits. Voicemail. She pressed END. A check of her voicemail registered no message.

If Tillie knew LeRoy as a friend's half-brother, a conflicted Aria faced a double dilemma. LeRoy's chin scar at Union Station exposed him as potentially one of Aria's casual teenage boyfriends memorialized in an inaccessible scrapbook forever lost. If she confessed this to Tillie, her friend might not look kindly on her because in Africa they'd promised every deep secret disclosed.

Then or now, Aria didn't wish to be shamed, or outed, as a liar, especially by her own words. But then again, if she teased LeRoy, no good would be served.

She tossed her blue blanket aside. With feet on the floor, she paused at the bedroom door and pressed her left ear to varnished wood. Nothing. Aria relaxed until she realized Mr. Breaux unlikely to answer her outreach until the morning.

The bed became her refuge. Yet, she couldn't fall asleep.

The room's window glimmered, an escape portal to glorified freedom. Yet, if LeRoy waited outside, she'd lunge herself into his arms. Her emotions ping-ponged from fear to despair. Logic designed her a plan. She'd lure LeRoy to her bedroom door, keep it closed and race to her pre-opened window. He'd never exit the house fast enough to tackle her dive to freedom.

While Aria schemed, an eerie quiet chill crept across her toes. Slipping into sneakers hadn't registered. She completed her second sneaker tug before she cracked the bedroom door and shouted, "LeRoy."

"Yeah. What's up?"

"Any chicken wings left?"

"I'll get them."

Better words for her purposes didn't exist. Aria depressed the bedroom door lock-button and dashed for the window. Not enough space between the raised sash and upper window to let her straddle the sill and duck her head to the night air. She reversed course to grab the window frame with both hands. First, her right foot and then her left momentarily rested on the sill until her thighs propelled her legs into the humid blackness. She sat on the window's threshold, arms extended overhead, and her forehead lower than the upper sash. With her fingers clasped to the inner framing, an inner spirit yelled go.

She obeyed.

Aria's feet slammed against the earth. Strong calves a balance counterweight to a forward body lean as her torso remained upright. Her gaze left and right unable to detect LeRoy. She ran. Grass tuffs padded her strides until she reached the gravel road. A right foot slip in loose gravel warned her of the ditch's edge.

Vehicle lights behind her too distant to cast her shadow. Yet, they approached. When low beams became high beams, she veered right toward the ditch. Should she dive and lay prone or try to find a tree? Her brain slipped into neutral.

The vehicle lights illuminated her path.

Aria bent forward to shrink her stature and breathe before a half-dozen pants depleted her lungs. A backward glance into stationary headlights blinded her.

A voice shouted, "You can't hide."

Aria recognized LeRoy. "Wasn't. Knew you'd follow."

Shadows obscured his facial features as he stood with his car idling behind him. "Then what's out here?"

Aria swabbed the inside of her cheek with her tongue tip. "Freedom." It wasn't the entire truth, but satisfied Aria's need to give a reasonable answer.

"In these parts young people on the Freedom Trail ended up in pine boxes, and worse."

Overheated to her bones by nerves plus exertion, Aria shuffled her feet unable to shuck being bathed in garish light. "That to scare me?"

"Not my intent."

"Then to get revenge for me and you years ago?"

"I've tried to move on. Remember those crazy photos we took at that mall booth?"

Aria shook her head.

"Well . . . kept mine. You know, that strip with four photos. Kept it for years. Threw it into a basement box at my mother's two years ago. It might still be there. Who knows? Why not let me give you a ride to the house?"

Aria tugged at her left ear lobe. "It'll be fine."

"If you say so."

She refused to be baited into expressing a sliver of doubt by a non-answer. With conviction she said, "I do."

LeRoy hesitated. His twist to a profile no longer showed him to be a scrawny teen. "Your chicken's still in the fridge."

Chapter Eighteen

Aria finished the chilled chicken breasts at breakfast, When LeRoy entered the kitchen, Aria's breaths labored to squeeze air from her lungs. Reason resolved her physical disability temporary and unrelated to LeRoy.

Aria closed her eyes and slowed exhales until it subsided. "You okay?"

She pushed her coffee cup aside. "Fine."

"Mr. Breaux rung. He expects to be here shortly."

Aria shuffled her four note pages. "I'll be ready. Only need my sneakers."

And, true to her word, Aria stood on the porch when Mr. Breaux arrived. LeRoy squelched grass tuffs into the red earth as he paced, then scurried to Mr. Breaux's vehicle. He imitated a high-rise doorman when he flung wide the front passenger door as a courtesy to Aria. She forced a smile and rotated her head to Mr. Breaux.

"I've been thinking."

Mr. Breaux coughed. "About what?"

"Yesterday proved to be a dud. Are we distracted? Galloping, so to speak, down the wrong road."

"Not if we believe that guard."

"That's just it. I've stretched my mind and don't believe he's honest. I keep putting him together with the other guards. Fan them a wad of cash and any one of them will try to convince you the moon crumbles like bleu cheese."

LeRoy leaned toward the front seat. "That's really poetic. Is there proof?"

"My word," Aria replied.

"Hadn't planned to locate that guard again, but, if what you say has a grain of truth, we've chased him to where we first found him." Mr. Breaux keyed the ignition.

In the daylight, without her darkness-inspired drama, the road Aria had run strayed from Shakespearean tragedy to pedestrian, accented by kudzu. If the Louisiana landscape outside Calhoon once appeared fresh and inviting, today for Aria the flowers its luster faded, clustered insects exposed. She buried her gaze and counted her sneaker eyelets. While far from exciting, the mundane exercise didn't conjure up or encourage nightmares.

When Mr. Breaux slowed and turned right off the asphalt highway, the laurel oak swing hung motionless.

When Aria opened her door, the humidity that had perspired her forehead after her run engulfed her.

She waited until Mr. Breaux stood at his car's front bumper to comment. "You said he's here? If they play poker inside, where's their vehicles?"

"Don't be distracted by poker," Mr. Breaux replied.

LeRoy's sneaky closeness distracted Aria. His fingers hadn't tickled her waist nor had he touched her, but his breath on her neck presupposed an intimacy she despised. Her left-hand swipe to her neck's nape, coupled with her steps after Mr. Breaux toward the white clapboard building, undertaken to influence LeRoy's thinking and to dispel all ardor lurking in his mind.

Mr. Breaux didn't knock. He pushed the hunting lodge door inward and shouted, "Anyone home?"

Aria waited for a vocal response that didn't materialize. A chair's crash alerted her to shift her feet and be ready to trip the first human across the threshold.

A scared tabby didn't qualify.

"You see him?" Aria asked.

"Not yet," Mr. Breaux said. He twisted toward LeRoy. "Get my back."

"Huh?"

"Watch my back."

"Okay."

LeRoy's left shoulder brushed Aria's right. She stifled a protest and hugged her arms to relax. The interlude amplified time to let her sort harbored doubts. Her tally predicted this quest doomed.

Mr. Breaux marched forward to shout, "Anyone home." After silence ruled, he threatened, "We know you're here. Let's not play games."

We? Aria mulled Mr. Breaux's word choice. Was this him plus her or LeRoy? She scurried to the protection of Mr. Breaux's advance. A second thought convinced her his "we" exaggeration trumpeted as a ploy to multiply her trio's debatable strength into an undefeatable invading force.

Her internal confusion less jumbled when the guard appeared, a double-barrel shotgun cradled by arms frozen at his waist. His gaze flitted from its polished stock to encircle Aria while his right index finger rubbed the trigger guard. "Why bother me again?"

"Your information proved wrong," Mr. Breaux said.

"No guarantees." His voice dry, scratchy.

"Not here to ask for a money return." Aria shifted her glare from Mr. Breaux to the guard. "I've a feeling you know more about me than you've owned up to."

"Never tricked you."

Aria clenched her left fist and fought hard not to fail a threatened contest of wills or who'd blink first. "But you've already admitted knowledge of prison stillborns."

The guard grimaced. His trigger finger continued to stroke the trigger guard.

Mr. Breaux leaned forward. "What about that infant you and your wife adopted three years ago? You want me to start asking questions to social services?"

The guard's eyes bulged, then relaxed. "You can't threaten me. Adoption records are confidential, sealed. My lawyer told me that."

Aria's private investigator confused her with a subject change. "You got a bill of sale for that shotgun?"

"Notarized."

Aria covered her mouth as she tilted her face toward Mr. Breaux. "Does that mean he can shoot us?"

Mr. Breaux shook his head. "No. Means I can't be a pain and report him for carrying an illegal gun."

The guard smiled. "That's right. See ya."

"Not yet," Mr. Breaux said. "You're correct about the general adoption rule, but there are exceptions or else Louisiana wouldn't have a state reunion registry to reunite children with parents."

"My adopted child wasn't born to this woman." He lifted and pointed his shotgun at Aria.

She gasped and then composed herself. "If that's so, you've admitted you're hiding information." Aria thought hard to bolster her bluff. "What if your child's biological mother carried a hereditary disease? Wouldn't you want to know? Of any interest to your wife?"

"Yeah," chimed in Mr. Breaux. "I know for a fact that here in Louisiana the courts will unseal adoption records at the slightest hint an infant's life or public safety is at risk."

The guard smirked. "Don't you dare bring my wife into this?" His gaze flitted left and right, a slight left-hand shake noticeable. His voice volume decreased by half. "Just because I lost the cream of a young dude doesn't mean my wife's at fault. Neither can you scare me my child was, or is, damaged goods."

Aria exhaled slowly. "Your wife's health isn't my concern."

"Don't be ornery."

Aria shuffled her feet. She modulated her voice so not intensify the group's unease. "Perhaps your baby's mother inherited corrupted genes she passed on to threaten your adopted child?"

"That's absurd." His gaze restarted an awkward and slow across-the-room survey. "Anyway, we've not been told."

"Maybe because you didn't use a legitimate adoption agency." Aria interlaced her fingers and tapped her thumbs to allow time for her words to magnify their impact. "If that's true, I'll pray for you."

As Aria spoke, a skeptical expression floated across the guard's face. She skipped LeRoy's whisper that he'd be outside to concentrate her attention on the guard's altered expression.

Without an announcement, Aria edged forward, each one of her two steps to prove his shotgun no longer controlled her. "If you don't wish to answer, I'll still pray for you."

"Heard you. Crazy."

Mr. Breaux strode to Aria's side. "Let's go."

Aria refused to budge. Shotgun or not, she didn't cotton to being the butt of a colossal joke when the guard emptied a lunchtime coffee pot with behind-bars-workplace buddies.

"C'mon."

The pressure of Mr. Breaux's fingertips on her left elbow didn't alter her stance, physical or mental.

112

"He's lying to us. Playing us for fools."

"We'll speak outside. Trust me, he can't hide anywhere." Mr. Breaux's unexplained half-smile emerged and melted into a hardened stare within seconds. "LeRoy's taken care of that."

Her investigator's fingers tugged at her until her backpedal eased the pressure.

"That's good, Aria. Now a few more."

She gasped when the guard's right arm arced the shotgun towards them. "You're a bastard," Aria shouted.

The guard chuckled. "See ya, later. Maybe laundry trustees washed your soiled sheets. Your pillow, even."

"Don't flatter him with a reply, Aria. Come with me."

Mr. Breaux punched the hunting lodge's front door clear of its jamb. It'd been the one they'd entered.

Aria inhaled a full gulp of humid air less smoky than inside. Its tension molecules unfiltered.

"Tires flat, anything else?" LeRoy asked.

"Not yet," replied Mr. Breaux.

Aria squared her shoulders. "Why'd we leave him? He stole my money and . . . ."

"Dear, you need to learn southern ways. If you'd challenged his honor more direct than your family mention he'd react madder than a bayou snake fighting a garden hose or wake up tomorrow and whistle for his buddies."

"The guards never respected our honor."

"Maybe so, but you ain't behind bars now. Rules change. You gotta change with them."

Aria ducked LeRoy's arm aimed for her shoulder.

"He's right, you know."

"Not you too, LeRoy. Don't side with him. Beginning to think the males I meet only exist to pocket my money."

Mr. Breaux shrunk back. His eyes shimmered with indignation. "Your aunt doesn't think so."

"Aunt Maggie isn't here."

"True. But I phoned her last night. Offered to refund her retainer after our futile traipse through the cemetery."

Aria relaxed her balled fists. "I've been a bit harsh. Reading in those infant gravestones marking babies not given a chance at life freaks me out."

LeRoy raised his left arm, let it drop to his side. "We should go back to the house. Rest." He focused his gaze on Aria's forehead. "Find another person with information."

"My exact thoughts," Mr. Breaux said.

Mr. Breaux's vagueness puzzled and deflated Aria. She couldn't discount his three words of agreement hid a subterfuge to expand Aria's costs. How LeRoy now fit in left unclear. She turned away from the two men.

"We need to explore every supposition," continued Mr. Breaux. "Best way, I figure, will be for me to drop you two off and go ahead to my office."

Halfway to Mr. Breaux's car, Aria asked. "What's your idea when you agreed with LeRoy?"

"Need to check out official adoption agencies. That's the only way the guard legally adopted."

"What if he didn't?"

"Let's not worry about that yet."

Aria bit her tongue and didn't fight LeRoy for the front passenger seat. On their drive LeRoy convinced Mr. Breaux to order at a Popeye's drive-thru.

Aria voiced personal disgust with spicy chicken, but didn't press her objection.

At Aunt Maggie's rented house, Mr. Breaux promised to return at 8 a.m. with positive news.

When LeRoy joined Aria in the kitchen, she faked a yawn. She planned to survive another night with a locked bedroom door between her and LeRoy. A shiver convinced her maybe not.

Chapter Nineteen

LeRoy spread three food containers on the kitchen table.

Aria slid one po'boy sandwich onto a plate.

"We got more than water?"

Aria's total response a pointed right-hand finger at the refrigerator. Her left hand searched the paper bag for the expected whole-wrapped pickle.

"There's beer." LeRoy swiveled his face to her. "Last chance for me to crack you one."

"Not tonight."

"You planning to keep your senses for our little party?"

Without a peek at LeRoy, Aria bit into her po'boy a second time after a liberated bottle cap pop re-agitated the air. Her swallowed third bite accompanied LeRoy's shuffle and the creak of a chair forced to accept his body weight.

"You didn't answer my question."

"Mouth full." Her words garbled.

"Many a man could fantasize all night with the enthusiastic and slow way you suck that pickle."

Cheeks warm, Aria yanked the once-bitten pickle free of her lips and tossed it onto her plate. She dialed up her LeRoy dislike. *Why did I ever twice date him years ago?* She caulked it up to teenage isolation and refused to waste her time digging up greater distasteful memories or to ferret out what he plotted.

While LeRoy had added sculptured physical muscle since his teen years, Aria graded his emotional maturity as undeveloped. If he now waited for her to articulate her thoughts or re-insert the pickle, he'd be totally disappointed.

"Sorry," LeRoy said. "Just popped out."

"I'll bite quicker next time."

LeRoy shook his head.

Aria castigated herself for traipsing into the past. She ignored the pickle and devoured her sandwich. Her water glass empty, she rose to deposit her, with pickle, plate and glass into the sink. "I've got to call Tillie. Aunt Maggie, too."

Without waiting for LeRoy's permission, she hustled to her bedroom and locked the door. To take no chance, LeRoy spied on her, she peered through the clouded windowpane into the fading twilight. With a cell phone in her left hand, her right pulled the shade.

Tillie answered on the second ring. "Tell me you dug up a secret life?"

Aria sat cross-legged on the bed, stared straight ahead at the door and shook her head.

"Hey girl. You still there?"

At Tillie's plea, Aria snapped out of her semi-trance. "Sorry. Won't bore you with details except to say the lead to find a grave a dead end."

For three seconds, silence prevailed until Tillie's voice cut through a static burst. "Cute."

Thus alerted by Tillie to her own words, Aria skipped a chuckle at her unintended pun.

"What now?"

"Mr. Breaux's searching for added info."

"Huh?"

Aria squirmed to stretch out on the bed. Bent at the elbows, her arms formed a V to keep her head and shoulders raised. "He says he needs state agency records to pressure the guard, you know, the guard you saw at the hunting lodge."

"Don't remember who you speak of, but why?"

"The guard today claimed he and his wife three years ago adopted a child, a child they maybe obtained illegally."

"Over my head. Hold on."

Aria twisted onto her back and waited as Tillie asked.

"Aunt Maggie wishes to speak to you."

Faced with a second wait, Aria flipped onto her elbows.

"Aria, honey, you okay? Hope you're eating, and not just junk food."

"Fine, auntie." She hesitated to ask when she planned to return to Harmony Square. "Be nice to see you again."

"What can you tell me about my niece or nephew?"

"Nothing so far." Aria swallowed hard rather than utter the two words "dead end" again.

"Hasn't Mr. Breaux helped?"

Three taps on her bedroom door so soft Aria challenged her brain to prove she hadn't hallucinated.

"Can't be that hard a question. Is he still helping?"

"Yes, yes. Don't know if it should relieve me, but he led me to a prison cemetery with clues to inscriptions where I, or should say we, didn't find a grave to confirm my fear."

A second static burst distorted Aria's hearing what her aunt said until she heard ". . . that must be positive, right?"

"You could say that."

"Balderdash. Don't portray disbelief like my sister. To search for a grave and not find it is a blessing, believe me."

For a second time Aria bit her tongue, not willing to ask the date of Aunt Maggie's Harmony Square return.

"Now don't you dare give me the silent treatment?"

"Wasn't." She couldn't divulge prison cruelties, lest she unsealed her paralyzed emotions that would encourage Aunt Maggie to ditch hope. "Trying to remember what exact records Mr. Breaux chases after. Can't."

"LeRoy there?"

"Not in my bedroom!"

"Not prying, dear. Meant in the house."

"You wish to speak to him?"

"No. Just checking he didn't run off. Now you impress upon Mr. Breaux he's paid dearly to do everything he can."

"Yes, Aunt Maggie."

"Good night and I pray every day my precious niece will return safely. Your mother had a box of stuff Tillie will try to bring home for me. God bless and don't you worry."

Aria hesitated to press REDIAL. Nothing her mother saved likely to reverse every refusal when alive.

Sharper knocks banged her bedroom door.

"Go away, LeRoy."

"Mr. Breaux called. He'll be here at 7 a.m."

"I'll be ready. Good night, LeRoy."

Aria heard no footwear shuffle. What if she needed to use the bathroom and LeRoy lay in wait?

Aria strived to convince herself that, while prison overburdened her worry defenses, she coped.

She'd force sleep; her tactic worked, sometimes.

Chapter Twenty

Zippered closed, Aria's blue slacks fit tighter and restricted her first breaths more than she would've favored. LeRoy's third glance convinced her to shoo him off the porch toward Mr. Breaux's arriving SUV.

His face lit with a smile, Mr. Breaux announced, "Y'all should expect exciting things today."

Aria latched on to the rear passenger door handle and asked, "Like what?"

"Guard's adoption wasn't legal."

"How's that help?" LeRoy asked. "Bet loads not kosher?"

Mr. Breaux slid behind the wheel. LeRoy slammed his front passenger door as Aria slid onto the rear seat to hear Mr. Breaux continue. "Perceptive and right you are. Doesn't mean we can't run a bluff to our advantage."

"How?" Aria asked.

Mr. Breaux keyed the ignition. "Just wait, Aria."

"That hunting lodge gives me the creeps."

Without a turn of his head, Mr. Breaux said, "We're not going there. Have a better idea."

"What?" LeRoy asked. "Doesn't that guard ever work?"

"He's at the prison today. His wife isn't."

The landscape that no longer cried out with newness didn't distract Aria's attention this day. "Makes little sense. She never saw me in prison. She can't know anything."

"Hold on," LeRoy pleaded. "Mr. Breaux says he has a better plan. Let him explain it."

Aria waited a minute, then thirty, before she smothered her anxiety. The miles between Aunt Maggie's rental and Mr. Breaux's unannounced destination sped by.

"Here we are," Mr. Breaux announced.

Aria breathed deep. In crow miles, they weren't that far from Calhoon. She hadn't counted the turns, but they were roughly opposite enough to create a circle.

"Those window blinds moved," said LeRoy. He glanced at Aria and Mr. Breaux and shrugged. "Are we expected?"

"Not really. No matter."

Aria trudged after the two men. One knock and the household accepted visitors. An obese woman smeared in pancake makeup wearing a blue smock filled the doorway.

"Yes."

"Mrs. Hebert, may we speak for a moment?" The woman nodded after Mr. Breaux's soft enunciation.

Aria gazed at the claustrophobic front room. Muted brown upholstery, accented by subdued greens, struggled to ward off the oxford-gray walls' visual advance. A corner table cluttered with framed family photos. Parents holding an infant front-n-center.

Mr. Breaux gestured for LeRoy to stay outside. He pointed Aria to an upholstered armchair and seated himself on the sofa's far end.

A standing Mrs. Hebert asked, "Is this about the prison?"

"No." Mr. Breaux swallowed. "Adoption."

Mrs. Hebert's right hand grabbed an interior doorjamb. "You'll have to speak to my husband. He's at work."

"Spoke to him yesterday."

Aria couldn't challenge Mr. Breaux's utterance. He hadn't lied when his content-vague assertion elevated an off-the-mark conversation to gain a yet-to-be revealed advantage.

"Am I right to assume he doesn't carry your daughter's adoption certificate to work?"

The woman's ruddy color paled. "Well . . . well, no."

"We can wait for you to show it to us."

Aria expected Mr. Breaux's direct, not-so-subtle approach to stiffen Mrs. Hebert's rejection of their request. It didn't please her to be correct.

"Need my husband's permission."

Mr. Breaux stood. "Let's not bamboozle each other. I've had all state registries double checked. There's no official adoption record in your name. Obviously, you can prove my research wrong if you let me see a valid certificate. Since you've chosen not to, the authorities can take the next step."

Mrs. Hebert's fingers against the doorjamb whitened.

Aria's palms scooted her forward and pushed her erect. She glanced at Mr. Breaux and, without a verbal stop, nodded to Mrs. Hebert en route to join LeRoy.

She didn't hear Mr. Breaux or a door close behind her.

"So, what did I miss?" LeRoy asked.

"Really nothing. Guess the adoption we learned about yesterday from the guard may have happened, but not processed through legal proceedings."

"So, where'd the baby come from?"

"Who knows? I don't."

"Hasn't Mr. Breaux told you?"

"Nah." When LeRoy stepped toward her, Aria frowned and he retreated. "Let's wait."

"For what?"

"Mr. Breaux. He may floor us with a secret."

"You know he has one?"

"No. Just crossing my fingers."

Thunder cracked and rolled behind her; she jumped uncertain of where the lightning bolt struck. The sheen on LeRoy's brow a tribute to the summer humidity.

He motioned for her to get into Mr. Breaux's car.

"He's locked it."

Mr. Breaux's voice sliced through the stillness. "It'll be unlocked. I'm right behind you."

A single audible click alerted Aria to the internal release of the door's locking mechanism. Her second door handle squeeze confirmed.

Mr. Breaux's quickened stride looped wide right past her. His double-time incited she'd no recall he'd ever done that.

Her westward glimpse to locate the horizon blocked by a black-cloud swarm. It motivated her to half-jump onto the front passenger seat.

Mr. Breaux jogged past the front bumper, his torso a blur beyond the windshield that protected Aria from well-spaced lazy rain drops.

Behind her, LeRoy snapped his seatbelt. She swallowed hard, her mouth's dryness mimicked the Sahara sand dunes. Even if possible to utter words, her glance at Mr. Breaux quieted every urge.

"That was that," muttered LeRoy. "Wasn't it?"

"Intriguing," Mr. Breaux replied.

"Huh?' Aria asked.

"We've narrowed the options. That's encouraging, even if I say so myself."

Aria didn't understand what he meant. "What options?"

"Well. You hired me to find your child. The body's not buried in the prison's nearby cemetery as far as we can determine. Nonetheless, there's been adoptions. Not of your child by the guard, since the timing's off, but circumstances may foretell events that will achieve greater clarity."

"The wife told you that?"

"Not in so many words. The photo frame off to her side spoke to me while she didn't."

"Whoa," LeRoy interjected. "What frame? Plastic, ceramic or wood can't speak."

"Official southern Louisiana adoption agencies give the adoptive parents with a framed photo to both document the adoption and to encourage the parents to keep the agency in mind and recommend it to others."

LeRoy voiced skepticism. "So?"

"I have a superb idea where the scrolled silver frame Mrs. Hebert displayed came from. And we should go there, but I can't go in."

"Huh?"

"I'm known. The Azalea Flower Shop owner won't admit the open secret she brokers adoptions."

"What about the staff I saw in your office?" Aria asked.

Mr. Breaux sighed. "They're local, well-known."

"LeRoy isn't."

"I was thinking of you."

Aria sat silent. "I'm convinced I'd make a hash out of undercover." Her unwillingness to rely on LeRoy an absolute. The fewer favors she owed him the stronger the wall she could build between them. She added, "The guard and his poker buddies saw me and gossip may have filtered out."

"Besides Mrs. Hebert never saw LeRoy."

"Not certain of that," Mr. Breaux said. "LeRoy was visible on the path from my car to the house."

Aria lacked a foundation to argue the point, even if she tried. Instinct told her LeRoy's lips upturned into a smile. She refused to angle her gaze to the rearview.

"Why can't Aria put on a disguise? A floppy or feathered hat?" LeRoy asked.

Aria pursed her lips. If LeRoy retained any of his high school thespian skill, he'd pull off Mr. Breaux's scam.

She gazed toward Mrs. Hebert's home. The depleted rain-shower clouds now scattered and pierced by blue sky. A lacy curtain on the nearest front window fluttered. Was Mrs. Hebert describing their vehicle to her husband?

"Please, is it time to go?" Aria's voice soft.

"Let's do a trial run," Mr. Breaux suggested.

The two-second engine whistle obliterated by the crunch of rolling tires.

Aria gazed at Mr. Breaux. "What? Where?"

"Just wait."

Aria tried to force herself to count passing telephone poles, gave up at six.

LeRoy sparked her attention when he asked, "Where again is this flower shop?"

"Calhoon," Mr. Breaux answered.

"There's no flower shop there."

"Sure is. The old livery hides it from Main Street. Was a tack room in bygone days when horses and wagons ruled."

LeRoy mumbled something Aria missed.

Mr. Breaux stretched his shoulders. "Now listen. Best way we can do this is if both of you act like a young couple unable to have children."

This yet-to-be-scripted scenario with two lying Yankees waltzing into a Southern lady's shop flouting the state's human services apparatus flawed to Aria's thinking. "Why? We're in this state without an actual address or even a pop-up trailer or a mobile home, whatever you call it."

"Happens all the time. Believe me."

Aria remained skeptical and, with her inner strength concentrated, refused to vocalize her greater misgivings. Her and LeRoy paired crumbled the wall she visualized between them. Aria's right hand gripped the seatbelt to ease its tension against her chest, but this act no salve to her mental torment.

"Am I going to be wired?" LeRoy asked.

Mr. Breaux shook his head. "This isn't the FBI. No blazing guns. Nor a violent script written by Tarantino."

The misgivings spawned within Aria doubled. When Mr. Breaux's vehicle brakes slowed them to a stop, Aria fixed her gaze on the old livery. "This isn't going to work."

"Give it your best," Mr. Breaux replied.

"I'll do the talking." LeRoy's dab of confidence unequal to the task of quelling Aria's fears. Yet, he continued, "Any ideas, sir, that'll help me with your plan?"

"Be natural. Know that's hard, but if you're nervous that won't be a failure. Just learn all you can. If stymied, press on. Consider it a test where your first effort will be repulsed."

Aria exited Mr. Breaux's SUV and shunned LeRoy's attempt to grab her left hand as they marched toward the rear of the old livery. Two hanging baskets may have announced a flower shop, but in Louisiana shiny or rustic planters adorned structures of every description.

A bell's tingle announced their entrance. Multiple fresh cut flower fragrances overwhelmed Aria. She allowed LeRoy to guide her by his grip of her right elbow.

"Welcome, y'all."

Aria couldn't but notice LeRoy's gaze drop from a lightweight blue blazer to blue jeans tension-wrapped to well-proportioned legs. She kept her gaze elevated. Honey-brown hair tinted by a salon, not the summer sun. A toothy smile practiced for beauty pageants gnawed at Aria's memory. She hadn't strutted the pageant stage, but the smile she'd seen flashed often to ward off prison guards, if but for an instant. The memory blurred when LeRoy jerked her arm.

"Haven't seen you in here before." The shop's saleslady's eyes aflutter in LeRoy's direction.

"No ma'am. We just visited Mrs. Hebert."

The saleslady didn't react to the name-dropping.

LeRoy continued, "She and others all very appreciative of what you do, or did for them."

"That's right. Best flowers in Louisiana, either fresh or bulbs. You must have a celebration upcoming."

"We do." Aria tried not to wince at her lie.

"That's right," LeRoy cut in to reassert his conversation command. "We've been told you can help. Is that right?"

"If I knew your budget."

"We haven't thought in terms of budget."

"It's open-ended then?"

"How can I say it?" LeRoy gazed at a row of vases. "We'd like a large family someday, but one infant is all we're able to contemplate right now."

The saleslady flipped her gaze to Aria. "If you're pregnant, it's not showing."

"Lost my baby." Aria didn't have to fake the glistening in her eyes. "Can't have another."

LeRoy interjected a second time. "That's why we're here. We've been told you can help."

A smile tugged at the saleslady's lips. "Don't reckon how, unless you're interested in flowers."

Aria's throat muscles tensed. This woman's vocabulary not unfamiliar. But where and when had she seen her?

"Understand you have to be discrete," LeRoy said, his voice quiet. "If you can't help us find a child to love, can you refer or tell us who might."

"Let's go, dear." Aria's last word an improv addition she truly believed she'd regret; sooner, if not later.

LeRoy hesitated.

Aria rotated her face away from the saleslady. The once pleasing fragrances tinged by a rising aura of decay ground into the wooden planks they trod.

If she recognized the saleslady, the opposite also true.

As she had verbalized her intention, Aria strode to the flower shop exit with the hope LeRoy caught up without a huge delay.

Chapter Twenty-one

Mr. Breaux's shadowed profile cast eerie shadows from the driver's seat onto the curved padding of the rear seat. Aria's sidestep blocked the sun's projection as she and LeRoy approached the SUV; she, as the distance diminished, ever more hesitant to volunteer their experience.

After LeRoy held the front passenger door for Aria, he unlatched the rear door and slid in.

From her left, Mr. Breaux asked, "Well?"

"Lady didn't go beyond flowers," LeRoy replied.

Aria didn't augment. To be sure, she clasped her right hand to her mouth. Her head twist left endured the chill in Mr. Breaux's voice when he spit out, "You try?"

"We did. Aria can vouch I'm telling the truth."

He flicked his gaze in her direction.

"LeRoy's right. Maybe this will help?"

"What?"

Aria fought not to shrink from Mr. Breaux's steely gaze. "I glimpsed a woman sweeping in an adjacent room that tripped a remembrance. Haven't seen her for a year. If I could speak to her, I'd know if she's who I remember."

From behind her came one word, "Huh?"

"Double that 'huh' for me," responded Mr. Breaux. "But, then again, I'm at your service."

Aria clung to her doubts about that. His professed service guaranteed to end, if as what transpired with mother, his invoice overdue seven days.

"Don't either of you have enough respect to even hear what's on my mind?"

"Yes," said Mr. Breaux, which became LeRoy's rear seat enhanced echo.

Aria straightened, then twisted her shoulders toward LeRoy. "That dark-skinned reed of a woman who carried a stack of pots into the far room reminded me of a prisoner paraded repeatedly in shackles along a connecting corridor. She kept shrieking she wanted her baby. I didn't see no baby. Buried her grief with my own sobs."

"You're not in prison now," LeRoy said.

"Partially correct. I'm not in a particular prison cell. Neither is this woman if she's who I think she was or is. Opens a pathway to truth."

"What truth?" Mr. Breaux asked.

Aria's entire body shook. "The truth. . . ." Her stutter clamped words against her throat walls and controlled her very being until her engrained tenacity steadied the quiver in her breast. "The truth . . . the truth about my baby."

"We chased every lead," Mr. Breaux replied. "You yourself matched coded dates to tombstones."

LeRoy slapped the shoulder of Aria's car seat. "We should hogtie that guard. Stomp the truth outta him."

"Doubt he knows much more than what he's revealed."

"If that's so, Mr. Breaux," Aria interjected, "I'm going inside and confront the one I recognized." She reached for the interior door latch, pushed the door wide.

"Wait for me," LeRoy said.

"No." Aria, her feet on the ground, twisted her torso toward LeRoy. "Better I go myself. If she's who I think, she'll shutdown if ganged up on."

"LeRoy," said Mr. Breaux. "Aria's right."

"I'll not go in, but, if you yell loud, I'll bust through that flower shop door and propel that stupid bell into the Gulf."

"Chill, LeRoy. This isn't prime time TV."

Aria wished it were; there'd be a resolution within the hour. Or, at the least, a continuation to a second hour. The psychological tension gripped her nerves tighter than male guards teasing sexual provocation and pawing her body.

Afraid her fears seeped through her buried casket of repression, Aria quickened her pace to the flower shop. Her entrance rewarded with a bell tinkle.

"Knew you'd return." The saleslady beamed.

"Not exactly what you might think."

"Edmee recognized you. You weren't stopping in to buy flowers or arrangements."

Aria shifted weight to her left foot. The door behind her closed and she didn't see a second person leave the shop. "Don't know no Edmee."

"Said she recognized you, not the guy with you. He didn't cotton to be from around here."

Aria repeated, "Don't know no Edmee."

"We pronounce it 'ed may' not 'ed me.'"

"No difference. Don't know either."

The saleslady glanced toward the rear room before she spoke to Aria. "How about I guess, for whatever reason, you two shared a life in our women's state prison?"

Aria shuddered. Truth generated her deepest fear. "I must speak to her."

"Sorry. Not possible."

"Huh? You just said."

"She's gone. Only works here part time."

Aria corralled her wits. "She help with adoptions?"

The saleslady grimaced. "That's for the state."

Aria didn't believe a word spoken. "C'mon now. You know I'm a Yankee. Born and raised in Chicago. What appears on the surface isn't what happens in actual life."

"Not here."

"C'mon." Aria advanced toward the saleslady before her better judgment mandated she halt and retreat two steps. "If I could speak to this Edmee, bet there'd be a consensus between us that babies don't always stay with their mothers."

"Can't say. Only say she's not here."

"Where's she live?"

"Can't say."

"Or won't?"

"Employees, even part-time, have a right to privacy."

Aria burst from the flower shop and ran, head down, around the corner.

"Whoa."

The command didn't slow Aria until her uplifted gaze spied LeRoy in the gap between buildings.

"We've got to hurry. You see, a lady coming this way?"

"You?"

"Not me. Dark-haired, skinny, maybe Cajun."

"Oh."

An exasperated Aria shouted, "C'mon. Answer me. You see this woman, either slow or fast, go past here?"

"Maybe."

"What's this, maybe? Either you did or didn't."

"Didn't exactly come this way."

"What's that mean?"

"A woman like you described came my way, then hurried off the way she came."

"Like to where?"

"The flower shop."

"But I was inside and no one rang the bell."

"Positive she appeared after you left the SUV and happened before your return just now."

"Oh." Aria hadn't contemplated Edmee ran out and then re-entered the flower shop through a door not the front.

"We going in again?" LeRoy asked.

"Let's wait." Aria braced her shoulders against the red bricks of the closest building. The four feet between her and LeRoy discouraged casual touchy-feely contact. Mr. Breaux was not visible inside his SUV. Aria surmised he either napped or strode off for coffee.

"How long?"

LeRoy's reasonable question simple enough. The answer as murky as the building's shadow pooled at her feet. No fog levitated from the darkness surrounding her sneakers. Nothing deterred Aria from confronting Edmee, yet she counted the ways it wouldn't be helpful. One, the state had never imprisoned the woman. Two, the woman had never given birth. Three, the woman lacked mental competency. Four, the woman lacked a connection to adoptions.

LeRoy cleared his throat. He'd jettisoned his circumspection gaze and replaced it with a derisive stare that harshly encouraged, no demanded, her immediate answer.

Aria shrugged.

"There's a better answer than that."

A head shake preceded Aria's heavy sigh. "How's the truth? Don't know. Never told the business this woman wants to attend to. You ever think of a family emergency?"

"She may wish to avoid you. Strive to evade you and hide out until you disappear." He swung his gaze to the street. "Where's your investigator, anyway?"

Her second shrug proved to be no impediment to LeRoy.

He flicked his right forefinger against his clothed right thigh. "Year-round ants and slimy critters grosses me out, if not do me in."

If either Aria's heritage had linked to a noble's crown as a refined lady of yore or she'd been blessed with inherited self-sufficient means, she'd have responded with disgust at the mere mention of centipedes or six-legged creatures. But she stood there with neither respected heritage nor an ability to write checks in six-figure amounts. The past left Aria with her mother's oft-repeated adage that no sleight of hand could or would squander her daughter's destiny.

While Aria never understood the adage's full ramifications, she comprehended her mother never let one opportunity pass without an expression of her love, even as hereditary maladies coursed through and racked her body.

A young, hand-in-hand, mid-twenties couple, dodged LeRoy, bypassed the livery entrance and headed between the buildings, possibly en route to the flower shop.

LeRoy's swat at a flying insect missed. "Should we follow? I've had enough of being a standing target."

"Hold on. If the woman doesn't appear by the time Mr. Breaux returns, I'll ask him to track down a home address."

LeRoy gazed past her. His lips twisted slightly. "What's the odds we end up in the hospital with yellow fever?"

Aria swallowed hard. Her street scan failed to locate a pharmacy. She'd seen magazine pictures of Paris where lighted green crosses dotted street after street to draw in passersby. "Let's get insect spray later."

"Great. You agree then they'll swarm the rental home eventually?"

"Must be water nearby, although have seen none."

"Let's ask Mr. Breaux." A shadow engulfed LeRoy.

"Ask me what?" Mr. Breaux halted next to LeRoy.

"LeRoy needs insect spray. He's a magnet to the strangest creatures, especially those that fly."

"There's a can in my trunk. But why are you standing here? My car's unlocked."

"Thought I recognized a woman who worked in the flower shop."

"And . . .?"

LeRoy spoke up. "She left and then returned before Aria could speak to her. She's hoping the woman leaves and we can intercept."

"Was she, say, small and dark-skinned?"

Aria chimed in, "Yes."

"We know her. Lives outside of town."

LeRoy slid both hands into his front pockets, rocked onto his heels and then stabilized himself on the balls of his feet. "Could we eat first?"

..*

Aria withheld her right hand from knocking on the strange door. LeRoy's request to eat had added two hours to their quest after Mr. Breaux had visited the flower shop only to return and suggest they not confront the woman at work.

She glanced past the uneven flat limestone she'd walked to see LeRoy and Mr. Breaux still in the latter's SUV.

Even after a deep breath, shreds of repressed guilt gripped Aria before her intrusion into another's world. When the white front door opened, the dark-skinned woman's green-eyed gaze penetrated Aria's soul.

"I know you," said the woman.

Aria froze. Up close, the woman's coppery skin struck Aria as amazingly moisturized.

The woman's repeated assertion she knew Aria threatened to blast Aria into a hasty, if disheveled, retreat across the irregular stones.

Faced with silence or flight, Aria surprised herself when she uttered, "Your cries penetrated my cell."

When embarrassment scars creased the woman's brow, Aria chided herself for inflicting needless hurt with unnecessary detail. She avoided the woman's direct scrutiny with an upward gaze to the steep metal roof on the single-story house, its porch triple the front door's width with a half dozen assorted terra-cotta pots not yet planted.

"Women's prison, two years ago."

"Yes," Aria replied, her voice soft. "Sorry to re-open wounds. Can we talk?"

"Will have to be out here. Baby's sleeping."

"That's fantastic. Congrats. Boy or girl? How old?"

The woman recoiled. She steadied herself and closed the door behind her within an inch of its locking. "Earl wanted a boy, and we waited eighteen months."

Conflicted thoughts lifted Aria's gaze to a roof that hadn't changed within the last few minutes. "Didn't know."

"That's okay. He's thrilled now."

The misgiving within Aria subsided. If she quizzed Tillie, there'd be no pushback about phrasing or the speed of multiple questions.

Her prior clashes with Louisiana culture, especially prison guards, confirmed Aria's belief Cajuns slower to accept outsiders, whether or not standoffish. A slow inhale uplifted her strength; she could do this. "Was labor long? Mine, so long ago, seemed to last days."

"Not when you adopt."

The unexpected expression of a natural occurrence jumpstarted Aria's attention. Should she try to be coy or straightforward? Be a casual friend or a shrewd investigator and summon either Mr. Breaux or LeRoy to be a witness to the woman's words?

Aria shunned perfection and blurted out her instant feeling. "Fantastic. I was told the saleslady in your flower shop could help me adopt. Guess she gave me wrong information as she said she only sold flowers."

"Don't be."

"Huh?"

"My boss never . . . ."

"Never what?"

"Helps without the big man's okay."

"Who's that?"

"Can't say."

"Can't or won't?"

"Both really. Since blessed with a baby girl I've dedicated my life to her and Earl. They come first." She stared at Aria. "And, I'm not destroying everything by blabbing or turning my back on my raisin'."

Aria tried not to escalate her presence into a stare-off. She sought information, not confrontation. The assessment scale in her head tipped between the woman acting from deep self-protection to having a strident reaction ignited by an unknown Yankee disrupting her daily routine.

"Let me explain. I'm not here to cause you pain."

The woman's gaze sagged, as did her entire face. The grim lines around her eyes magnified. "Then why?"

Aria sensed an emotional appeal would benefit her. "Like you, I'm seeking my child, but, unlike you, I've been unsuccessful. And, I have questions."

"Like what?"

"Did you lose a child in prison?"

Tears welled, turned what had been angry eyes into the saddest ones Aria had ever seen, words unnecessary to confirm the truth.

The woman struggled to speak. "Buried . . . laid to rest in the cemetery outside the walls."

"Sorry, so sorry for your loss."

"Prison midwife the next day said the baby's round face showed Down's. Didn't see. Saw only the blue blanket when one matron snatched my baby and handed the bundle to another who disappeared." Gravity launched a tear from her left eye. It skid to her chin.

"Happened same to me."

"Your baby sick, too?"

"Said dead. Can't find a grave." Aria dreaded her deceit when she said, "State agency won't let me adopt because they say I'll abandon the child when I go back to prison."

"Told me the same."

"But you have a baby."

The woman wiped two tears from her left cheek. "Earl knows a guy at the hunting lodge."

Aria tried to smile. Quit when the woman revitalized her painful stare. "Maybe, your husband could introduce me to this guy he knows. I promise to keep it a secret."

"Might . . . could."

If there existed a trick to change the woman's reluctance into a positive, the tack eluded Aria. She reverted to a question devoid of personal disclosure. "This hunting lodge. Can you tell me where it's at?"

The woman fidgeted, rubbed a pinch of cotton dress fabric between her right thumb and forefinger. "Don't reckon there's an address. A white building. Only one Earl ever say he drives his pickup to. Near here from what he say."

That was enough for Aria. Lucky, too, for a baby cry escaped the house.

"Please tend to your precious baby girl. My apology for any inconvenience. You think Earl might talk to me? I can call again?"

"Might . . . could."

The woman grabbed her front door knob and the open space swallowed her before Edmee spoke another word.

Aria stared at the closed door.

LeRoy shouted, "You gonna stand there 'til supper?"

Aria waved a shaking right hand at LeRoy; her strides toward the SUV short and deliberate. As she hugged herself, she imagined a healthy, smiling boy that may not be alive. A scared Edmee added credence to Aria's search that an answer existed. An answer she may or may not favor.

She strained her mind to determine an identity; who was this 'big guy' Edmee protected and cowered to when he wasn't even present?

Chapter Twenty-two

Tillie answered on the third ring. "Yo girl, you calling to tell me your arrive time? Pot's ready for a tasty gumbo recipe."

Aria laughed and shifted her shoeless feet, one lifted to rest on the rental home's living room sofa's crest rail. Five minutes before, when LeRoy left with a subtle smile, she half-expected he'd return with a surprise in addition to pizza.

After the door banged behind LeRoy, Mr. Breaux's stoic expression unreadable as he claimed his office summoned him, although Aria hadn't heard his cell phone ding.

Alone with the groans of an aged house, Aria, uplifted by Tillie's spirited voice, teased, "Can't find crawdads."

"Whoa there. No way you're to fool me. You date crawdads. Gumbo filled with deveined crawfish. Don't tell me Chicago isn't a windy city, Etouffee?"

"Yeah, right." Aria hadn't realized Tillie had crafted her a new nickname. "Can you put Aunt Maggie on?"

"What? No new hunk news?"

"Later. Now, is my aunt there?"

"Hold on."

The distant door creak and a shout that traveled the airwaves convinced Aria her aunt hadn't been eavesdropping.

"Honey, you okay? Tillie's eyes a little downcast."

"No worries. I'm fine. Search is still a dead end. But there's a question I have that Tillie can't answer."

"Yes."

"Met a woman today who I'd seen in prison." Aria repositioned herself to rest her left forearm on the sofa's arm. "She's convinced her baby born behind bars suffered from Downs Syndrome."

"That's so sad."

"Caused me to think. Did mom or my grandparents have anything I should be worried about?"

Static blips interrupted the phone connection silence.

Aria stood. "Aunt Maggie, you still there?"

"Yes, honey."

"Well?" Aria plopped her butt on the sofa. The cushions reacted to bounce her. "What's the answer?"

"You mustn't hold me to this."

"Won't. But, if there's something important I should know, you can't treat me as if I'm a little girl."

"Never."

Aria's question interrupted by the invading static.

"Don't know a thing about your father's family. Your mother's is different. Your mother's DNA included an abnormal TTR gene. While nobody told me it killed her, it's inherited. She could've been a carrier."

"And me?"

"Can't say."

The pitch in Aria's voice rose. "And me?"

"Honey, believe me when I say 'can't say.' That's the truth. Believe me I wouldn't lie, not to you."

"You have this, whatever you mentioned?"

"Not years ago when liver tests showed no unusual amyloid deposit buildup."

"Then I'm spared. Safe to live my life?"

The annoyance of repeated connection static denied Aria an understandable answer from Aunt Maggie. *Can't be intentional.* Aria waited. Drummed her fingers on the sofa's arm. Counted to ten. "Aunt Maggie?"

"You hearing me?"

"Yes, Aunt Maggie."

"Thank goodness you're still there. I said my long ago liver tests showed me to be normal. However, the doctor cautioned he could only guarantee that my positive results applied to me, no one else."

While Aria's nerves quaked, ready to explode, she struggled to subordinate and hide her deep-seated angst with a soft spoken, "I'm happy for you." Inhaling a deep breath, she asked, "Any Down's Syndrome in my ancestors?"

"Heavens no. Thank goodness."

The crunch of tires on the gravel outside announced LeRoy's return. "Would you do me a favor and search around if there might be another inherited disease I should be worried about." Aria didn't wait for the expected promise. "I'll ask Mr. Breaux if he knows of any prison-related outbreak I might not be vaccinated against."

"Tillie's here. Will you call tomorrow?"

"Yes."

"Here's Tillie."

A car door slammed beyond the living room window.

Aria sped up her words. "Remember our pledge in Africa not to speak secrets in front of refugees while, if you could, help me research what TTR is."

"Sure. LeRoy behaving?"

"So far." Aria pressed the cell phone against her stomach. She gazed up at LeRoy, two pizza boxes in his hands. "Let's eat in the kitchen."

He nodded and departed the living room.

"Sorry, LeRoy interrupted. What'd you say?"

"Good girl. Don't want you to return here leaving a stricken lover behind."

Aria's involuntary shriek followed by "Tillie!" The remark struck Aria too close to home considering her husband died in a Louisiana cabin.

LeRoy dashed into the room. "What's happening?"

"Nothing, LeRoy." Her voice boomed, loud enough to be transmitted to Tillie via a burst through the open channel airwaves and transform LeRoy's grave expression into an inscrutable gaze Aria failed to decipher. "I'll join you in the kitchen after a word with Tillie."

"Give her a shout out from me."

Aria lifted the cell phone to her right ear, listened.

"Sorry, Etouffee."

Aria cringed. "LeRoy says hello."

"Tell him not to fritter away your aunt's money. Now, you're returning what day?"

"Three, maybe four." Aria squirmed to find a comfortable sofa position. "No use, I guess, to dilly-dally here if there's no answers to be found. Leaves open booking our flight to Africa where we abandoned unfinished tasks."

"Doubt I will. Not safe, but, while you're pragmatic, tell me today, or when your return, that you'll agree to focus on living, to bring enjoyment into your life."

"Yeah, yeah."

"Well, anyway. Hide LeRoy's little blue pills."

"What?"

"Teasing, girl. Call the instant you crack your mystery."

Aria's left forefinger pressed her phone-screen's red circle to gag Tillie's voice with silence. Aria fought the urge to again scrutinize the gravestones she'd visited. Someone wiser than who she'd met must exist.

"Anybody home? Pizza's chilling."

Halfway to the bathroom to wash up, Aria shouted, "Be right there." to promise LeRoy she'd not forgotten.

Still rubbing her hands as she stepped into the kitchen, Aria faced LeRoy's table preset of two blue paper plates, two metal forks, and fanned white napkins next to two pizzas centered on the kitchen table. A pepperoni aroma streamed up and sideways from the cracked-open oven.

Aria considered a bow, right forearm at the waist, but thought better of it. *Don't antagonize, nor flatter.* "You could've started. No reason to suffer at my expense."

"How can I be a chef if I never witness my offerings being enjoyed?"

"Chef? Where's your hat?"

"Don't be old-fashioned. Have a seat."

With a chair-leg screech and an awkward plop, Aria did.

Politeness overwhelmed LeRoy when he cut short his smirk at her obvious ineptness. He lifted a butter knife. "A chef displays his skill by exquisite cuts. Watch me. Right before your eyes this whole pizza will be one slice for eight."

"Even with a sharp knife, I'd challenge you."

LeRoy dropped the butter knife to squeeze the wooden handle at the end of a chef's kitchen knife's eight inches. Four swift cuts and Aria counted eight equal pizza slices.

Aria hesitated, amazed. She accepted a slice scooped onto the plate he presented to her.

"Must I say start?"

Aria shook her head, grabbed a fork and savored a bite.

LeRoy led her in consuming four slices before she'd finished two. No problem. Slow eating provided a semblance of nourishment and, most important, safety from clumsy conversation separated by a bedroom door lock.

"You have a fruitful day?"

"Not really." Aria's words amplified by her head shake.

"I've not known you long, but there's a question."

Off guard, Aria could only respond with "What?"

LeRoy placed both palms on the table. "I've dated a girl or two and before night's end they've crossed their fingers and withheld their heart. Maybe that's my fate."

"Will be if you remain that pessimistic." Silence and nibbling equal parts cheese, pepperoni and pizza crust diverted her internal debate. She squelched the idea to bring forth from her family a further "mother" quote.

"What inspired you to get married?" LeRoy's question couched in a lowered confidential tone. When Aria offered no prompt answer. He filled in the silence with the supposition: "Assume you fell in love."

"You could say that." Her inflection flat and steady.

"And?"

Without an injection of anger or sarcasm, she parroted him. "And, what?" She poked her fork into the pizza slice in front of her. "My father didn't threaten Brad with a shotgun."

If she'd desired to rile or put him off, neither happened.

His closed lips soundproofed his chewing. She pondered whether his travails with the opposite sex rightly lay at the woman's threshold. He'd been courteous to her that first day at the train station. Since then he'd added a dash of flirtation plus honest concerns the night she jogged after an ill-advised window escape. She'd not promised him a reward for his driving her across the Louisiana landscape. What he inferred remained his innermost secret.

"We can put that second pizza away unless you've invited store or delivery friends."

LeRoy smiled. "Just us. Maybe I went overboard, but better leftovers than want." He gazed to the ceiling. "There's always the possibility of hunger pangs before breakfast."

"Not from me."

"Then how's 'bout my question. What inspired you?"

Aria weighed whether an answer, or not, would end this. Thinking too long about Brad elevated her grief. When the man who killed her husband faced justice, then, and only then, did she expect closure and eternal peace.

"Kindness, multiple little things."

He smiled. "What things?"

"Let's not embarrass ourselves."

LeRoy's shoulders swayed an inch left, then double that right. Aria suspected he required these seconds to digest her evasive answer and conjure a response.

She wouldn't press. Make him angry and she'd have to scramble for transportation, even with Mr. Breaux on her payroll. "Let's forget this. No use for either of us to play head games with the other."

"How 'bout you tell me what the flower lady on the porch told you while I sat in the car."

"Real sad."

LeRoy gazed at the unsliced pizza. "How so?"

"Woman's baby afflicted with Downs."

"That is sad. Must be difficult to raise."

Aria shrugged and struggled to speak. "Child died."

LeRoy sorted the napkins. "Well then, Tillie have news?"

Appreciative of the subject change, Aria reached for her third pizza slice. She scrapped off three pepperoni circles. "Not really. Wants to know when we'll be home."

"Whatcha tell her?"

"Like we promised, except I hope I can persuade you to extend our stay here if necessary."

LeRoy smiled. "You like the pizza or my company?"

Aria understood the Hobson's choice. "As was said earlier, let's not embarrass ourselves."

LeRoy jumped to his feet. "Damn women!" He spun his body on the balls of his feet, completed a full circle. "Never trust one and expect you won't be kicked in the teeth."

"Huh? Who kicked?"

"Figure of speech." He hiccupped. "When did Tillie blab I'd served two years in Joliet Correctional?"

"She didn't. Cross my heart."

"Ah, c'mon. Tillie wouldn't share her hoity-hoity townhouse digs if you hadn't inherited a fortune or she and you shared something else. Don't know what, but do know I don't do drugs anymore. If you're a mule from the New Orleans docks, don't want nothing to do with you."

"Tillie and I met as missionary workers in Africa. We don't shoot up or deliver drugs in either the Congo or Wriggleyville and, while my mother graced me with an inheritance, I ain't no heiress with a fortune. So there's no gain for you to be hurtful."

"Dirty laundry blackmail not my style. There's no way I'll clench my hands against bars again."

Aria internalized her kinship with these words muttered by ninety percent of ex-cons, even her. Tonight's revelation of LeRoy's criminal record offered Aria a stepping stone yet unrealized. She treaded carefully to capitalize.

"That tight-lipped flower-shop woman you asked about explained little more than her enduring heartache."

"Yeah." LeRoy's skeptical tone progressed. "So what does that supposedly tell me?"

"Intuition tells me you should have a talk with her."

"Me?" LeRoy rubbed his forehead. "Why me?"

Aria skipped a long, detailed theory to cut to the chase. "Ask to see the baby. Claim to be the father. It'll be denied, of course, but get Edmee or Earl to admit they adopted the baby without using a legal state agency."

"Do I need additional lies to spare being shot?"

"You're free to ad-lib."

LeRoy frowned.

"You can do it." Faced with defeat in not locating her own child, Aria forfeited her internal struggle to avoid words she might later regret. "I'll owe you."

A glint popped into LeRoy's eyes. "You will, promise?"

Chapter Twenty-three

Aria scrambled to escape her bedroom after a car engine's vroom. Then a soft backfire. She peered out the front window. Yes, LeRoy. Now gone without her.

She'd verbally pleaded with him the night before to let her go with him to no avail. She expostulated at length on her ability to avoid detection. Even with her offer to hide in the car's trunk, she lost.

Hungry and forlorn. She reheated pizza and sat at the kitchen table. Brainstorming generated no action plan. The Mardi gras ringtone jingled inside her bedroom.

Still she sat. If important, the on-duty voicemail primed to digitalize the caller's message. Aria swallowed the last pizza crust sliver. Her trust incomplete. She racked her brain for a logical thread to support why she broached the subject of LeRoy attempting to extract information when she failed.

In a haphazard circle she strolled from the kitchen to the front window, peered at an empty driveway and pivoted to her bedroom. LeRoy's question the night before about heterosexual attraction wasn't brazen, yet, after a restful sleep it prodded her to admit to herself that since Brad's funeral she'd spayed her desire to love again.

She lifted her suitcase to the bed. The clean clothes pickings were slim: a blue cotton blouse, black slacks, white socks and intimates, enough to make do, plus sneakers.

Voicemail spewed out a message from Mr. Breaux that he might stop, no arrival time given.

Neatness and boredom drove her to repack her suitcase, perspiration-laced laundry on the bottom. Above she laid in the folded jacket and skirt purchased at the Chicago thrift store. While retro fashion wasn't hip in Louisiana, perhaps if she'd worn it to the flower shop she wouldn't be idly roaming a rental house eager to hear from LeRoy.

All kindness and nice in her presence, he dropped the ball with his phone communication skills. If a mother, would this self-pity be her everyday emotion self-imposed on her child? Aria bemoaned a definitive and satisfying conclusion.

Loud gravel-crunching sounds permeated the house. At the front window, Aria watched a familiar muscular figure alight from an SUV never before seen.

Aria opened the front door.

A second figure she recognized from the hunting lodge exited the rear SUV door. He stood rigid at the vehicle's front bumper.

"Aria, there's news you should hear."

Indecision swarmed inside Aria's brain. Here approached the prison guard who had misled her with gravestone information. What information now? She pulled the front door shut to block out a view if anyone else stayed with her.

From the porch she asked. "What brings you here? I'm expecting a guest so I've little time."

The guard who'd shooed her away on her release, halted his advance. "We need you to confirm a child's ID."

Knees weak, Aria almost collapsed. She steadied herself with a hand extended to a porch post.

"We know you visited the flower shop and the woman who works there. Ingenious on your part." He glanced at his compatriot who immobile stood as a gargoyle with a menacing gaze. "Disregarding our culture is dangerous to outsiders."

"What? You directed me to the cemetery tombstones outside the prison. Was that a ruse for your amusement?"

"Calculated risk."

"Come again?"

"Most people, if given a chance for a peaceful resolution . . . try . . . no become disheartened when expected results don't pan out. Not you, obviously."

"Quitters don't win."

The guard rested his right boot sole on the porch's first step. "You ready to pack up and head north?"

"Not really. If no one buried my child, there's a chance she or he lives. Until there's proof, I can't stop searching."

"If you feel that way, come with me."

The offer struck Aria as manna from heaven. Without a second thought she piled into the SUV's rear seat. While the second man's expression never changed, he kept his distance.

When the SUV stopped, Aria recognized the hunting lodge. "Why we here," she asked. "There's no cemetery nearby. Have you invited an adoption person?"

For a reason not clear to Aria, no response came from either the guard or his companion. She bit her lower lip as her eyes scanned the lodge parking lot. Was it unusual to be uninhabited at ten a.m.? "Who are we meeting?"

The two men shared glances before the guard spoke. "No one you'd remember. C'mon, get up and follow me."

The sharp-edged 'get up' sliced open a prison memory capsule Aria believed she'd buried. The sooner she escaped Louisiana the better. In lockstep between the leading guard and his companion, Aria complied in docile fashion to each speed-up request.

Inside the hunting lodge, Aria questioned the identity and whereabouts of the unseen third person.

"Come this way."

Past the poker table, the guard led Aria to a door she'd never seen open. The eight-by-ten foot windowless room outfitted with a carpenter's workbench to the left. Maintenance tools and brooms hung on the opposite wall.

Brawny hands from behind grabbed Aria's shoulders. She twisted to free herself to no avail. She shrieked, "Let me go!"

"Not yet," the guard said. "You must remember that shouts loud screams are no-nos." He pulled a handkerchief from his front pocket, extended its ends between his thumbs and forefingers and twirled. With a hand at Aria's ears, he jammed the rolled handkerchief between her lips and tied the ends tight against her nape.

Throat guttural sounds sputtered from Aria's mouth.

"Since she can't follow instructions, bring her here."

The gargoyle's hand in the middle of her back pushed Aria to a clamp and tilt foldable workbench. A splayed hand to her cranium bent Aria's head and shoulders forward until her forehead rested on the gritty saw-dusted top.

"Wait," said the guard. "Put her arms into the slot between the boards and clamp her."

Aria's biceps throbbed as the workbench's screw clamps squeezed the top boards together. She stifled moans to give her tormentor no reason to extend her torture.

Behind her, the gargoyle rubbed his hand from her inner thigh to her ankle. "Should we tie her feet?"

"Tie one. Use laces. We need to find the boyfriend."

Aria gulped.

"She's already killed a husband. Who's to say she didn't take offense when she caught the boyfriend fooling around."

"Great thinking, great thinking."

"Now let's go hunt up a Yankee boyfriend."

After footsteps, Aria watched a stream of light merge into the darkness on either side of her. The clink of metal against metal preceded a lock's closure.

The mixed odors of cleaning chemicals and sawdust assailed her nostrils. Mid-day heat promised to intensify her discomfort. She jerked the workbench. Rock solid. She guessed it bolted to the floor.

Think, Aria. Soft, phantom baby cries tormented her.

Chapter Twenty-four

In the ominous stillness, Aria promised herself she'd never send LeRoy to finish what she couldn't nor criticize him for pizza. She'd welcome cold pizza, if only to stave off hunger.

Questions swirled. Had LeRoy eluded the guard? Had he and Mr. Breaux abandoned her? Both had to realize that after hours of no communication she wasn't at Aunt Maggie's rental home. Would they consider she'd bolted for Chicago?

Her predicament defied explanation. They'd immobilized her, but they hadn't otherwise abused her.

Today wasn't a prison where weekly guard entertainment occurred when corridor surveillance cameras were looped with prerecorded sanitized footage, time-stamp stripped.

The confined quarters generated arm sweat to offer her hope. She pulled at her arms and grunted to no avail. Why this punishment? Unknowingly had she become a threat? If so, she dared not think of what lie ahead.

Sweat beads dripped from her forehead.

She'd marched through an empty main hunting lodge room to her confinement. If poker existed as the main amusement, was the hand dealt her foretold by the gargoyle's stroke of her inner leg? A freaky cue that her restraint meant as a temporary reprieve from physical debasement. While she recognized the guard, could the second man be there to examine her for future deprivation and/or to buy her for forced transport abroad?

Women danced or wiggled, nude or topless, for entertainment in men's clubs throughout the world.

The door behind her opened. An air gust shivered Aria's exposed skin. She bit her gag.

"What's wrong with her?"

Aria's nostrils belabored an inhale. Had LeRoy spoke? She turned her head as far right as she could. No LeRoy.

The guard paced in front of her. A scowl accented his stiff stride. She fretted she lived on the ledge of a great abyss. Had he taught or learned the intimidation techniques practiced by the prison guard majority? She visualized his fingers tight against her throat. She swallowed hard, even though no fingers compressed her pharyngeal muscles. If he tried, did his mind twirl with gaiety or did her present agony entertain him apart from the echoes of past prison injustices.

He spoke past her. "What you see is slight exhaustion. We're restrained her only to subdue her natural exuberance. Trust me, she's given birth once, many fruitful years ahead."

The baritone voice behind her asked, "My sources tell me there were two or three woman with Downs Syndrome births." An abbreviated snort interrupted his speech. "You'll regret it if you're covering up deformed births or nature's imperfections to fleece my honest dollars."

"Never. Her child would've passed prison protocols."

"You saying that many didn't."

"Her child as perfect as my own."

"Good. My clients desire healthy, picture-perfect babies. Unfortunately, current baby demand is greater than the number your pregnant inmates can supply or are predicted to conceive and deliver in the coming months."

"What can I say?" He scowled at Aria. "Babies aren't bayou insects. If you take this one, my debt's paid, right?"

"The boss will decide that."

Aria gasped; a hard swallow loosened the muscles that choked her throat. Her mind whirled. Hadn't the flower shop woman mused about a boss? Who? Wasn't it the guard, a Mr. Hebert, if his wife had taken his name?

Were these boss references to the same person? She listened for a further clue. The guard didn't speak as an underling. His companion acted as a compatriot, neither a servant nor a boss.

Already released from prison, what could an employed guard do? Her parole papers safe at Tillie's house.

The compatriot asked, "We gonna keep her here?"

"No way," the guard replied. "Not safe, too many eyes."

"What then?"

"We're going to take her to where no one will look."

Both ignored a rap on the door. "Where?"

"That rental cabin an hour's drive from here where she killed her husband. No will ever figure she returned."

Aria listened in horror.

"Brilliant. Did the boss approve?"

"Not yet, but whatever we do to her will not get us in trouble unless she dies."

Aria tried to scream. Feeble whimpers escaped her lips as her tight gag muffled one, then two, valiant efforts.

The two men hovered and surrounded her. With her arms freed, Aria's muscles relaxed until plastic restraints bound her wrists. When she flexed her unbound ankle, Aria fantasied her liberated feet skirted the poker table and dashed for freedom. Reality intervened. New plastic strips dug into her ankles and limited her mobility to hops.

Please remove the gag. I'll promise not to scream.

Aria's unarticulated plea lost in the darkness zipped around her by a bag best used to cart the dead.

The ride jostled Aria into endless delirium. Twice a welcomed peace jolted by the vehicle wheels beneath her. She steeled herself to the haunting vision of a cabin she entered in wedded bliss and was dragged from in agony.

How could the cabin be the same? Hadn't a mop scrubbed the vinyl floor, or a sponge wiped the papered walls to degrade or obliterate the blood splatter's streaks and dots?

Aria didn't want to believe her life's spiral. The grand promises sunk in life's quicksand.

Without validated answers, her entire being mired deep in borderless speculation. She trusted her DNA contained an inbred trait strong and sane enough to spur her breathing without hallucinations.

Virile fingers compressed Aria's flesh at her shoulders and thighs. She resisted until her body lay prone. From her pointed-to-the-ceiling heels, the metallic teeth gnash began faint and grew louder as it traversed her spine until one snap behind her hairline ended the sound's life.

Surrounded by darkness, unseen perspiration beads slithered diagonal across her forehead until one bumped her nose and the facial crevice sped it along.

After muffled voices stilled, masculine arms, like lift-truck prongs, hoisted her. The cocoon that imprisoned her swayed forward, then rearward. If a baby she would've enjoyed the gentle pendulum rock.

Now into adulthood, she feared a slow descent to a lake's bottom. Her gag prevented shouts. Yet, who listened, even if she escaped her cocoon? Bindings suppressed her legs' ability to exploit the exponential power of her knee when flexed as a common fulcrum.

How long did she have until the wicked unknown crashed her reality? Yet, what could she do?

Chapter Twenty-five

A drowned corpse in a tailspin terrorized Aria's mind, although no lake water invaded her zippered bag, and nothing except her profuse sweating glued white cotton blouse fabric to her breasts.

Her bag's jarring thud against a solid surface rattled her nerves. Jittery, Aria's stream of consciousness wandered a familiar path. Why kill her? What information did she have that threatened her prison guards?

She convinced herself no one dared ask.

Voices, once clamorous, now silenced or departed.

Aria counted thousand one, thousand two until she, for no rational reason, paused at a thousand eleven. Panic regained its hold. Calf shivers diverted her from the pain of self-pity where she dwelt on not being able to cuddle her child, a child who starred in frequent apparitions more real than fantasy.

If she waited, who'd unzip her? A person who'd owed her a favor or a fiend? Inmates oftentimes sold themselves or sold out others. Had she been the latter? She doubted that.

Prison economics, as explained to Aria, were based on simple principles. One gained an advantage if one possessed a value desired by another. Sex headed the list. With a growing baby bump, Aria opted for loose-fit garments. She then never endured lascivious glances flashed to inmates by guards who ogled half-naked skinny feminine bodies.

The urge to stroke her abdomen today stymied by plastic ties that abraded grooves into her wrists.

The accelerated zipper rasp heightened Aria's anxiety.

Had they commuted her drowning? If the zipper release meant to scare her, it partially succeeded. Forever cautioned to be careful, what encore physical or psychological indignity crept closer, ever, ever closer?

"Aria, you alive?" LeRoy's voice shaky.

She wiggled her shoulders.

"Mr. Breaux, she's alive."

"Step away. There may be an explosive."

Unexpected danger chilled Aria's moisture-filled pores. A burning-arrow fear she'd never thought of. She breathed deep and called upon her brain to be analytical, not driven by emotion.

The foot shuffle indicated more persons than LeRoy and Mr. Breaux. A canine scent pervaded her claustrophobic environs. Fresh thoughts of her dog pawned off in the days before her incarceration flooded her brain cells, but today's scent different.

A dog barked.

Aria shivered and bit hard against her gag without the knowledge of whether a bark signaled safety or danger.

LeRoy's call of her name welcomed as a positive sign.

"Finish the unzipping, LeRoy." Mr. Breaux's command direct and firm. "Aria, don't move. Let us do the work."

The joyful glimpse of LeRoy's face wiped away every negative thought she'd attributed to him. She'd eat pizza for life. She suppressed her irritation at his roughness when removing her gag.

"Thank you, LeRoy. How did you find me?"

"Ssshh." He smiled. "Let me look at you."

Aria's cheeks warmed. Fright had added a tautness to her nipples. Her glance convincing that sweat and a cotton blouse offered neither modesty nor a disguise. "Get me out of here. I'm fine. Let me stand."

"We will, Aria," Mr. Breaux said. "LeRoy, crouch behind her head and lift her by the armpits. I'll yank this bag away."

Once completed, Aria sighed. Her bound feet restricted her movement, but LeRoy's strength kept her upright. On his cheek next to her left ear she identified the Axe fragrance.

"Hold her," Mr. Breaux said. "I'll unfasten this ankle restraint and then the gag."

Aria steadied her body on separated feet. LeRoy's hands loosened their grip on her shoulders and freed her wrists.

"Thanks. How'd you find me?"

"After the hunting lodge, Mr. Breaux suggested this building existed as the weathervane that pointed to your prison walls. Didn't object. Judged his paid engagement meant that others with greater insight than I acknowledged his greater deductive powers."

Mr. Breaux flashed a sly smile.

Aria scanned the room. Nothing struck her as familiar. "Is this the cabin where I supposedly killed Brad?"

"Indeed," Mr. Breaux replied. "Was a reason it remained on my radar to find you. Pieced together the bounty hunter with an abduction and the underlying connection radiates to your imprisonment."

LeRoy stared at Mr. Breaux. "What about the husband?"

"Collateral, I'd say."

Aria tapped her toes to speed oxygenated blood to fill foot capillaries. Her gaze active. On neither wall nor floor did she detect faded blood spatter. An unknown person had steamed and removed the wallpaper she remembered. Red paint applied as a not-so-subtle choice to camouflage human blood that may have seeped through the wallpaper seams or onto the drywall's outer layer.

"Was this place chosen to scare me?" Her question directed at whoever saw fit to answer.

"Doubt that," Mr. Breaux said. "Suspect they chose it as an unoccupied summer rental."

Aria stiffened. "What did I do to be a target?"

"Can't be sure." Mr. Breaux's gaze narrowed to Aria's face. "But best guess relates to unexplained baby deaths, and you being observed strolling from one grave to the next in the adjacent cemetery."

"Then why this cabin?" LeRoy asked.

Aria chewed on her right thumbnail as she awaited Mr. Breaux's factual recitation or reasoned judgment.

"One can conclude or suppose a nervous person or persons required to check if this cabin might still expose secrets and upset your conviction."

"How can it?" Aria asked. "Anyone can see they have scrubbed, repainted. No doubt others rented this place and swept DNA into cracks or crevices since Brad and me."

"Everything's not lost," Mr. Breaux said.

LeRoy's dumbfounded expression didn't deter Aria, although unsettled questions crept into her mind. "How so?" She braced herself for a vague or jargon-laced explanation, if not a fully distorted, diversion from reality.

"I've secured photographs."

"Aunt Maggie never mentioned or alluded to photographs. What you say strikes me as convoluted."

In a departure from his normal stoic mien, Mr. Breaux wrinkled his nose.

If exaggerated tenfold it would've replicated her mother's wrinkle of 'well that's that and now let's forget we even mentioned it.' Although her mother rarely forgave, Aria survived. Today stood as no different.

LeRoy interjected, "What photographs?"

A sour-faced Mr. Breaux, with a restricted lip movement, slowly enunciated his words. "My associate has the crime scene photos admitted into evidence after introduced by the district attorney." He reached into his pocket, pulled out a cell phone and pressed two numbers.

Aria watched, her voice still, as his phone remained pressed to his left ear.

He switched his gaze from LeRoy to Aria. "What other ones do you think I'd own?"

Put on the defensive, Aria answered in a quavering voice: "Ones to prove me innocent?"

"Right, put Remy on." Mr. Breaux lifted his right forefinger. "Middle drawer of my credenza. Dig out the Gleason trial photos. Bring'em to me. Ginger knows where I'm at. And, hurry."

He lowered his cell phone to his hip. "Now, I'm sorry dear, what did you last say?"

"Can you show me these photographs? The ones that prove me innocent?"

"Yes, ma'am. That's my view."

"Can I get a look, too?" LeRoy asked.

"If Aria agrees. She's my client and her file privacy remains with her. Wait here until my associate arrives. Shouldn't be long. Put the pictures on the front room coffee table. In the meantime I must run the dog to its kennel."

Aria nodded and smiled. She cooled her heels until Mr. Breaux exited before she strode to and sat on the davenport next to the table Mr. Breaux spoke of.

LeRoy, allowing a companionable-plus separation, plopped to her right. Aria lauded his chivalry with no intent to tell him so.

She tried, with no clock visible, to count the seconds in repetitive tens. After she guessed three minutes, Aria rose and paced.

"Won't get those pictures here faster," LeRoy said.

Aria halted her twirl halfway, happy to perceive his profile, not a flush-on-full face. "I know that," she hissed, sufficiently loud to make her point, although soft enough to avert a duel's forty paces at dawn, a cocked pistol poised.

"Testy doesn't become you."

"Neither does this wait."

"Think this cabin has pizza in the freezer?"

Aria shook her head. Something glittered in LeRoy's left eye. Was he being cute or good-natured hostile? Aria had lived by her wits too long. Although she struggled to divine LeRoy's scheme, his increased speaking rhythm convinced her he harbored one ready to be hatched.

She stood stiff, her muscles tensed as if she were a champagne flute balanced on a rickety serving tray.

"If you check, don't blabber I agreed."

An engine whined outside. Drawn curtains stymied her vehicle and driver identification. A sharp kitchen clang, not the sound of an oven's rack being shoved in with frozen pizza, accented LeRoy's unseen clumsiness. The myriad sounds pricked her inner ear nerves and distracted her from parting the front window curtains.

"LeRoy, you okay?"

His mumble drowned out by sharp door raps.

Chapter Twenty-six

Aria flinched and ducked four red-tinted knuckles leading a fist initially aimed at her forehead.

"Sorry," said a plaintive voice weak in contrast to a tall rugged man in a pale-blue dress shirt, dark-blue denim pants and boots straight out of a western oater.

Aria caught her breath to scrutinize, almost inhale, the sculpted Hispanic facial features darkened by a hat's brim. His left-hand fingers clasped a black attaché handle.

She grasped the front doorknob. "May I help you?"

He bowed ever so slightly. "Mr. Breaux summoned me."

"You've missed him."

"He forbade me to leave."

Heel-clicks on hardwood announced LeRoy's entrance.

"Who's he?" the visitor asked.

Aria half-turned. "My friend, LeRoy."

"Can we trust him?"

She glanced toward LeRoy and muttered, "Of course."

LeRoy, to Aria's left, squared his frame and jerked his head toward the door. "Are we to invite him in?"

Aria addressed the visitor. "Please enter."

Before he advanced, Aria angled her steps to the davenport. "I apologize for not knowing your name."

"Remy." The visitor bowed. "Remy Jayden." With a halting gait he strode to the open chair where he remained standing. "Did Mr. Breaux tell you when he'd be here?"

"Exactly, no."

Raised to shoulder height, LeRoy waved his right hand at Aria. "Is your suggestion we twiddle our thumbs? There's no food in this cabin. Water's cloudy, if not murky."

"First, let's all sit." Aria followed her own advice. LeRoy plopped onto the davenport.

Remy squared himself on a chair with his attaché on his lap. He stretched his gaze to three corners. "First time I'm sent here. Am I to assume something important?"

Aria stared at Remy. "Can we see what you brought?"

"I'd lose my job."

"Who'd know?" LeRoy said. "We're no snitches."

"Don't know." A chill lined Remy's face. "Can't."

Aria squirmed. It wasn't Remy's presence. Mental flashbacks of Brad's injuries rippled through her as she gazed into the kitchen through the door left open by LeRoy. Today's memories of what transpired in uncountable seconds no sharper than when she sat at the defense table before the judge announced the jury verdict and her incarceration.

Perhaps if she called Tillie. No. She'd be at work. Aria gazed at LeRoy. His left hand flattened his hair. Was he reacting to Remy's straight hair part? Could be? Yet, Aria didn't register a past or present reference to judge whether Remy's presence lit LeRoy's jealousy.

Remy's right forefinger rubbed the attaché latch.

Aria waited for its click. And, waited.

"You from around here?" LeRoy asked.

"Born on bayou stilts thirty years ago. Guess you could say near here."

"Ever leave?"

"College a few years ago."

Aria elevated her gaze from the attaché, convinced his firm jaw excited greater physical interest. "They graduated you when?"

"Fell short when my father killed."

A spirit of parental kinship filled Aria's breast.

"Can I pry?" LeRoy asked.

Aria's facial muscles tightened. She feared a frown and wiped her right hand across her mouth.

"Nothing the world doesn't know," Remy replied. "Father shot during a bank robbery. Left me, mother, and a brother."

"Tragic," Aria whispered into her palm.

As if ESP operated, Remy said, "While sad, no one should feel sorry for me. While it has been years, I'm ready to meet the prosecutor's demand for provable evidence to convict my father's killer." He glanced sideways as if to determine if the three remained alone. "If not, I've gathered an unregistered revolver and a box of bullets that'll do more than send my father's killer to his otherworld justice."

Aria lowered her hand. "Pray tell, is that why you work for Mr. Breaux?"

"Originally, but he treats me well."

"He tell you about me?"

"Somewhat, but not how beautiful."

LeRoy jumped to his feet. "We should see what's in that briefcase. You aren't Sherlock Holmes. If you don't, I just might yank it free."

On her feet, Aria issued a caution. "Whoa, LeRoy."

He glared at her. "Isn't it your money that's paying for this? We're halfway through the week. If it's nothing, we can scram. Maybe not you, but this place gives me the willies."

"Me, too." Aria hated her admission of vulnerability after her release from being terrorized two hours before.

LeRoy stared at the seated Remy. "What say you?"

"Can't. Not my instruction."

"You a toady? No ability to stand on your own two feet? That you?" Exasperation a heavy coat on LeRoy's words.

"LeRoy, don't threaten. It'll not get us anywhere."

"Thank you, ma'am." Remy's exhale audible.

Aria, unprepared to referee a tussle between LeRoy and Remy, heaved a sigh of relief when a knock at the front door required an answer.

LeRoy strut towards the door. A second rap and he raised both hands, palms up, while he gazed at Aria.

"Open the door," she said.

LeRoy yanked the front door toward him.

Mr. Breaux entered. "Sorry I'm late. Oh, Remy, glad to see you're here. You bring what I asked?"

Remy nodded; his right hand slapped the attaché.

"Great." Mr. Breaux underlined his vocal approval with four steps into the room. He gazed at Aria. "Please accept my apology if what I show you offends."

Aria swallowed hard. She'd been strip searched multiple times by prison guards and, if any pictures of the demeaning process existed, she'd shiver and close her eyes.

Mr. Breaux hesitated in front of Remy. With a bowed head, he whispered, "You bring the photos?"

Remy nodded.

"Aria, you must give me written permission to have this other gentleman stay."

"You mean LeRoy?"

"Yes. This may be extra cautious, but . . . ."

Aria locked her gaze with LeRoy. It had been only days, but she weighed whether to trust him given his quick aversion to be jealous of Remy, a complete stranger.

"Am I threatened?" Aria asked of Mr. Breaux.

"Not this minute, but who knows? Getting out of one scrape usually doesn't extinguish the fire. Then, the guard's out there plus, as you know too well, bounty hunters."

"There's no way I can leave Louisiana without LeRoy. If I can't trust him, who can I trust?"

"Me and, of course, I'll vouch for Remy." Mr. Breaux smiled at his associate safeguarding the attaché. "Others, problematic. Totally your decision. I'm at your mercy."

"What choice? I'm punished every day in new and unexpected ways."

"Client pessimism not a surprise. Happens often."

LeRoy stepped forward. "You okay, Aria?"

"Would be better if Tillie were here, but, I know, that's impossible. Mr. Breaux says you're not to be trusted."

"What?"

"Hold on," injected Mr. Breaux. "I said it wrong. I've evidence, court evidence, which requires me to record whoever views it other than Aria, who was the defendant."

"I'll sign anything, if it helps Aria."

"That all, Mr. Breaux? I can trust LeRoy. Aunt Maggie wouldn't have left me here with him unless she had confidence his presence benefited me."

Mr. Breaux gazed at Remy. "Open your attaché. Hand me that top sheet, the consent form."

Remy complied. His wink at Aria a gratuity.

LeRoy signed his name as did Aria.

"That enough, Mr. Breaux. Now tell me what I need to see. I promise not to faint."

Mr. Breaux spread six photos on the davenport cushions and Aria dropped to one knee for a close look. She flipped the color photo of Brad lying on the kitchen floor, blood pooling near his head and right side.

"Aria, isn't that your name on the wall?" LeRoy asked.

Mr. Breaux pointed to photo stickered with the number two in the bottom left corner. "Not completely. There's three letters scribbled in blood. They begin with an 'A' and end with an 'I' but there's no second 'A' or other mark."

"Don't remember that," mumbled Aria.

"You shouldn't."

"Why? Could've blacked out."

Mr. Breaux shook his head. "Prosecutors told the jury that Brad wrote those three letters in his own blood seconds or minutes after mortally wounded by a lamp. False."

Aria's right forefinger slid photo number two nearer. "My public defender didn't voice one objection."

"Look closer," Mr. Breaux said. "See the wall's blood spatter. Transcript shows lab technicians testified the wall splatter dry when the three letters were scrawled over it."

"And that means what?" LeRoy asked.

"Put that into context with Brad losing consciousness shortly after being stabbed. Therefore, unlikely he could have raised his arm to name Aria. And, there's more. The cabin searches by authorities found no lamp or other moveable blunt object, except a Tennessee whisky bottle. The lamp displayed neither blood nor bloody fingerprints."

LeRoy pointed at a photo numbered three, a whiskey bottle, and gazed at Mr. Breaux. "That all?"

"No."

"Right," Aria interjected. "Brad never drank Tennessee whiskey." She refused to wilt under Remy's stare. "And, I should know, because no whiskey of any kind crossed my lips. I wanted to tell the jury that until my public defender threatened dire consequences if I testified. He claimed northerners never fared well in front of a southern jury."

Remy rubbed his hands. "I'd say his jury advice spot on, although I can't say he represented you well."

"He didn't," Aria said, her vocal volume doubled.

Mr. Breaux raised his hand. "Please, please, be calm."

Aria inhaled deep, exhaled slow. From behind her, LeRoy pressed his fingers into her right shoulder. She gasped and turned on him. "What's this?"

"Needed your attention."

"Can't see why," she whispered.

"You're wrapped in the past. It'll eat you alive."

A second whisper, this time between her teeth, released her inner passion. "Resolve injected the antidote."

Chapter Twenty-seven

Pain burst deep into Aria's pelvis. She forced her abs to contract and release, then repeat. An accelerated contract/release rhythm matched her chest-induced pants. Together, on a prison mattress, had subdued and blunted pain throes, if not the mountain of mentally scaled shame.

Alone in Aunt Maggie's rental for at least one more night, Aria conceived no solace for unanswered questions. Fresh underwear saved for the car trip to Chicago offered no incentive for a brighter future. She'd will herself to embrace, yes endure, a life defined and doomed by miserable events outside her control, one after another piled upon a cumulative deliberating effect.

Double knocks vibrated her bedroom door. The door's stillness and two simple words: "Pizza's ready." placated her jitters that she'd left the door unlocked

Aria swung her legs off the bed; two palms propelled her erect. She steadied herself as her pelvic pain migrated to her heart and pooled there, unable to dissipate.

"Give me a minute. Trust me, cold pizza lacks pizzazz."

LeRoy reinforced his presence. "Don't be long."

A blouse change for dinner would've uplifted her, but with only LeRoy, Aria tucked her wrinkled pink blouse into tight blue jeans, grabbed the doorknob, pushed the door wide and marched into the kitchen. LeRoy's table setting, his pizza choices and the Spartan environs all too familiar.

LeRoy swallowed open-mouthed. Tomato sauce painted his upper lip; melted cheese dangled off a pizza slice edge.

A pulled chair permitted Aria to grab the seat and position herself at the table across from LeRoy. "Don't expect you'll let me catch up?"

LeRoy lowered the slice to a plate and wiped his mouth with a folded napkin. "Been thinking." He gazed upward.

Aria trained her gaze on him without being able to discern his full expression. She forced herself to wait.

"Been thinking," LeRoy repeated after he lowered his gaze. He wiped his chin as if his brain needed time to assemble the thought he labored to express.

His hesitation crept to the border of rudeness. She didn't crave artificial thrills. Honesty never existed behind bars. Fear and deceit ruled. "C'mon, let me take a bite."

"Tillie's said the past has been difficult for you and today's photos with the blood and Brad." His elongated inhale shortened by a noisy exhale. "To me it's easy to see you were framed, framed by a professional."

"That's the nicest thing you could've said. Sorry, if I acted like an impetuous brat just now."

"Thanks, but here's a deeper, more important question."

Aria chewed and swallowed the pepperoni circle she'd peeled off the pizza slice in front of her. "What?"

"With twenty-four hours left, you must either scramble to reverse your conviction or continue the baby search? Doesn't seem you've time to do both."

"My perception agrees with you."

LeRoy shifted left in his chair. "And?"

"My heart isn't whole. Knowing grief would be better than the hole I live with. Perhaps that's not understandable, but it's the best I can do." Her gaze followed LeRoy as he stood. She braced for his approach.

"Aunt Maggie told Tillie and me we shouldn't press. I can see by your taut facial skin my selfish desire to fathom you better has backfired."

"No, no." She lifted her gaze. "Your question on choice is one that desperately needs an answer."

"I can help?"

162

"Let me figure things out first. Remy volunteered to stop by at sunset." LeRoy's head drooped; his reaction akin to a sunflower head too heavy for its stalk.

He rebounded. "What's he know that I don't?"

"He claimed he hadn't seen the photos before we did and wished to study them. He said he hoped to match what happened to me with other unsolved cases."

LeRoy's grimace proved his neck muscle strain revived. He sat in his original chair. "If nothing ain't dawned on Mr. Breaux, don't get your hopes up that this Johnny-come-lately will sweep you off your feet." He raised a pizza slice chin high. "That's all I'll say."

"Ain't wearing rose-colored glasses. Never have." She bit into the pizza slice before her, unconcerned if LeRoy answered or not. Her peek showed him with greater interest in pizza than conversation.

A dropped fork clinked against the tabletop. With her attention drawn to him, LeRoy spoke with a stoic expression. "Anyway, you can forget I said anything."

"LeRoy don't . . . ."

"Don't is a suitable word. Let's turn it around, shall we? You don't owe me. I'm the one who charged into your life. Remember the bus station. Aunt Maggie promised to pay me to keep you safe. Doubt she told you. Messed that task."

Aria stared at him, long and hard.

"Thought so."

A weak appetite for pizza morphed into no appetite at all as Aria swallowed her third and last bite. Silverware crossed, she pushed away her plate.

"I'll telephone her within the hour."

"Fine by me."

"Cozy on up to Aunt Maggie if you want. Remember it's my mother's inheritance we're spending."

"Know that." LeRoy cleared his throat. "Why do you think I've lived on this gawd-awful pizza? Ops. That came out wrong. Meant that, while we're getting the best pizza Louisiana offers, it's far from Chicago deep dish."

While sincerity encircled her aura, Aria cautioned, "Don't apologize. You must excuse me."

LeRoy nodded.

Aria pushed her bedroom door closed and reached for her cell phone. After a speed dial press, she listened to Tillie ask straight out, "You doing okay?"

"Conflicted."

"Don't tell me it's LeRoy?"

"If it were only that simple. Earlier today Mr. Breaux showed me pictures of where Brad killed. If I'd seen them at the trial, I'd lived in a haze. Couldn't have been me that struck or stabbed him."

"Know that. So what's this I hear in your voice?"

Aria skipped the pain of being abducted. Not that she didn't trust Tillie, but if Tillie never knew, there'd be no slip up to worry Aunt Maggie. She paced bed to door, paranoid that LeRoy's ear pressed to the keyhole.

"Let me check something." She strode to the nightstand and rattled its one drawer. "Can't find them."

"What? Condoms or a pregnancy test?"

"Knock it off. This is a crisis."

"Whoa."

Aria glanced past her right shoulder as if Tillie stood inside the door, seven feet away, shouting a command that required immediate obedience. "You heard truth."

"Yeah, I know. You're so tense you can't take a joke."

"Be a friend. Help, not jokes, is what I need now."

"Ah . . . you know, I'm always on your side. What's stressing you?"

"Indecision. Can't choose. Pursue my innocence or find my baby. There's no excellent answer."

"Let me ask Aunt Maggie."

"Noooo." The elongated vowel echoed inside Aria's brain, or was it the weak undecipherable response from deep within her heart?

"Okay, okay," Tillie said. "I get the picture. You and LeRoy still plan to head north in two days?"

164

"Yeah. Let me speak with Aunt Maggie and I expect your lips will stay sealed. I'll let you know what I decide."

Tillie's shout for Aunt Maggie jolted Aria's ear. She shook her head and deluded her feeling of dread with the melody and lyrics of happy days are here again.

"Aria, Tillie says you're coming in days."

"Yes, Aunt Maggie."

"You find what you've searched for?"

"Not yet."

"God speed then." Aunt Maggie's disconnect barely offered Aria time to say good-bye as a nagging question gripped her.

What was going on with Aunt Maggie? Wasn't like her to be cryptic and then religious. Aria gazed at her cell phone. No doubt the hang-up deliberate, not accidental.

Aria interpreted the exterior kitchen door loud bang as LeRoy's departure. Whether to the backyard or beyond, she knew not. She ditched her slippers for white sneakers. She chuckled. If her blouse had been red, not pink, she'd be a Yankee Doodle Dandy deep in the bayous of Dixie.

After quick steps through the house, she stood on the front porch, LeRoy nowhere to be seen. A black SUV with a dented front fender turned left off the main road and slowed to a stop. Overhead, an orange streak emerged beneath the blue heron's wings. Aria anticipated the sun's full glory to be splashed across the low gray clouds stretched to the horizon.

"Am I late?"

Although he'd dressed up his appearance from jeans to black khaki slacks and a white dress shirt, Remy's rugged Hispanic features unchanged. The wide-brimmed hat preserved his allure from earlier in the day.

"If you haven't eaten, sure I can offer a pizza slice."

"Very gracious, but excuse me if I pass." Remy advanced to the bottom porch step.

For the first time Aria glimpsed his eye color, intrigued by the intense brown shade darker than an almond's shell. "Where we off to?"

165

"Nowhere tonight."

A gulp filled Aria's throat. Once cleared, she launched her second question. "Thought you had a plan?"

He squared his feet on the first step; his left hand on the nearby rail. "Definitely, however, Mr. Breaux said I had to explain the risks and obtain your permission."

"I have paid him. What more?"

Remy gazed at his spit-shined boot toes. "If you were a Cajun lady, perhaps I'd find it easier to explain."

If he designed his comments to belittle, no degradation crept or fluttered within Aria's thoughts. Whether for blows or embrace, her restraint kept them two steps apart.

"Do you wish to see the intercepted communication?"

Her chest tightened. "What's this communication?"

"Mr. Breaux entrusted it to me and I promised not to break the seal until you did. I only know of the embossed flower shop return address."

Chapter Twenty-eight

The early morning road bumps, softened by vehicle suspension and Remy's deft steering wheel jerks to miss potholes, added little to Aria's vague notion of where they headed. The lines Remy drew on a road map the prior evening forgotten. Okra fields non-existent. A swampy bayou landscape predominated.

Forewarned by Remy that there'd be a walk, Aria grabbed the interior door handle as Remy slowed, steered off the gravel onto the left shoulder weeds and braked.

Remy glanced at her. "Meet me outside."

Aria refused to allow her thoughts drift from the present as she scurried to the car's front. Yesterday's clouds swept north by a wind that clung to their grayness. Mid-morning humidity predicted a suffocating afternoon. The thrum of critters naked to the human eye hastened Aria's desire to learn what Remy promised before she joined LeRoy for their thousand mile Interstate 55 journey. She swatted the ephemeral moisture wisps.

"It's not far," Remy said. "Bridge may be scary."

"What bridge?"

"The house we seek rests on stilts." A sly grin parted Remy's lips. "Can you swim? Not for me, unless . . . ." His turned head obscured his smile and her ability to read lips.

"Did you mention a boat?"

He gazed at Aria; his expression stoic. "No. Doubt there'd be one. Authorities never venture out this way."

He stretched his right hand to encircle her left wrist. Aria strode forward to ease Remy's tug. She spoke aloud to his shoulder blade. "But, you claimed this house relates to the two who restrained me at the hunting lodge."

Remy squared his shoulders to her and displayed his dexterity to walk backward. "More the flower shop owner."

"Watch out! A branch."

Remy stopped in his tracks. His forward step and pivot unleashed a swish on the recoil. "Thanks." He stared into her eyes. "If I let go, you'll follow?"

"Why not? You've pocketed the car keys."

His sly grin returned. "Bright you are."

"Go back. Finish what you said about the flower shop owner. Is that the woman I spoke with or another?"

"Never told who you met."

"Saleslady with honey brown hair and a toothy smile. Wore blue blazer. Skinny woman named Edmee, hard to describe. Don't remember a distinctive facial feature."

"I'll need time to research."

Remy restarted their walk after he again grabbed her wrist. The path wandered right. On both sides Spanish moss dangled without a flutter to obscure what nature or man built behind the greenish curtain. Aria stepped on larger rocks exposed by erosion. Brackish water appeared, she estimated, a hundred yards ahead. She braced her free hand against Remy's shoulder blade as the terrain sloped forward.

"Almost there."

"Don't see anything."

"Behind the copse there's a bridge."

"Really?"

"Trust me."

"You sure someone will be home?"

"If plywood covers the bridge gap, we're in business."

Aria pulled her hand off Remy to wipe at the dampness on her forehead. *What a place, deodorant hell!* She hadn't counted her steps, nor activated the step-counter on her cell phone. She thought a moment. Did burners have counters? Not her worry.

"We there, yet?"

Remy glanced past his right shoulder. "See that Bald Cyprus? I'm told it's a marker we're on the right path."

Aria took in a tree that had to have been six feet in diameter. She remembered others, but never one she couldn't hug and touch her fingertips. She gazed upward in awe. A red lantern hung twenty feet above her. "Is that lantern significant?"

"Tells us we're expected. Otherwise we could be shot at."

"Is that neighborly love?"

Remy halted his advance and let go Aria's wrist. "In this bayou it is." He gazed left, right and at the path they'd traversed before he cupped his hands around his mouth. "Red lantern, red lantern," he shouted. "Safety we seek; no weapons we keep."

A light flashed. From where it came, Aria knew not. "What was that?"

Remy bent close to her face. "We're welcomed."

Around the tree, Aria gazed past Remy to see a three-foot wide wooden bridge, the ends of a plywood sheet laid across

2x4 inch planks. She thanked its builder for handrails, even if rickety and not guaranteed to prevent a tumble into the water.

Remy offered a suggestion. "Best way to reach the house is to look straight ahead and move fast. Dilly-dally and fears build. I'll go first or you may. Your choice."

No smile, grin or smirk existed on Remy's face. Aria pondered her decision. If she went first, Remy had a chance to catch her backward fall, but not a face-plant. If she went second, he might miss her fall until he heard her splash. "I'll go first."

Aria quickened her pace across the plywood, slowed it on the weathered boards and skipped a decayed board ready to split. Safely on a second plywood sheet, within touching distance of a door, she breathed a sigh of relief.

The bridge beneath her sneakers swayed.

Remy grasped her waist from behind.

Aria's body tensed.

Remy's breath upon her nape. "Sorry."

The weathered one-story clapboard house on stilts impressed Aria as a hovel for gators. "Do we knock?"

"Doesn't hurt. Should be open."

Aria pushed the door. It swung inward. Four cribs surrounded a rocker with a woman cuddling a child.

She screeched, "Remy, how dare you!"

Aria cowered, her upright stature reduced by a third, Remy at her back. Two black cats jumped from a shelf along the far wall. They circled two cribs, cast a sentinel wary eye at Aria and sat on their haunches, tail swipes hitting the wall, twenty feet from a covered diaper pail's pungent odor.

Voicing concern, Remy said, "Edmee, don't be upset."

Aria twisted her torso toward Remy. "You knew she'd be here." She twice struggled to inhale. "You knew."

"Let's say, suspected."

Aria scanned the cribs a second time to conclude that two, or half, were but sheets and blankets. Unable to speak for several seconds, she finally mumbled, "That baby you hold, was he or she born at the women's prison?"

"Yeah. So what? Every child deserves a chance to be loved, and that's what I do. Better here with me than fondled by good 'ol boys who ogled or groped their mothers."

Aria battled the pain of her constricted throat to eke out a mere three words. "But the mothers . . . ?"

"Aria," said Remy. "Don't be sidetracked."

"But . . . but." Internal emotion choked off her words.

"Focus. You wished to find a child, not overrule a jury verdict. That's why we're here."

Aria coughed. "What, what about Mr. Breaux?"

"He's busy today."

In a whisper she asked, "So, he's given up on me?"

"Not so. I convinced him I'd be better to find this place."

Of what Remy claimed, Aria could form no judgment. Here she was. What positive could she make of it?

Aria stared at Edmee. "Do the babies have names?"

Edmee uncovered the face of the babe she cradled against her breast. "Only in my heart. If one stays two weeks, that's a long time. If I attached names, there'd be greater heartache."

"Who brings the babies here?" Remy asked.

Edmee shook her head.

Aria leaned forward to catch a glimpse of the baby's face. "You can't do this yourself."

"I've done it two years and four wives help."

"Who?" Remy asked.

Edmee renewed her head shake.

Aria's hand touched Remy's shoulder. "We should go."

"You sure?"

"Yes." Aria twisted her gaze to Edmee. "Thank you for cuddling, keeping each baby safe, wrapping every child in your boundless love."

Aria completed her pivot before leading Remy to the door and their escape from this house and the water that threatened to jump up and claim them should a step be missed.

At the car, Remy's brooding expression caught Aria off guard. "What did you expect that poor woman to tell us?"

Aria gazed into the bayou. The faraway mist, without the hint of being scared, as enlightening as Edmee.

"Aren't we searching for your child?"

"Stop it. Just stop it." Aria stepped away. She heard Remy's footsteps behind her. She threatened to walk the gravel roadway's entire length, if that's what it took.

Remy shouted out, "Aria, don't forget it's your goal."

His last word imprisoned her stronger than any steel chain or leather cuffs that had bound her wrists and ankles. She twirled. "Being strong unleashed me. Yes, I've always had a goal, more than personal. Babies can't be stolen."

"Didn't see that."

"C'mon. Don't tell me the prison laundry marks on the sheets and the blankets were invisible. Those items didn't float across the bayou to be plucked and dried."

"Wasn't close enough to inspect the cribs. Anyway, not my big thing. Did you notice there wasn't a records cabinet?"

"Well, no. Baby thieves unlikely to keep records."

"Birth certificates important, especially for adoptions."

"Granted, but Edmee can't help us. She's scared." Aria paused with no wish to offer a lengthy explanation. "She said two years. My baby . . . ." She fought to dispel the emotional catch in her throat. "My baby, if alive, more than twice that."

The splash of a wave combined with a motor boat engine's *brr-brr* snatched Aria's attention away from history to a possible present danger. Did she really hear a boat's motor or was it a dream?

Remy jerked his gaze in two outward directions. "Can't see anything between the tree trunks."

Aria heard the sounds repeat, only closer. Remy's left hand clasped her right wrist.

He spoke in a hushed tone. "We need to get out of here."

Remy's abruptness puzzled her. "Where to?"

"Trust me."

Chapter Twenty-nine

Aria fingered the velvety black satin, slithery against her skin. The scalloped white lace tickled her cheek as she sat in the passenger seat of Remy's SUV.

A burst of ire flooded her being. She tossed the blindfold onto Remy's lap. "If you don't want me to see something, I'll close my eyes, okay?"

"Suit yourself." He sat on the blindfold.

He shifted the SUV into gear and drove below the speed limit. A brief glimpse of the Deputy Dog statute settled Aria's fidgeting. Nearness to a walking trail, rather than a bridge, brought her comfort.

Then calmness took a hike.

In drier times, the two-lane asphalt road they turned onto may have had ditches, but today the water lapped the shoulders. At one juncture Aria had perceived a vehicle behind them, but it never tried to pass and no longer filled her side mirror.

"You said earlier we're headed to an isle called San Marie. Is that it ahead?"

Remy uplifted his gaze from the road surface. "If we outrace climate change before it's submerged, it will be."

"Is this our only access?"

"Yes. So, unless we find an isle high point wide enough to execute a U-turn, suggest you cross your fingers and steady your heart because backing up isn't my strong suit."

"You sure we'll find what I seek?"

"Hold on." The car's front suspension dipped and bounced. When Remy and she stilled, Remy said, "If you wish to close your eyes, now's the time. Expect a bump."

"That's okay. I've survived worse carnival rides. Tell me why we're headed this way."

"My boss said the hunting lodge guard makes a trip this way twice a month on average. Often it matches activity at the flower shop. Last week a rental box truck visited this isle and stayed overnight."

"How can you know these things? One can't sit on this road without being observed."

"Eyes don't have to blink human. Two of those bald cypress trees have hunter cameras. Until last year I rowed a boat to retrieve the photo chips. Wireless technology upgrades beam the images to my boss's network computer."

"Amazing."

"It is." He flicked his gaze at Aria. "Like you."

Her right-hand fingertip touch confirmed her cheek skin warmed by a dilated capillary blood rush. While her intense involuntary reaction threatened to expose a hidden deep-seated embarrassment, she hastened to hide her reaction beneath palms and spread fingers plastered to her face.

She appreciated that neither spoke until Remy's car braked to a stop at a planked walkway to an island large enough to prevent Aria from seeing its opposite shoreline. Beyond the walkway and the water beneath it, similar to a moat, stood a house constructed in basic concrete block.

The bayou stilts she'd expected elevated a four-foot round steel water barrel.

Whoever had designed and built this one-level house with a gable roof feared neither low nor high tide to swamp its interior. If Tillie had questioned her on how to describe it, Aria would've directed her friend to picture a shotgun house she'd first seen in a travel advertisement for New Orleans.

With his driver door partially open, Remy encouraged Aria to get out with the words: "We should go in."

"Anyone inside?"

"Expect not, but records are what you seek, right?"

Aria nodded and reached for the car's door handle to exit. Her choppy steps to miss the plank cracks caused her to lag behind Remy, although he twice paused to reach for her wrist. While she accented her discomfort with scrunched facial muscles, she swung her arm behind her butt.

Without acknowledging her reluctance, Remy strode ahead, neither a turn nor slowing reprised his outward action to lockdown Aria's physical contact.

Aria maintained her pace until she joined Remy on the front stoop. When Remy unlocked and cracked the solid wood door three inches, Aria's nose detected no whiff of rancid diapers. To her, this proved she'd see no babies and implied no babies visited or slept inside in recent days.

She gazed at Remy. "Shouldn't there be at least one person out and about? Sure it's hot, but flowers and a side garden need periodic watering, if not weeding."

"Parish climate experts predict this island will be submerged. They don't say when, but it's not an if."

"That's sad. This house and the two-story across the lawn spark recollections of vibrant yesteryear plantations."

Without an answer to her implied question, Remy knocked on the ajar door twice, his second rap harder than the first.

His yell, "Anyone here?" unanswered. His right elbow pushed the door wider. The soft door creak gave way to an unrestricted inward invitation. "There were file cabinets here last time."

Aria peered into the front room. "None here now." An intrepid Aria strode forward without a rearward glance. "Kitchen's gutted, no appliances, shelves bare." A closed door twenty feet distant blocked Aria's visual inspection of what she perceived to be a rear bedroom. "That's weird."

"What's that?"

"Door lock clasp on the outside." When she shifted her gaze, she felt his on her face and turned away when her psychic sensitivity morphed from odd to creepy.

"There's no lock," Remy said. "I'll watch the front door."

Aria's curiosity overwhelmed her alarmist hesitation. The oiled hinges let the door swing with minimal force applied.

Daylight streamed through the room's window to scribe multiple rectangular, almost square, boxes across the floor. Stagnant air offered brief buoyance to suspended dust particles against gravity's heavy pull. One by one a mote rocked ever lower, ready to bond with compatriots and add a further layer to the floor's dusty crust, the bayou's snub at a volcanic upheaval.

"There's a ratty mattress on iron springs littered with papers." Aria tiptoed toward it. She shouted over her right shoulder. "Want to see?"

"In a sec."

Aria breathed deep. The floor's light-created boxes existed as a monotone chess board. She stifled a cough. Without pawns, she harbored no illusion of being a queen. Box lines crossed her sneakers. No magic extraterrestrial force or windowpane created them. Steel fencing affixed to the house's exterior bespoke but one answer.

She tried to push her right hand upward against the window's frame. Her fingertips stuck where she put them. Even engaging her palm generated no window movement. Consistent with the door lock clasp, Aria deduced the person who scavenged the kitchen nailed the sash tight. Unmoved by this conclusion, she suspected the room served as a makeshift storage vault or a jail cell.

Stymied by the reluctant window, Aria wandered to the bed and lifted a yellowed, 8x11 inch, bordered sheet of paper. The faded words "Louisiana birth certificate" left no doubt what it purported to be, yet, it wasn't an original. No half-inch blue border surrounded the typed-in information. The name Jindal she'd heard, but other names were foreign to her.

"You found records to help us?"

A startled Aria flinched at Remy's voice behind her. She steadied herself as she faced him. "Maybe."

"Reminds me of a high school scavenger hunt into an old abandoned house that scared every girl with us."

While high school hijinks a distraction, she accepted a two-minute diversion as a minor irritant. "How's that?"

"Six of us agreed the last item on our list had to hide in an abandoned house's attic."

"You win?"

"Hardly. We disturbed a bearded man with shaggy hair."

Weary she'd even asked, Aria tried to divert attention to the documents found. "Doesn't sound terrifying."

Remy flexed his fingers and in a deadpan tone said, "Twelve-gauge shotgun was." He gazed toward the room's closed door. "We all froze, except Emma who convulsed with the loudest gasp I've ever heard."

"You obviously escaped."

"Wasn't easy. This weirdo barricaded me and three other boys into a bathroom after he forced two of us to bind the hands and feet of Emma and Riley."

Her interest aroused, she asked, "No one shot?"

"Emma said later she wished she'd been. And, that was the clearest part of what she said. This weirdo called her a 'box' and said he'd the powers of Pandora."

"Pandora didn't have any powers."

Remy shifted his weight from right to left, then left to right. "I used to believe that too."

"What changed?"

"After two hours, the weirdo released us from the bathroom and, with his shotgun cradled by his right arm, told my buddies to run to see if they'd outrun the blast pellets. His left hand clamped itself on my arm. I expected to be gator lunch after thrown into the nearby bayou."

Aria shivered as Remy's eyes narrowed. "The girls?"

"Best as I could see beyond the sofa that blocked my view, he'd stripped and retied them. Saw little blood."

"So he attacked them, let you guys off?"

"He did, if you believe Emma. Still, I have nightmares, wake up with sweat beads clinging to my skin, red marks on my left arm. His curse stares at me."

"Dare I ask?"

"He claimed a voodoo chief priestess gave him Pandora powers to seduce women to conceive warriors. When I challenged him, he pinned me to the floor, unzipped my pants and jabbed a syringe needle into my scrotum. He threatened me I'd die a painful death within three years if no born warrior carried my DNA."

Aria shaded her head with her left hand, stopped. She convinced herself Remy narrated a sci-fi fantasy, yet didn't wish to belittle him if he believed. She pivoted to extend her gaze for other birth certificates.

Hand pressure on her left shoulder stiffened her. She shuffled right to disengage, half-turned on the balls of her feet while her legs kept their restlessness. Her right hand extended the birth document.

Aria didn't understand if Remy's sheepish grin radiated guilty embarrassment or was an attempt to appear silly.

"A birth certificate?" Remy snatched the document. "An obvious copy." He stepped to the bed. Rustled though fifteen to twenty documents. "All birth certificate copies, unique names, boys outnumber girls."

"Could they be frauds?"

"Fifty/fifty would be my guess." He raised one document to his face for a closer examination. "What I see likely began as a doctored original, then copied. Come closer."

With a hesitation in her step, Aria advanced and kept an arm's length distance. "Even if I looked, I'd not know how to recognize whatever shouldn't be there."

"Your mind must be open. Think of us."

Aria shook her head. "What of us? You're confusing."

Remy ripped in half the document he possessed. "Please don't get me angry. That's not true. When I held your hand, you didn't pull away."

Aria swallowed hard. She'd once allowed Tillie to lead her by the hand through an African jungle without expecting Tillie to assume they were anything but friends.

Remy knelt on his right knee to swipe his forearm across the stained mattress. Papers flew. "You squeezed my hand.

That was deliberate, far from an accident." He stood to kick away a landed document that draped his shoe.

"Thought I'd fall." Although she hadn't exclaimed this reason at the time, Aria believed in its truth.

"You know, as kids, we're cautioned not to hide away; trained to seek or welcome the intriguing people the world brings to us."

"But I'm no kid, no naïve girl."

"My eyes definitely see that."

Aria's cheeks warmed.

"And, it's much more. It's being engaged for fresh experiences, being ready to accept someone who can offer closeness plus an exciting future."

Aria shook her head.

"You don't believe that?" The skepticism front'n'center in his tone as he leaned his right shoulder forward. "I doubt it. Of all the persons who pass into and out of our lives, who doesn't believe this procession may include a soulmate, a unique person to spend their life with."

She fixed her gaze on his face. She'd never vocalize he wasn't handsome, but he'd popped into her life yesterday and now he probed to expose her deepest emotion, a love she'd given whole-heartedly to Brad. Her physical reaction to Remy she wished to categorize as a loneliness craving, light years from flipping an intimate attraction on-switch.

Aria tried to relax and sought to re-channel their conversation. "What do we learn from these forms?"

Remy distanced himself from the bed with a circular route that left him alongside Aria. "Best guess, someone started with a copy of the official birth certificate, whited out child and father surname and typed in substitutes."

"Don't see that done here."

"You'd be right."

Unconsciously, Aria stiffened as Remy eased behind her. He continued, "This is likely a transfer point."

"Transfer what?" Aria squatted to begin a frantic effort to pick up each certificate. She crawled to a half dozen, at first unreachable. "You could help."

"There's no purpose. Whatever information exists is either fake or so generic it'd lead us nowhere. And how will this help you? The one birth certificate I read dated this year, not the years ago you seek."

Without rising from her knees, Aria stacked the documents she'd gathered. She cocked her head left.

Remy pulled a folded business-sized letter, its edges slightly frayed, from his back pocket.

"What's that?"

"Overdue rent notice." He jammed the envelope into his rear pocket without offering her a confirmatory inspection. "Time you threw away those stupid forms." His hands clasped her hips.

"Don't need help to get up."

"My pleasure."

Aria didn't fight against the hand pressure as it continued to retard her ability to stand erect. Her ears struggled to isolate Remy's vocal rhythm hum from the insect thrum and shrieking bird calls on the concrete wall's exterior side.

"Long time since I've been here."

This vague untethered admission skidded through Aria's consciousness like gravity zigzags rain droplets through the bark crevices she'd seen on thriving bayou bald Cyprus trees. She continued to be alert.

"Good times," he sighed,

Aria steeled her back muscles to ward off collapse.

"We could enhance our adventure, pass a good time."

"Not pinned to the floor."

"There's a bed." His right hand inched up her side. "If I tie you up, I'll promise not to strike you."

His words, especially their lack of subtlety, ripped at her being. She possessed no physical weapon. Break through the window and she'd run to splash into swamp waters without the faintest idea what disease or monster awaited.

"It's an awful time for me," Aria pleaded. She hoped he'd comprehend her clue to feminine functions, but she discarded her misconception as his right hand groped her right breast. Evil demons danced in her brain cells.

"Let me go!" Her scream's intensity surprised even her.

"Calm yourself. I've seen you size me up. Thinking I didn't notice. Understand you concocted this crazy scheme to convince your aunt to release money to you."

"Not that way." Aria's voice soft while defiant.

"You should share."

"Never." Aria inhaled to refill her lungs.

His right hand rubbed her breast contour.

"Ouch."

Remy's clamped-on fingers squeezed.

"Don't think I haven't endured worst."

"Know you have. Prison guards keep few secrets."

Aria glanced at the bed. No sharp corner she'd be able to slam Remy's head against. Even MacGyver couldn't fashion paper documents into a sturdy club, and paper cuts never disabled an Ian Fleming villain. She strained to craft a question that would give her greater information on the whereabouts of her baby, if not dead.

"So you're part of the conspiracy to profit from babies born to locked-up innocent women?"

"No way. The only babies not pampered are those stillborn. There's no money in digging graves."

"Then you'll let me go?"

"Maybe later. At the hunting lodge they remembered you forced a miscarriage upon yourself rather than lose a second baby. You deny that?"

Aria remained silent. When the prison doctor had pronounced her recovered, they had wheeled her on a gurney into a medical storage room for three days. Hands and legs bound, eyes blindfolded, mouth gagged, her ears heard multiple male grunts and hearty laughs. Only one comment still haunted her: "Should we bet on who will be the father?"

"Don't remember," Aria said. "Really don't."

"Let's ignore your past. Our pleasure is, and should be, now. I'll show you a high I've given others. I'll be the new Pandora. My touch will build a warrior legion."

"I'll rat you out to Mr. Breaux."

"Just try. He'll blame your disappearance on the multiple bounty hunters. Trust you've met one?"

Aria gulped.

"Now let's get you onto the bed, it's softer than the floor and, if you don't struggle, I'll try to not hurt you."

If she screamed, who except bayou insects would hear?

Remy's overpowering grip lifted her shoulders and knees as she struggled. Her dropped butt dented the naked mattress before the unexposed springs moaned as he pinned her arms.

Remy bent close to whisper into Aria's left ear: "The blindfold's in my rear pocket."

The scream inside her brain reverberated against bone. *Please, please. LeRoy wouldn't do this.*

Chapter Thirty

The footstep thuds on the walkway planks outside the concrete house intensified Aria's physical fright. With her wrists taped behind her back and a knee lifted from her stomach, Aria squirmed on the bed. Neither a rock left nor a rock right enhanced her ability to differentiate plank squeaks to count how many attackers advanced.

The first interdigital space of Remy's left hand compressed her throat. Confident her throat's flexible skin capable of stretching without permanent scaring, she dared not contemplate the irreparable damage the base of Remy's thumb threatened to do to her thyroid.

Aria bit her lower lip to test her pain tolerance. Her shallow breath expelled all thoughts to bite his hand. She rated the consequences of enraging him would outweigh her fleeting joy for he'd unhooked her bra and advertised his eventual goal when he'd unzipped her slacks.

"That's right, bitch. You'll enjoy me."

The bunched cotton fabric at her knees temporarily acted as a makeshift chastity belt until the cohorts she expected added their gropes to Remy's right-index-finger probe for her exposed flesh.

The outside plank squeaks stopped.

"Remy, you there?"

While uncertain, Aria thought she recognized the masculine voice.

Without a door knock, the voice repeated his summons. "Know you're in there. This ain't no party shack."

Remy whispered to Aria. "If you know what's good for y'all, you'll close your casket."

He pushed himself away from her, stood and rubbed both hands from shoulder to knee across his clothes.

He shouted, "Wait. Need to rearrange these papers. Can't have them trampled on. Hold on to your po'boy a sec and I'll unlock the door."

Aria sighed. *What a lie.* She tugged her slacks to her waist and rolled right. When her toes touched the floor, she gripped the bed's edge to propel herself erect. She tugged her waist band and zipped her slacks. *Bra, you can wait.*

Remy cast a grimace in her direction as he shuffled birth certificates in a manner Aria believed masqueraded his awkward attempt to hide one in particular.

Latent irritation coated the muffled yell from outside. "The timed road camera images of your SUV uploaded to my office document you've been here longer than anyone should be. Hurry, damn it, or you're fired!"

Road camera? Aria hadn't seen one. A fuzzy memory of Remy's mention of hunter cameras mounted on Cyprus trees jibbed as the only plausible explanation. What confused her was how could a prison guard fire Remy? Her emergent thought left unexpressed as Remy jogged for the door lock.

Aria tucked a birth certificate into her pocket and stood by the room door.

A gust of warm humid air breached the weave of her blouse and deepened her skin perspiration with a moisture layer iced onto her physical fear sheen. Her toward Remy gaze disjointed. The walls didn't join the floor. She backpedaled into the room to steady herself against a wall before dizziness and nausea ruled.

"Took you long enough." The vocalized agitation coincided with Mr. Breaux's first step into the room. He gazed at Aria. "Oh, you're here."

Aria's muscles froze; her closed lips clamped an elongated sigh deep within her throat. Speechless, her brain forged no image or thought easily melded or crafted into intelligible words.

As she stood there, feverishly trying to slip her hands under her blouse and hide her effort to refasten her bra, she counted Mr. Breaux's five second glare at Remy. Neither flinched. With a sufficient infusion of courage, she masked her fear to ask, "Can I see those papers Remy has?"

"Why?" Mr. Breaux's retort expected.

"They're birth certificates."

"Let's see." His direct command both proper and adept in its misdirection to defuse his earlier threat to discipline. His right hand reached for the documents Remy's forearms crumpled against his chest.

As if he thrusted an iron in hesitant and jerky motions, Mr. Breaux's waggling fingers approached Remy's chin. The younger man's arms relaxed to display the documents his hands supported.

Mr. Breaux flipped through the pages.

Aria doubted he read more than a dozen words per page.

"These have this year dates. Thus, of little value."

"How can you dismiss them that easy?" Aria asked.

"Remy hid one from me. You see that one?"

Mr. Breaux's gaze darted to Remy and, with equal speed, reversed direction to latch onto Aria. "No, but I may have spoken too quick. The original birth certificate date has no relevance since a new one will be entered onto the certificate that is but a template for the all-important forgery. Does that make sense?"

"Sorta."

Mr. Breaux's standing within the room tamped Aria's fear in approaching Remy. "Show me the one you hid."

Remy reached into his front pocket and withdrew a folded paper document. He lifted it waist high.

Aria grabbed it. Ripped an edge in her rush to undo the folds. Wetness lined her lower eyelids.

"What's there?" asked Mr. Breaux.

"My name." Aria's head shake did nothing to free the lump in her throat to release further words nor did it compound her current woe. She stared at Remy and imagined him to be less evil than guards she catapulted into a surreal hinterland while on her mystical hero journeys.

Outwardly perplexed, Mr. Breaux asked, "What name?"

Tears rallied behind Aria's eyes. "Gleason."

"Name not uncommon," Remy said. "If I researched Illinois, I might find hundreds so named, if not thousands."

Aria struggled for a full breath. Deep within the crevices of her mind, dark, twisting thoughts zigzagged forward toward doors spray painted with "no exit" admonishments. Each wood-framed portal connected by time and space. An expansive wormhole exposed when she approached. After she fell into a matrix glitch, she grew mentally exhausted and pitched her frustration into an alien world.

"Are you feeling okay?" Mr. Breaux raised his brows. "Guess you are if you don't complain."

"She's fine." Remy edged toward the door.

"Perhaps, she should say so."

Aria fought off further scrutiny to mutter: "I'm fine."

Mr. Breaux reached his right hand towards her. "Please give me that birth certificate."

Aria clutched it to her right breast.

"Can you trust her?" Remy asked.

Mr. Breaux twisted the exterior door's knob. "What choice do I have?"

Chapter Thirty-one

A birth certificate in her left hand, Aria's thumb pressed the pilfered precious copy into her palm. She glanced left as she directed Mr. Breaux to drop her at Aunt Maggie's rental.

LeRoy waited on the front porch. "Expected you earlier. Too late to get an early start north."

Aria waved to the departing Mr. Breaux before she turned her complete attention to LeRoy.

"We need to make a side trip."

"Huh?"

"Speak again to that Azalea Flower Shop employee."

"Is that the Cajun lady with the baby we visited?"

"I need to ask her about a birth certificate."

"What birth certificate?"

Aria pointed LeRoy to a porch railing as she backed her butt into contact with a post. "Found this birth certificate today." She stepped forward. "Be careful with it."

From the onset of LeRoy's scrutiny until he finished two minutes later, Aria stretched her gaze to the inactive road.

"Recognize last name Gleason, but otherwise it's hard to make sense when no words fill the boxes." LeRoy raised his gaze to pan her face. "I saw my birth certificate years ago and remember it listed my birthday, my parents and an unreadable signature scribbled beneath the hospital's address, presumably the gynecologist who slapped my cute ass."

He laughed and clapped his hands hard. The certificate fluttered left and right and ever downward. Aria gasped and lurched forward as if she envisioned a white, lonely moth attracted to a flame. She ignored the hypothetical moth's eventual demise when first her right hand, and then her left, hit the porch planks before her abdomen anchored her body's forward movement.

Aria's uplifted gaze watched the certificate settle, first one edge, then a second, onto LeRoy's shoe. She elevated her shoulders. "We can go now."

"Let me grab water bottles from the fridge. It'll be hot this afternoon." He secured the certificate in his left hand, straightened his shoulders in line with his hips and reached out his right hand toward her. "Need help?"

Aria shook her head. Coordinated toe and hand effort thrust her torso skyward. When her hips reached an extended-limb apex, she walked her hands until she stood.

"I'll take that certificate."

He handed it to her and entered the house.

She waited for LeRoy two strides away from his car's passenger door. When he approached, she relieved him of two water bottles and fastened herself in, ready to go, but uncertain of her first question to Edmee, or her second.

"Ready?"

"Yeah." Aria swiped one bottle against her cheek. The car's AC struggled to exhaust the built-up heat of a closed sedan parked in Louisiana's midafternoon sun. "Let's try the flower shop first."

Aria endured a blurred landscape until her cell phone rang. Screen showed 312 area code. "Tillie, we ain't left yet."

"Aunt Maggie's antsy."

"Why? We're on schedule?"

"She found an old letter."

"What old letter?"

"Your mother's. And don't ask. She won't tell me when written, its topic, or why it's important."

"I'll wait to see it. Can't be more important than my searching for birth certificate information."

"What do I tell her?"

"I'll be home in two days and I love her."

LeRoy tapped his right fingers on the steering wheel.

Aria pocketed her cell phone; tilted her head left. "Aunt Maggie's found a letter she claims is important, but refuses to tell Tillie what it says."

"I'll be cool." LeRoy stopped his Buick near the livery. "Stay here. I'll see if what's-her-name's working. If so, I gather you'll wish to chat outside."

"Tell her it's urgent."

"Don't I know? We're set to leave today." Before he departed, LeRoy shifted into park, let the car idle and dialed the AC fan to high, which pleased Aria.

Aria wiped the second bottle's condensation against her cheek as she gazed in the direction LeRoy took. Fearful she might miss something, she jerked her head in the opposite direction. A youngster on a bicycle raised her awareness of youthful freedom which merged into the Freedom Trail and Deputy Dog. Fleeting mental images of no practical value in her current circumstances.

A shadow across the car's hood tensed her muscles. *Had LeRoy locked the car?* A flick of her gaze calmed her nerves.

She exhaled as LeRoy slid behind the wheel. "That lady was nicer today. Edmee's at home is the promise I got. You can give me a water."

Aria extended her left hand.

"Thanks." He uncapped the bottle and tipped it to his lips. "Ahh, nothing better." He gazed at Aria. "Can you tell me why this Remy didn't drive you?"

The simple question grated on Aria's sensibilities to tell the truth to the extent she pretended her left hand blunted an oncoming sneeze that didn't occur. "Mr. Breaux directed him elsewhere. Guess I'm not important enough."

LeRoy smiled. "You are to me."

Aria lowered her gaze and quickly raised it to engage his continued smile. She couldn't be as haughty as a French court mistress nor acknowledge the warmth in her cheeks. "Thank you. I shall definitely tell Aunt Maggie of your kindness in offering your car."

LeRoy flipped the empty water bottle into the backseat. "Help me remember the way."

"Take this street out of town, turn left and we should see the house." Aria tried to smile. "If not, we'll turn around."

LeRoy drove as she'd suggested. With no need to reverse direction, Aria braced herself to reunite with a former prison inmate, not that she herself deserved greater acclaim.

After she'd alit from LeRoy's Buick, she tossed the unopened water bottle on the front seat, closed the car door, and steadied her gait on the uneven stones.

"There's nothing more I can tell you," the voice said.

Aria hesitated until the woman emerged from a porch shadow. The woman's right arm supported naked baby legs, his or her chin resting on the woman's shoulder.

"Edmee, I apologize for my intrusion. We've both suffered enough. I wish to share your joy."

Edmee screamed. "You're not stealing my baby. Earl, help. Get out here."

A brute of a man in a white t-shirt and dark green trousers burst through the screen door opening. "Git, git out now."

Aria gasped for breath, humidity weighed on the silence. "Won't . . . didn't plan . . . to steal your baby." She inhaled until her lungs hurt. "I'm sorry. You misunderstood. I'm interested in my baby, not yours."

"What then?" The man rubbed his knuckles. "Why scare my wife? She's suffered enough turmoil in her life."

Edmee murmured, "So has she."

When the man displayed open palms where fists had been, Aria's flight reflex relaxed until a door creak and footfalls behind her elevated caution to alarm. Tense neck muscles strained to increase her lateral vision rearward.

"What's going on?" LeRoy yelled.

"Calm yourself," Aria said, her rigid torso not heeding her own admonition.

"Is he the father?" Edmee asked.

The question alone enough to shock Aria. "No, no."

"Who's this big dude?" LeRoy asked. "Know him?"

Aria shook her head. "Save it for later."

LeRoy halted his advance. Aria hoped her audible exhale didn't blunt her soaring relief that her and LeRoy's arrival hadn't erupted into fisticuffs or anger-fueled taunts.

"Can I start again?"

Edmee nodded. Her left arm gently tugged the baby's outside shoulder to prevent the baby from slipping out of her grasp and off her shoulder. Earl folded his arms.

"Will you share your child's birth certificate?"

"Oh my God. You're not thinking my child is yours?"

Aria flinched, recoiled onto her heels. LeRoy's hand to her shoulder blade reversed her momentum, offered stability. Had prison trauma dulled or pilfered Edmee's memory? A static expression offered Aria little clue. Could she expect a mild episodic loss of short-term memory to be a halfway station between normal aging and dementia? Aria steadied her balance; she'd ruminate about prison and her mental health another day. Critical she secure what she came for.

She tried to minimize her harsh, "No." At the same time, she reached into her pocket to extract the birth certificate she'd taken from Remy.

Earl jerked forward to snatch the document from Aria's extended right hand. His summer sweat overpowered the sweet water-lily scent from a nearby make-believe pond.

"Need to compare the one Earl has with yours."

Earl interrupted. "Why? This here one's blank."

Aria leaned forward. "See why you can help."

Earl grimaced.

"Dear, be nice and get it from our desk drawer."

A grunt escaped Earl's lips. "If you say so."

Edmee smiled. "If he does that, you'll leave us alone?"

"Of course," Aria replied.

LeRoy whispered to her, "Maybe you should get a copy."

"Ssshh." Aria believed that if Edmee's certificate proved legitimate, there would be an invaluable adoption number to facilitate her request for a copy from the state registry. If illegal, she didn't wish to know where that would send her.

Aria glanced at the lily pond until Earl reappeared.

He unfolded an official appearing document. "Here."

Aria bent her shoulders forward to exam the document in Earl's meaty palm that he safeguarded by clamping the paper tight to his palm with his thumb. The wording looked authentic. However, the surname "Gleason" ignited fast-paced recycled heart throbs.

"Your . . . your certificate says 'Gleason'. Why?"

Edmee flicked her gaze to a tight-lipped Earl and then to Aria. "Agency said that was the child's birth name."

Aria swallowed hard. "Can't be."

"You calling us liars?" Earl screamed.

While Aria struggled to find the words sufficient to repeat her protestation she harbored no baby-stealer desire, a clenched left fist inaccurately forecasted her wish to attack. She inhaled. "That's my married name, but the baby's age, the darling you hold, when compared to my prison dates, means I'm not its mother. Can't say more."

Edmee gazed at Earl. "Believe her, honey."

Earl groaned. "Don't spend all day trying to read this certificate. It's like others I'm told."

Aria tried to comply. She scrutinized the address. "This says Calhoon followed by the initials 'I' and 'A'. Isn't that a mistake? Shouldn't it be 'LA'?"

LeRoy tugged at Aria's left hand.

Chapter Thirty-two

LeRoy repeated his tug at her arm.

Aria glared at him. "Stop squeezing me. I gotta stay."

When Aria rotated her gaze, she caught Earl closing the front door. Edmee and the baby no longer in sight.

Aria spit out her words. "Now you've done it."

"Why?" LeRoy arched his brows. "You read the birth certificate. There'll be a copy filed with the state."

"Not that simple, LeRoy." Aria rapped her fist on the wooden door. As she expected, no one answered. A white lace curtain to her right fluttered with no face or hand visible.

She tripped and recovered, not to be conquered by an uneven stone in her retreat to LeRoy's Buick. An imaginary burden, no longer LeRoy's grip, weighed on her. Capturing a light's radiance amidst her pain, now an ever fading hope she'd ever find her child.

"Can we drive straight through to Chicago?"

LeRoy, his right elbow bent, held his car keys aloft. "Without stopping to eat?"

Without a bite in her words at LeRoy's repeated reference to stuffing his mouth, Aria unleased her real meaning. "Only meant we skip the motel." Met with a shrug, she continued, "I know how to drive. My license expired because its renewal date skipped by while Tillie and I worked in Africa."

"Knew that." His tone expressed a growing lack of patience. "I'll start. You'll be safer driving on I-35."

She interpreted his "you'll" as "we'll be safer," but a snippy retort she'd save for Tillie. "Let's go then."

Aria tried not to squirm on the front passenger seat to distract or interrupt LeRoy. She counted cows huddling under a lone field tree, precious shade from the sizzling sun.

Her distant gaze interrupted when a double honk diverted LeRoy's Interstate 35 entrance onto the right shoulder rumble strips until a courteous driver allowed a proper lane return.

"You okay?"

"Yeah, yeah. Stupid idiot." LeRoy's deflection didn't calm her heart beat until they glided down an exit ramp after a billboard advertising Popeye's. After the parking lot dinner of a spicy-chicken order, Aria offered to drive. Her second request answered with: "Guess shuteye an enjoyable thing."

Thirty minutes later, Aria relaxed her fingers one hand at a time. She considered the engaged cruise control a godsend, even if vehicles whizzed by and blotted out the setting sun.

At a rest area she didn't wake LeRoy. Adrenaline fueled her choice to reach Chicago. When LeRoy jerked awake two hours later, Aria relented and relinquished the steering wheel.

LeRoy drove and her sleep effort, head propped against the passenger door, flunked. Darkness circled the passing light. With Tillie in the Congo they dreaded the curtain-like darkness drop with unseen animal growls less nettlesome than the malaria net draped against moist skin to ward off an insect's sucking probe. There she'd been the brave one. The rock of their bonding existence.

The image of Edmee twice cuddling a baby now haunted Aria after her prison cemetery search proved futile. Sinister forces cloaked with the authority to mete out justice presented her with a scary opposition not yet vanquished.

Nonetheless, her physical strength and artful or beguiling behavior great enough to propel her toward escape. Chills radiated from her abdomen.

Babies required mothers. Her baby needed her.

Chapter Thirty-three

Tillie waved her upper extremities faster than an inflatable arm-waving tube-person as LeRoy guided his Buick into an incredible vacant Chicago-street-parking spot. Two kitchen chairs, set on the street, flanked Tillie.

Overlapped live oak leaves blocked the late-morning sun's warmth as Aria darted to hug Tillie.

"What's up, girl?"

Aria sighed. She'd prepared no elevator speech. Life's rejuvenation required she sleep in a bed, don clean underwear and avoid male ears. "How about I catch you up after a shower and a nap?"

"Best you let Aunt Maggie speak with you first."

Regret invaded Aria's psyche. For the endless hours of the trip north she'd shut herself off and wallowed in her own misfortune. Others endured heartbreak or worse fates, and they included her Aunt Maggie. "Yes, yes, absolutely."

Tillie gazed at LeRoy. "Can you bring all the bags inside? Aunt Maggie is dying, well, not really but you know, to learn about Aria's last week."

LeRoy shrugged and tramped to his car's trunk.

"Perhaps I should help," said Aria.

"LeRoy's good." Tillie winked. "He loves to grab the luggage of arriving females."

Aria chuckled with the memory as she followed Tillie up the front steps and into the living room.

Aunt Maggie squeezed her fingers against the armrests of her wheelchair. "Aria, darling," she gushed. "So happy to see you. You mustn't wheel me into Harmony Square. Love trains, don't you?"

Bending forward, Aria arm-hugged her aunt. "Don't wish to get too close. You can probably smell the bayou. We'll fix everything. You'll see."

"Nonsense, darling. Mr. Breaux treat you right? He called yesterday, said you were on your way home, yet he left what you learned in terms not understandable to tired ears."

Aria decided badmouthing either him or Remy neither fruitful nor calming. "While he rescued me from a bounty hunter, his guidance on my search encountered dead-end after dead-end. Can't help but think he knows more than what he lets on."

"Isn't that life?" Tillie interjected from her position on the sofa. "We should all know more than we actually do." Her left-eye wink struck Aria as a not-so-subtle hint to abandon Louisiana and engage Aunt Maggie.

Aria returned her gaze to her aunt. "What's new, Aunt Maggie?" Without a reply, Aria pressed her point. "There must be a TV comedy that tickled you. Never saw your colorful blouse before."

"Oh, this old thing. Tillie was kind enough to bring me one or two boxes that I'd stored."

Aria's gaze darted from her aunt to Tillie. "She's always so thoughtful."

Tillie shrugged. "Aunt Maggie, you should tell Aria about the letters you found?"

LeRoy burst into the room; his hands clutched the handles of two suitcases and one smaller bag. When he let the two suitcases drop to the carpet, he punctuated the resonating thunk with an audible grunt. "No tip required." A sly smile creased his lips. "Here okay or do I lug them upstairs?" He glanced at Aria. "A bedroom perhaps?"

No woman spoke.

"I'll grab my suitcase and head home."

Tillie and Aria rose.

"Thanks, LeRoy," Tillie said. "We'll manage."

"Yeah, thanks," Aria said as LeRoy, a suitcase in hand, strode toward the front door and exited. Tillie's plop squeezed the air from her sofa's cushion.

With no comprehension she'd snubbed LeRoy since she crashed there as a guest, Aria gazed at Aunt Maggie. "What letters did Tillie refer to?"

"Do you think LeRoy's hurt?"

Aria chafed at Aunt Maggie's avoidance. She bit her tongue while she reseated herself.

"Have no worries," Tillie said. "He may at times act forward, but trust me his day-after memory will bypass today and hopscotch into fresh adventures tomorrow."

Aria crossed her fingers for Tillie's faith to be true. With no wish to repeat her question, she stared at her aunt who, in the week of Aria's absence, had slumped into a frail creature hidden beneath the plaid blanket wrapped snug from armpits to toes. The mummy-styled fabric belted in to prevent Aunt Maggie's catapult should her wheelchair tip.

"Should I leave you two alone?" Tillie asked.

Aunt Maggie shook her head. Her thinning hair free and wild. "Remember those letters, Tillie?"

"The ones you found this week?"

"Bring them to me. I need to share."

Pleased that either her patience or the head shaking had unscrambled her aunt's memory, Aria waited for Tillie.

Two letters, each the rectangular size of birthday greetings, appeared in Tillie's right hand with dime-sized brown stains and cut and frazzled top edges.

Aria stiffened. From six to eight feet away, the address writing appeared to be her mother's.

Aunt Maggie slid a folded sheet of writing paper from a pastoral-flower-scene card. "Your mother always sent the most beautiful cards. I've missed them these last four years."

"As have I," murmured Aria. *Why can't I just read them?*

"Good, I've got the right one. There's no splendid news."

Aria tightened her right hand into a fist. "What news?"

"Brad's parents years ago contacted your mother concerned their grandchild would have Marfan syndrome."

"What?" Aria stood. "Let me see." She snatched the letter from Aunt Maggie. She read. "This all relates to Brad's family, not ours."

"That's what I thought, too, until your mother's next letter. She said she traced the syndrome in our family and believed she carried the mutated gene identified by that French doctor named Marfan."

Tillie interrupted. "You saying Aria's kin diseased?"

"Not a disease, a genetic defect."

Aria slumped onto the sofa. When would her bayou catastrophe end? *I may as well just die.*

Tillie cradled Aria's right hand between her palms. "How could you have this thing? We both underwent extensive physicals before Africa. We both received top-notch reports." Tillie shifted her gaze to Aunt Maggie. "Aria's exhausted, not sick. That's fixable by a good night's sleep."

"I'm not a doctor," Aunt Maggie said as she tucked the letter into its envelope. "My sister struggled with the idea we inherit this Marfan syndrome, which may skip a generation, and then reappear in either a son or a daughter."

"What's say we do research tomorrow, right Aria?"

With her last ounce of strength, Aria nodded to Tillie and stood to give her aunt a hug. Aunt Maggie wished her goodnight before Tillie guided her wheelchair into a bedroom Tillie commandeered from an absent roommate. When Tillie returned with a sheet, pillow and blanket, Aria helped spread the sheet and blanket on the sofa before her shower.

Her fretful sleep filled with multiple pillow punches and body turns, Aria rebelled to kick off the blanket and will her eyelids closed. Startled, she awoke to stare at dark compassionate and calm eyes she recognized to be Gloria, Tillie's roommate. The furrowed brow deepened by captured concern while her eyes sparkled with innocence.

"Sorry to disturb you. Shoulda slipped off my shoes."

"No worries." Aria flattened her torso to prop up her shoulders with vertical biceps atop elbows. Gloria's wrinkled outer garment, a white frock, pointed to a night shift return rather than one prepping to leave for work.

"Your aunt quizzed me a couple days ago about a letter. You haven't suffered heart problems, have you?"

"What?" Aria jerked her bare feet from underneath the lifted tangled sheet, swung them left and let the carpet cushion her soles. "Why?"

"Marfan victims open to mitral value leaks."

"Leaks what?"

A penitent expression flashed across Gloria's face. "My bad. Often forget I'm not always seated with fellow nurses. The mitral value is in the heart, left side. If it doesn't form a tight fit during heart beats, blood will leak. Let me say that's not good for a healthy heart. Can cause breathing difficulty."

Aria barricaded from expression the negative thought landslide invading her head. "No one ever told me my heart not normal. Had an EKG before volunteering to serve in Africa. They didn't derail me before I flew across the Atlantic so I assume my health then, and today, was fine."

Hesitation dominated Gloria's eyes.

"You think it should worry me?"

"No, no. Ebola and fevers plague African visitors. We inherit Marfan via the FBN1 gene. You have it or you don't."

"And . . . I don't?"

"That's complicated. You've heard of carriers. Persons who carry a malady but aren't disabled by it."

Aria's right hand squeezed folds of sheet. "Guess so."

"Let me see your hands."

"Huh? Which one?"

"Either."

Aria extended her left hand. Gloria grasped Aria's fingers, tried to stretch them and fizzled in her effort.

"Elongated fingers are one Marfan sign since the affliction affects the connective tissue. If I were an expert, I'd give you a definite opinion, but I'm not. My best guess is you exhibit no elongation."

"That's good?"

Gloria nodded.

"So, what worried my mother doesn't apply to me?"

"Can't go that far."

"Huh?" Interstitial tension within her breast inched toward an anger that, if not clouding, engulfed Aria's ability to think straight. "What's it you're not telling me?"

Gloria cleared her throat. "Hear me out first. Then ask your questions."

Aria nodded.

"Like I said, individuals inherit Marfan. There's two autosomal streams." Aria studied Gloria's lips for a hesitation hint without discovery of even an inadvertent twitch. Gloria continued, "One is classified as dominant. The other, recessive. With me so far?"

Aria nodded a second time.

"If dominant, the parent passes the defective gene to the next generation without the need to pair with a second gene from the opposite sex. If recessive, one parent's gene needs to be paired with the same defective gene of a sexual partner to pass the defective gene on to their offspring of either sex."

"Not entirely clear, but does that mean this defective gene can skip a generation?" Aria coughed into her right elbow. "Excuse me."

"No worries. But as to your most recent question, the answer is absolutely. More likely with recessive genes."

Aria gazed past Gloria's right shoulder. "Is your, or this, answer the same if, by chance, I have a baby somewhere?"

"Yes, and no."

"Well what?" Aria folded her arms across her chest. "Isn't there anything . . . any way to get an answer? Before I married Brad we both passed mandated blood tests."

"Apples and Oranges. Marfan is not a communicative disease like herpes." Gloria lifted her gaze to the ceiling for a second. "How can I say this?" Her right hand rubbed her chin and cheek. "Marfan exists because it's an inherited DNA trait with negative or harmful attributes."

Torn between not finding a grave marker where she could offer a prayer to her child's spirit and being advised that infants who appeared sick or deformed weren't adoptable prompted Aria to ask, "With this inherited trait is there a way doctors can know the baby has this Marfan at birth, or they will within days thereafter?"

"Simple answer is no."

Aria's shoulders slumped. *I'll never have an answer.*

"Remember when I checked your fingers?"

"Yeah."

"I was looking for tissue elongation. That requires time to develop, or appear. It's a condition more visible than mitral valve leaks or breathing difficulties that researchers associate with many physical maladies."

"You're saying this Marfan hides?"

"Never expressed it that way, but, yes, you're right. If they examined your child, you'd be advised on what steps needed to mitigate adverse consequences."

An escalating slow burn strengthened its grip on Aria's psyche. *What good was knowledge without hugging her child?* She knew her question's answer. Absolutely zero.

Heel clicks on the stairs upset Aria's concentration.

Gloria pivoted.

Tillie, dressed in beige Capri's with a navy blue top, maintained her railing grip at the last step. "Where's my invitation?" Tillie smiled. "Kidding."

"If you're on the way out, I'd better tidy up." Aria lifted the sheet to fold it.

"Gloria here filling you in on the latest 'Gray's Anatomy' hospital gossip or the latest bachelor doc?"

"Nothing like that," Gloria interjected.

"My friend sick from gumbo too spicy?"

"If she wants to answer, that's her business. Since you're here, I'll assume the bathroom's free. See ya both."

Tillie stepped from the stairs to give Gloria a wider berth to pass. After Gloria turned the upper hall corner, Tillie whispered, "Gloria's great at teeny scrapes and bruises, hope she didn't give you serious advice."

"Talked to Aunt Maggie about my mother's letter."

"If she told you to worry, I'd brush it off. Good gracious, girl. There's a blush in your cheeks and a dazzle in your eyes. Sleep blessed you with the best medicine."

Doorbell rang, then again.

"I'll hide in the kitchen."

"Stay. If it's LeRoy. I'll shoo him."

"What if he won't go?"

"He'll go. Then we'll find a laptop, the nearest café and find out what your mother's letter really means."

"You sure? I might emit death rays."

"Knock it off."

Aria believed Tillie to be serious, but not to the extent they'd be traveling to Louisiana. Positive LeRoy would volunteer to drive, Aria gagged at the signal she'd send.

"You okay?"

"Yeah. I'll wait upstairs until Gloria's out of the bathroom. Promise me LeRoy will be gone."

Chapter Thirty-four

An unexpected glimpse of LeRoy's smile beyond two café tables impelled Aria in mid-sentence to clamp her lips tight.

She stared at Tillie. "Tell me you didn't."

"No way. Never invited him to this café."

"Greetings, ladies." LeRoy's gaze dropped below Aria's eyes to scrutinize the laptop screen.

Aria slammed the cover closed.

"What's with the secrecy? All dating apps do is promote scams and heartbreak."

"Who's saying we're scrolling dating profiles?"

"C'mon, two provocative women in a café with coffee and a laptop, that's a given, wouldn't you say?"

"Shove it." Tillie's first words to LeRoy both unequivocal and laced with a take no prisoners confrontational tone.

Aria refused to believe their verbal banter subtext a jousting match or sincere posturing easily forgotten.

"C'mon, Tillie," LeRoy pleaded. "We have history. This isn't your apartment where you control who enters."

A server approached to ask LeRoy if he wanted coffee.

"Not today, thanks. Gotta run."

Aria's right-hand forefinger traced the laptop's outer edges, ever thankful LeRoy's departure announced.

"Ciao," Tillie said.

Aria, uncertain if Tillie's foreign word masked a secret code, nodded before LeRoy turned toward the doorway.

Convinced the café's buzz drowned out her words, except to Tillie, she flipped open Tillie's laptop. "All this medical jargon and the only conclusion is that what Gloria explained is true. Plus, mother wouldn't have written to Aunt Maggie unless pressed with an urgent concern."

"Any heart problem is serious," Tillie said. "Shouldn't your mother or aunt have warned you in prison?"

"She could've forgotten. Anyway, that's behind me. I'm now worried about harm to more than just me."

"Don't tell me, this child you can't find?" Tillie sipped coffee. "Ever entertain this child lives as a figment of your imagination. A coping mechanism during a hard time."

Aria pressed her right hand against her chest. "Don't go there. I'm not insane."

Tillie's saucer rattled when struck by her cup. "Not saying that. Tell me about this birth certificate you got."

Aria slid her fingers off the scroll bar. "One had my surname, nothing else. Of greater interest to me is one Edmee, a flower shop lady who'd adopted a baby, had."

"How so?"

"I realize mistakes occur in official documents, but the Louisiana Public Health Department has an online copy of what Edmee showed me." Aria paused, rubbed her forehead. "You remember Calhoon. Aunt Maggie rented the house near there. That's where LeRoy and I visited the flower shop."

"Go on."

"Well, the birth certificate said 'IA' not 'LA'."

"Doesn't seem to be an enormous deal."

"Could be. There's a Calhoon in Iowa."

Tillie raised her right forefinger. "LA is also short for Los Angeles and bet there's a street named Calhoon there?"

"Nope. There's a firm named 'Calhoun' but it's not the town spelling. No. Gut tells me no typo. Adopted babies from the Louisiana prison share a connection to Iowa."

"How you gonna get there without LeRoy's car?"

Chapter Thirty-five

Aunt Maggie, in Tillie's front room, quizzed LeRoy on his family tree as Aria gathered drink spoons and listened from the kitchen. When her aunt asked him why he visited Tillie's so often, Aria hurried the third coffee cup onto the tray. If LeRoy answered, the refrigerator's hum drowned it out.

As Aria entered the front room, Aunt Maggie derisively asked, "Don't *YOU* have a job?"

"Tomorrow I do."

"And that's what?"

"Driving to Iowa."

The three carried cups jangled against their saucers.

Aunt Maggie jerked her head to the right. "What's got into you? If you make a mess, I can't help clean up."

Aria, at her aunt's wheelchair arm, steadied the tray. "Don't worry. I've got it." Her visual sugar cube count showed two short. She'd do without as she didn't dare leave her aunt or trust LeRoy not to embellish her plan.

With a stare at LeRoy, she handed him her tray's second cup and saucer complete with two sugar cubes. She lifted the third saucer with its cup, set the tray aside, and sat.

Aunt Maggie sipped. "Thanks Aria. It's nice you've returned. Have you thought where you'll live?"

The unexpressed undercurrent didn't escape Aria. Aunt Maggie expected they'd live together.

"Not really."

"We can't impose upon Tillie. It wouldn't be right."

Aria fully understood. "Hopefully my predicament solution will start to emerge tomorrow. Mother's money helps, but I've planned to search out a job."

"And a husband?" Aunt Maggie winked.

A grimace stretched Aria's facial skin and deepened pre-existing shallow furrows within her soul.

LeRoy piped up, "Your aunt's a fine traditional woman."

"Thank you," Aunt Maggie said.

Aria gulped, coffee residue lingered in her mouth.

"While you were in the kitchen, LeRoy said they have employed him to be a chauffeur. Isn't that nice?"

"Yes, Aunt Maggie."

Aunt Maggie extended her empty cup and saucer to Aria. "It'll be so nice. You and me." She smiled at Aria. "There remains another box of things we can sort through together."

"I wouldn't want to invade your privacy."

A pale blush consumed Aunt Maggie's fleshy facial complexion. "There's not what you think. No love letters."

"Interesting." LeRoy glanced at Aria. "More coffee?"

"Sorry." Aria disconnected her gaze from LeRoy with a desire not to leave the room. "Only brewed three cups." She'd chastise herself later for this teeny white lie.

"So." Aunt Maggie cranked her attention to LeRoy. "You working downtown Chicago, or the suburbs?"

"Going to Iowa. Don't know where, actually."

"Gracious, me. That's a lengthy drive."

"Aria said that's where we're headed."

"What? No way."

"Not . . . not for ever, Aunt Maggie." Aria stammered, unable to express a fuller or palliate explanation now that LeRoy had exposed her plans.

Aunt Maggie fussed. "I can't approve, won't. Can't believe your mother wished you to use her money for galloping here and everywhere."

"But Aunt Maggie . . . ."

Chapter Thirty-six

Summoned by Aria's 5:01 a.m. phone call, LeRoy evoked her uproarious laugh when he exited his Buick dressed in a black suit with a green-tweed Scottish tam.

"Your carriage, ma'am."

Aria lifted her suitcase from Tillie's front steps. "Just open the trunk."

"Yes, ma'am."

"Stop it. And where did you buy that silly hat?"

LeRoy patted the tam's visor. "Believe the same store Tillie escorted you to to buy that retro suit you never wear. Is it in the suitcase along with your bikini?"

"Heavens no to both. And let's get started before Aunt Maggie realizes I'm not sleeping."

"She's such a gracious lady. You should respect she's been through hard times and treat her nicer."

"We can debate this once you get us to Rockford."

"Yes, Miss Daisy."

Aria shook her head. Neither did she plan to sit in the rear seat while LeRoy drove. Yes, she'd hired him; her promised payment due at their trip's completion.

Buckled in, the dense, industrialized suburbs within the hour replaced by cornfields, populated exits and soybean fields. When on Amtrak, grazing cows caught her eye.

LeRoy interrupted her daydreaming with a question. "Have you ever in your life seen such immense hog barns?"

"Is that what they are? Please remember society limited my outside view these past five years."

"Hog prisons. That's what's built."

Aria's entire body tensed.

LeRoy gazed in her direction. "My bad."

"I can take it. When I hug and kiss my child, I'll rejoice. Life will improve for us all."

"You're so positive."

"Wasn't always, but let's find you an exit for lunch."

The smile that erupted on LeRoy's face Aria knew well.

This first meal stop of two during a ten hour drive found Aria adjusting and readjusting her passenger seatbelt at irregular intervals. Once or twice she gripped the door handle as LeRoy bolted past slower Interstate traffic.

"Does this Calhoon have a motel?"

"Internet says a B&B."

"Wow, a creaky bed and a hall bathroom trudge."

"Let's wait and see. Another hour should tell us."

LeRoy eased off the accelerator. "That it?"

"Splendid. Sign says Calhoon ten miles. Let's go."

"Where's this B&B?"

"Description promised on a major street."

LeRoy chuckled. "How about this street? It's the only one they got." He again slowed.

Aria seized the opportunity to offer directions. "Sandstone brick house on the right. See the trellis?"

"Gotcha."

Aria touched her fingers to her seatbelt's retractor, ready to relieve the day's butt pressure. When the Buick stopped, she jumped to be the first onto the B&B's entrance sidewalk.

"Whoa, Aria," LeRoy shouted. "Your suitcase."

She stared at LeRoy until she realized acting rude wasn't her inbred nature. "Later. Let's see if this place rocks."

The duo walked into an antebellum parlor.

"May I help you?" A woman dressed in a black dress that reminded Aria of the Amish smiled at them.

"You should have a room reserved for Gleason."

The lady glanced at a ledger. "Yes." She elevated her chin toward Aria. "However, there's a minor problem."

"Which is?"

"You booked twin beds and that room's ensuite awaits the plumber. We apologize for any inconvenience. I've saved you our best room, The Explorer, at your lower booked rate."

"No twin beds?"

"King. Extra-sized room, marvelous window views."

"We can make do," LeRoy said. He gazed at Aria with a quizzical expression. "Can't we?"

"Since you've staying three days, I can add a portable cot starting tomorrow. I promised our only one for tonight."

Aria pondered a simple and bold straightforward step. Say no thank you and find another B&B nearby. Locating this one in Calhoon, Iowa, had struck her as destiny. While there'd be no bedroom door to shut out LeRoy as had existed in Aunt Maggie's rental house, a bathroom door existed.

"Best I can offer," the B&B receptionist said.

"Is there a tub or a shower?"

"Both. The original owners lived here and spared no expense for their comfort. It was their master."

"We can do this," LeRoy said.

Aria closed her eyes and forced herself to think about why she stood there. She and Tillie in an Internet search the night before had discovered three adoption orders, two girls and one boy, within the six months following her incarceration. For a town, population of 607, within a county of two thousand residents, mostly aged fifty-plus, the odds of three closely spaced single-family adoptions astronomical.

What had once been an emotional dream now consumed her as a resolute trek to save her child from inherited disaster.

"All right," LeRoy said, "Can we decide?"

Aria's eyes blinked. *How do I do this? What do I do? Loneliness or grief can't rule forever. If I do nothing, will regret burrow into my soul and sprout the rest of my life?*

"We'll take it."

LeRoy reached for his wallet. "Use my credit card."

Aria interjected, "Can we just pay for tonight and return tomorrow if we need two more days?"

"There's a pending request. You must decide."

"We'll do the three nights," LeRoy said. He extended his right hand with his credit card. "My car can use the break."

Key in hand, Aria unlocked the door decorated with two crossed spears, a feather dangling from the hilt of each spear.

She gasped. A leopard skin lay across the huge four-poster bed. She fantasied that if she opened the armoire door, she'd find Dr. Livingston's skeleton.

LeRoy set down their suitcases. "Cool. Awesome cool. Enough pillows on the bed to sleep a Girl Scout troop."

Aria agreed, although she envisioned piling half of them in the bathtub behind a locked bathroom door to escape any delightful escapade LeRoy harbored.

"Ta-daah!"

A jittery feeling overwhelmed Aria as she twisted her gaze toward LeRoy to learn what had excited him.

"See this coffee maker? Keurig. Full rack of exotic single-cup blends. We can wake up to heavenly aromas."

Aria shook her head. "This is a B&B. We get breakfast downstairs. The dining tables sat to the left of the reception desk. Didn't you notice them and the buffet line?"

"Of course. What if we sleep in?"

"Not happening. We need to find a café, assuming one exists. I'm surprised you haven't pestered me to eat."

"C'mon. Haven't I shown you I can be a gentleman? If you wish, I'll check out these armoire drawers for a leftover loin cloth. You can be a damsel-in-distress tied to one of these mahogany bedposts."

Aria shrunk away from him.

"Kidding, only kidding. Just trying to liven up this trip to be a marvelous adventure."

"Then let's explore. Need to see if we can find one of three addresses. If we find a café, great. If not, well . . . ."

The early evening humidity tested Aria's underarm deodorant, but deciding which travel direction to choose less worrisome. The town's business district existed to the north. Brick buildings dominated and four cars parked together three blocks ahead marked what Aria believed to be the town's hotspot, hopefully a café.

"We need not race," LeRoy said. "Where the cars are, I expect to be a tavern with bar grub if we're lucky."

Aria reduced the length of her strides. To ease the tension she felt between herself and LeRoy, she complimented him. "You're right. That is a tavern."

Curtains hung on a bar two-thirds of the way towards the top of two windows that bookended a frosted-glass front door left Aria, standing next to LeRoy, with no idea of what awaited. Her prior relief had been when LeRoy went into the bathroom to cast off his suit and resort to blue jeans and a red plaid short-sleeved shirt. No cowboy boots.

If a desperado spied on them, she didn't know from which direction or height. No rooftop rifle barrels glistened from the summer sunset's dying rays.

"Well, partner?" LeRoy stared at her. "We going in?"

A neon placard claimed the Tipsy Hog open. "Guess so."

Aria expected a creak when LeRoy twisted the doorknob. Didn't happen. Her prospect of a face-to-face showdown with Iowa-born John Wayne lost in a heartbeat.

"What youse waiting for? Come on in." The bearded man's invitation delivered as his right hand wiped a well-oiled bar. "There's bar seats. Or tables if youse object."

Aria pointed to a table separated from men playing poker. *How is Iowa different from Louisiana? Spears at the B&B. Hunt clubs sprinkled across the bayou. Poker ubiquitous.*

"Aria, there's a menu. We're in luck."

While LeRoy may have thought so, Aria tamped her enthusiasm, expecting disappointment until overwhelmed.

She read the menu while LeRoy ordered a burger basket. When it became her turn, she said to the bearded man, "I'll have the same, except can you put the raw onion to the side?"

"Will tell the cook. Can I bring you each a drink?"

LeRoy's eyes blossomed. "I'd like a draft." He altered his server gaze to take in Aria. "I'm not driving. Or am I?"

She smiled. "We're on foot, but water's fine for me."

The bearded man collected the menus. "Anything else?"

Aria waded in. "I'm searching for a family named Campbell said to live here. Know one hereabouts?"

"Half mile outa town, but you'd need a coon dog to smell out John Campbell's remodeled historic log house. He works at the hardware store, but it's closed."

Her heart skipped a beat. "Permanent?"

"Gosh, no. Most likely you'll find him there tomorrow stocking shelves. Why might you be looking for him?"

"Oh, nothing special. Might he have a child about five?"

"Can't rightly say child, but a rascal for sure."

"Oh!"

One card player gawked hard in her direction. Aria interpreted its length as ominous. Rather than reciprocate, Aria turned her gaze to engage LeRoy in trivial chitchat. She tried to tightrope between words embracing friendship without a slip into unintended sexual undertones.

She basked in her diversionary success when LeRoy asked, "Do you think they serve pie?"

He waved to the bearded man.

Chapter Thirty-seven

LeRoy snored. Aria kicked out. Missed. Her attempt stymied by two factors. First, human anatomy required a twelve-foot leg stretch and, second, the ability to plunge fourteen inches from the bed's mattress to the floor.

LeRoy's weight compressed pillows stacked two deep on the floor. The leopard skin, an impromptu blanket, let LeRoy doze in an animal netherworld.

Sunrays dripped from the top of window-darkening curtains to highlight widely spaced dust motes. A bathroom door whoosh and a lock's soft click scattered them.

Beneath a sheet, Aria clutched it to her chin. Her cell phone displayed 6:32 a.m., its alarm set for seven. She twisted onto her side, confident to let the alarm alert LeRoy his bathroom occupancy time expired.

"Rise and shine. Breakfast awaits." LeRoy's cheerful voice jolted her awake. Seconds later her alarm tweeted. Her right index finger swiped snooze.

"Guests who monopolize the mattress shouldn't dally."

"Shut up, LeRoy!"

Within two seconds, Aria felt ashamed. She peeked at LeRoy from above the sheet she raised to imitate an Arabian veil.

"Yes, ma'am. I'll hold your chair at breakfast."

"Please . . . ." Aria's unspoken words commanded no value within the Explorer Suite occupied by her alone. In her bathroom dash, she stumbled across a discarded pillow.

The soapy body wash and unscented shampoo advanced her preparedness to dress in jeans and a long-sleeved blue top. The B&B furnished hair drier provided a definite plus.

It wasn't prom, but she considered herself presentable for an Iowan breakfast, especially since no one knew her. Well, LeRoy, of course, but she'd paid him. Her prior evening's mention of this fact had short-circuited any squabble from LeRoy on who chose first to sleep in the king-sized bed.

LeRoy rose when she entered the B&B breakfast area. She asked, "Have you left a waffle for me?"

He lifted his right hand to show a plastic cup filled with almond batter. He smiled triumphantly. "Lift the handle, pour this batter on the plate and twist. Bell says you win."

Aria complied. When the timer rang, her upper-plate lift exposed a perfectly browned waffle. She forked it onto a paper plate, raised a ceramic pitcher and drizzled maple syrup across waffle ridges until the dimpled pockets overflowed. She savored her first bite. *Heaven, just heaven.* She alternated two waffle forkfuls with digestive coffee sips until the receptionist she'd met began clearing her dish.

"Let's get cracking."

LeRoy raised his gaze. "You mean hardware?"

Aria smiled, ready to depart with LeRoy in tow.

Morning foot traffic outside the B&B struck Aria with the loneliness experienced the prior evening when she and LeRoy explored the town's main drag.

"Have you researched this John Campbell?"

Aria shook her head. No toilet-repair visions filled her head as she strolled into the hardware store leaving LeRoy to window-shop a gift emporium across the street.

Her one step into a paint aisle exposed an eerie stillness bereft of the darkness. "Yoo-hoo."

A disconcerted voice disrupted Aria's concentration. "Who's there?" A second "Who's there?" floated in.

A shadow darkened the aisle's end ahead of her. "Are you, by chance, one known as John Campbell?"

"Who's asking?"

"I'm Aria Gleason. Perhaps you can confirm to me you adopted a child say four or five years ago."

A stooped man dressed in a plaid shirt, suspenders and blue jeans stepped into the breech between aisle endcaps. "Yes. Was God's holy will."

"Were you given a Louisiana birth certificate?"

"No. My wife, a nurse, knew the neighbor whose daughter died in childbirth. We'd prayed to have a child. This struck us to be God's plan, an answer to our prayers."

Struck by the sincerity of the man's expression, Aria asked, "Did anyone else adopt when you did?"

"Our community encourages, supports adoption."

"That's commendable." Aria refused to be thwarted by evasion. "I've seen an adoption certificate that lists Calhoon, Iowa. Is there an adoption agency here?"

"There's a Lutheran adoption agency for western Iowa. That I know from experience. Maybe two others between here and the Nebraska border. You'd be better off to search the Internet or telephone books then rely on my memory."

A whisper of internal dread tested her resolve to appear calm and collected. "I can understand you're well intentioned, but one of my goals is to uncover an insidious adoption agency. One that preys, with an 'e', on heartache."

"Is that why you're here? You brand me a sinner?"

"I didn't□" Aria choked off her words. She neither wished to be combative nor dismissive. "I'm happy for you. Wish my life so blessed." Her words not inspired by church attendance. She'd scarcely opened the unsolicited Bible Aunt Maggie forwarded to her while imprisoned.

"If I can't help you, I've an order to fill."

"Thank you. I'll not bother you further." Aria pivoted to confront LeRoy. His presence inside the store's front door hadn't registered. To him she said, "Let's go."

Outside on the sidewalk, Aria weighed her possible options to avoid exasperation. The day's expected heat yet to arrive. This pleased her, if LeRoy's facial contortions didn't.

"Where to now? A drive?"

"Let's walk."

"I'm up to it. A jog around this town equals a four-hundred yard track and field sprint."

A youngster's shout peaked Aria's interest. "Where did that come from?" Aria quickened her pace.

When LeRoy caught up, he mumbled, "Past the church."

"What?"

"There's a daycare. Walked past while you dithered inside the hardware store. And, your frown speaks volumes."

"This may be it."

"What turned you on?"

"Shut up! Pretend I'm paying you."

LeRoy charged across the street; Aria left behind. He pulled up at a white picket fence gate centered ten yards from a house porch decorated on high by Victorian scroll-sawn brackets. Three kids played in a sandbox and a fourth, a boy, swung on a board roped to a horizontal live oak limb.

Aria pondered if they should enter. Her need to decide evaporated when a woman about her age and dressed in a Little Miss Muffat costume called out from the porch. "If I might help you, stay where you are, gate closed."

A sideward glance at LeRoy elicited Aria's disgust that he'd stand there with his mouth agape. She'd never appear in public attired in a satin pink mini dress hemmed in white lace, a white apron and stockings fitted into gold-buckled black patent shoes.

And LeRoy's smitten reaction was exactly why. She wouldn't surmise what his brain cells imagined.

"Hi there." Little Miss Muffat trained her gaze on LeRoy. "If you're interested in child care, I'm sorry to say the only choice is this fall's waiting list."

"We're not married," LeRoy blurted out.

Aria rattled the gate lock without trying to cause it to open. "What my friend means is . . . well, I'm on a mission to locate my child."

"I can assure you your child is not here. I know the parents of all the children in my care." A girl behind her yelled, "That's mine. You can't take it."

"Susan, play nice. Give Cindy the shovel."

"Can I help?" LeRoy asked.

"'Fraid not. I teach the children not to be friendly or interact with strangers, although you appear harmless."

LeRoy smiled.

Aria shifted her gaze to the boy on the swing. "See that boy on the swing, how old is he?"

"Sorry, that's privileged information."

"Looks like five to me," LeRoy said.

"Good guess. Again sorry, can't confirm."

When the boy's right hand wiped his brow, Aria took note. The backhand brush against his chin caused her to shiver. She'd witnessed no one but Brad execute the double brow-to-chin move. She waited to see if the boy repeated the affect due to the warm weather.

"Do I need to get my registration form?"

"Aria, she asked us a question."

"That boy on the swing. Does he always wipe his forehead and chin like he just did?"

LeRoy interjected, "He did it again. Used the back of his right hand."

Little Miss Muffat tweaked her gaze from the sandbox to the swing. "Never gave it much thought. Why?"

"My husband, Brad, did that frequently. When questioned about it, he claimed it to be a simple reflex."

"Probably learned at home," LeRoy said. He smiled at Little Miss Muffat. "Isn't that so?"

"Caleb is quiet, well-behaved. He could just be warm."

Aria jerked her gaze to the girl grasping her shovel and returned it to the boy now known as Caleb. "His eyes blue?"

Little Miss Muffat nodded. "You're quite perceptive."

"Brad's eyes were blue. My mother's, too." She shook LeRoy's right arm. "I picture Brad in his face. He could be my son! He could be my son!"

"Hold on, Aria. Let's go slow here."

"Aren't parents required to provide a birth certificate to register their child? You must show me Caleb's."

"Like I said, I can't. I'll lose my license if the state finds out I've jeopardized the safety of any child."

Aria dropped her hand from LeRoy's arm. "Can't you see?" She rung her hands. "We're not here to harm any child. Could never do that."

"I believe you. The law ties my hands."

"Tied! You say your hands are tied!"

"Calm down, Aria. Don't freak out. You can't blame this lady for doing what she must."

"Doing what she must," Aria shrieked. "How can she stand there and deny me proof my child lives?"

"Ma'am☐"

Aria pushed up her right sleeve. "See these small scars above my wrist. That's where the guards shackled me. The stirrup clamp marks on my ankles testimony to when they immobilized me and shouted at me to push. Months later they hid their ravage by using multiple hands to clamp me to the infirmary cot. Where was this law you hide behind then?"

Little Miss Muffat shrunk back. Fear etched her face.

Chapter Thirty-eight

Aria twisted against LeRoy's grip on her shoulders.

She snarled through clenched teeth, "Let me go."

"Can't let you terrorize that boy or hurt yourself." He turned her toward the B&B.

"Let me walk."

LeRoy released his fingers, yet blocked her retreat.

The next morning at breakfast she explained that in her soul's deepest depths she believed Caleb was her son.

"You need to be smart," LeRoy said after a glance at a window splattered with ever-reoccurring raindrops. "Doubt the children will play outdoors this morning. Will impede your desired closer observation."

Aria swallowed a toast point. "You're skeptical."

"Feelings, gestures may be fine for you. Others would say facts and corroborated evidence must rule."

"Others? You mean you?"

"Well, you can't dispute logic needs factual support." LeRoy busied himself with a cream pour and two heaping spoonfuls of sugar, clumsily stirred.

"When the sun breaks through, I plan to hike past the church and trust Little Bo Peep will be tending her sheep."

"Wrong analogy. Bo Peep wears blue, not pink."

"Stuff it. When what eats you inside never goes away, you'll not be so god-awful flippant."

LeRoy bowed his head. "My apology, deepest apology."

"Let's finish breakfast□" The morning's oatmeal coagulated itself into a throat plug. Since paroled, the righteousness of suffering tempered Aria's heartbreak.

Yesterday's child sighting had inflamed her heartbreak.

They both hesitated on the B&B's front door threshold. Gathered storm clouds threatened a second outburst.

Aria tucked a newspaper under her arm. "We can always run to the hardware store."

LeRoy chuckled. "Or the Tipsy Hog."

With an elongated stride, Aria sidestepped a street puddle in front of the church and withheld her disappointment on seeing the childcare sandbox covered and the swing idle.

"We can return later," LeRoy said.

"I'm knocking to obtain a registration form."

"What?" His face fractured with disconcert.

"Not to fill out, but it's a reason to knock."

Little Miss Muffat in Capri slacks and a non-descript red top answered the door. "Hello, again."

Aria strained to peek behind her. A ground-level treehouse in a make-believe forest with rope lights looped across the ceiling enhanced a fantasy world Aria never enjoyed. "I've come to ask for that form you mentioned."

"Don't know. John at the hardware store cautioned me last night that you're here to cause trouble for families."

Aria pleaded, "You can't believe that."

"All right. I'll be back in a sec."

Four children marched into the forest. Aria shivered. Caleb resembled what she surmised to be a youthful Brad. She waved, her right hand no higher than her shoulder. The kids shied away as the sound of heel clicks grew louder.

"Here you go. I've included a pre-addressed envelope."

"Thank you."

"Remember to include a verified birth certificate copy."

"I will."

LeRoy held his comment until they'd walked a block. "You case the place so we can steal the boy's birth certificate when the clock strikes midnight?"

Chapter Thirty-nine

Clouds that Aria defined as stratus lazily streaked across the moon. A shadowy and indistinct landscape outside the Calhoon, Iowa, B&B bedroom window hypnotized her. The prison darkness she'd experienced hid undiscernible fears whose tentacles had often sapped her hopes.

Caleb's bright ray offered future joy. Like mothers described childbirth, his discovery masked her pain.

"LeRoy," she whispered. "LeRoy."

Scattered floor pillows obscured his ears and skull. Eyes closed, he muttered, "Don't have a tuffet."

Aria guessed he dreamed of Little Miss Muffat. She teased, "Curds and whey a dollar."

He rolled onto his right side, away from her. "No, no. Let's play first."

"Wake up, LeRoy. Stop dreaming. It's time to go."

He rubbed his eyes. "I don't have a ski mask if we're to break in. Have you really judged the consequences?"

"I'm no criminal. I'll rescue my son legally. Besides, Aunt Maggie can't bail out three of us."

"Three? There's you, me. Who's the third?"

"Caleb, who else? Not Little Miss Muffat!"

"Oh. Do you have time for me to shave?"

"Plus breakfast. Aunt Maggie would want my mother to get our money's worth on this trip, although, with finding Caleb, it's already priceless."

After breakfast, LeRoy carried their bags to his car. When standing at the open trunk, he asked, "Should we make childcare our last stop?"

"No. Last night's darkness fears awoke heightened torments. Let me nurture hope until it's replaced by my clutching a beating heart."

"Whoa. Can tell this drive to Chicago will be easy-peasy, even if I don't understand what the hell you say."

Aria tugged open the passenger door. "If you drive and I spot eating exits, we'll taste Tillie's cooking tonight."

"Deal." He slammed his trunk lid.

LeRoy's pedal-to-the-metal a far cry from Thelma and Louise's movie exploits and Aria appreciated that. Between watching for Interstate 80 directional signs or daydreaming about escorting Caleb to kindergarten, she kept up her side of LeRoy's chitchat. To her surprise, Little Miss Moffat entered their conversation just once when they passed a billboard displaying a huge mushroom. It didn't remind her of a tuffet, but then LeRoy's mind revolved in an entirely different contextual sphere.

"We going to do this again?" he asked at the midpoint.

She deciphered no subtext. In a strange way, she liked LeRoy. She interpreted his vagabond facade as a cover for an underlying insecurity. Tillie had warned her about his making a pass. Yet, that hadn't happened, even in their close proximity within one B&B bedroom.

Aria couldn't discount that Aunt Maggie, outside her presence, threatened him with the fear of God.

When they arrived in front of Tillie's home, Aria, standing on the curb, blushed when LeRoy, like a Scottish Lord, bowed and asked, "Will ye lady wish her bags inside?"

A voice boomed from the steps. "Oh, my God, Aria. Did your magic reduce LeRoy to a humble serf?"

Aria gazed left and upward. "Shut up, Tillie."

LeRoy joined in. "Yeah, shut up, Tillie."

Tillie bounced down the steps. She hugged Aria and whispered, "Was it feminine charm or did you use the electric prod cattle ranchers use on the prairie?"

Aria blinked her eyelashes. "If you want to lord it over LeRoy, tell him you recorded proof he snores."

"Really?"

"Yes, really. Now, is Aunt Maggie here?"

"She's in the front room." Tillie gazed at LeRoy. "If I order deep-dish pizza, that okay?"

"Magnificent."

Aria trusted LeRoy to bring in her suitcase. The same trust didn't equate with meeting Aunt Maggie in Tillie's front room. She expected her aunt's initial question.

"Do you bring wonderful news?"

"Not really, Aunt Maggie. My instincts tell me I have a son adopted by an Iowa family, but can't prove it."

Aunt Maggie rotated her wheelchair wheels forward and back; her expression stern, although loving.

"My attorney expected that."

Aria sat on the sofa. "You engaged an attorney?"

"Louis has been my estate attorney for years. He helped me obtain your mother's money. I'm sorry if I didn't explain his involvement earlier."

"That's okay." What else could Aria say? Her mother's money financed her Louisiana and Iowa search.

"He explained an adoption attorney in his office expressed doubt that you could ever reclaim a child."

Aria jumped to her feet. "What!"

"Calm yourself, please. I can't take turmoil as much these days as I could when I was your age."

Returned to a seated position, Aria coughed before she tried to speak. "Tell me what he said. I'll be calm. Listen."

"Well, major point against you is that you're a convicted felon, even if granted parole."

On her feet again, Aria screamed, "I didn't kill Brad."

"You know that and I believe what you tell me, but we're not the authorities. You need proof stronger than song lyrics about how the lights went out one night in Georgia."

"Louisiana, Aunt Maggie, Louisiana."

"Whatever. Who cares which southern state? I don't."

"Amen."

Aunt Maggie extended both arms. "Give me a hug, dear. I'm so glad you've taken to heart that Bible I sent you."

Hugging Aunt Maggie felt right and kept Aria's secret she'd rarely opened the Bible she received. *What next?* Elation and despair griped Aria in tandem and in turn. She castigated herself for being prissy and so scared she scuttled LeRoy's suggestion to burgle Caleb's birth certificate from the childcare center. She believed it a piece of cake for any certified document examiner to prove it forged and false.

Aria sat and released a gigantic sigh. Like leaning from a merry-go-round horse, the elusive gold ring tantalizingly close, yet unreachable.

"There's only one recourse," Aunt Maggie said.

Instinctively Aria had an idea, yet asked, "And that is?"

"Prove your innocence. That's what the attorney said."

The advice caught Aria off guard. "How?"

"Dear, he didn't offer a paint-by-number solution. He said you'd have to decide what trial testimony or crime scene photographs shown the jury to contest and debunk. That, he said, is the best, if not the only, way to convince a reviewing court the original verdict misguided or contrived."

"I didn't see Brad's killer."

Aunt Maggie wagged her finger. "Your mother told me."

"Okay." Aria's assent less than full-throated.

"She believed in you. Believed in your innocence."

"Oh." Her voice sounded strained. "You're just too nice."

"Never. While your mother battled her health issues, she never once expressed your life as subservient or unworthy."

Repulsed by this, Aria subdued her desire to express her outrage at Aunt Maggie's revisionist history lest it spill ill upon her earliest clutched thoughts of her loving mother.

"Let's set mother aside. Again, what did the lawyer say?"

Aunt Maggie clasped her right hand to her mouth. Within seconds Aria watched her aunt's hand slid southward. "Dear, I told you. Told you truth, real truth."

"What's going on?" Tillie sashayed into her front room.

Aria asked, "Where's LeRoy?"

"He left. Although he grumbled, said he'd return."

"About what?"

"Said he hadn't received his money. You give in?"

Aria shook her head. "Easily kept him at bay."

With a shrug Tillie said, "Can't fool me."

"Whatever." Aria expected Tillie's conjecture and moved on. "Aunt Maggie deserves my attention."

"Don't let me intrude." Tillie pivoted toward the stairs and didn't cast a glance rearward until the landing.

Aria let Tillie depart. She redirected her gaze to Aunt Maggie. "Let's forget mother. What else did the lawyer say that perhaps you're not telling me? You show him anything?"

"One photo."

"Which one was that?"

"I'd always wondered why the letters of your name were smeared in blood on the wall when the police first mouthed the claim the murder appeared to be by an intruder."

"Never heard that."

"Why would you? You're family and the greatest majority of homicides are committed by those dearest."

"Brad didn't write on the wall."

"What proof exists?"

"His love for me says it wasn't him. He'd only use my proper name if he was mad or upset about something."

"And, you'd try to convince a judge that bleeding to death didn't count as either one of those?"

"Well, no."

"What then?"

Aria's right index finger and thumb rubbed her forehead. *Dried blood, but what about it?* She gazed at her aunt. "It was the wall blood. Something about it."

Vertical creases stippled her aunt's brows. "You should be able to remember. You're not thinking."

"Trust me, I will. It's been five years."

Aunt Maggie rocked her wheelchair. "You're right, five years. Then maybe you should get on with your life. Stop fantasizing about a child that may never exist. You've searched and what did it get you? Tell me that."

Aria raised the finger and thumb that had rubbed her forehead. "I'm this close." She separated her digits by a half inch and rotated her wrist toward Aunt Maggie. "This close."

"Then why return empty-handed?"

She tried to keep her response level, even quiet, with no indication of the exasperation that swelled within her breast. "Didn't you say words to the effect that I couldn't be a convicted felon on parole if I wished to hug my child?"

"Well, that's what the lawyer said."

"Right, then an Iowa return must be after Louisiana."

"Dear child . . . ."

Aria silently ranked Louisiana as the last place she desired to visit. She preferred Amtrak, but LeRoy existed as her only practical transportation choice. She discredited his worthiness to shield her from Remy. "I'll need to obtain a debit card if traveling with cash is ill-advised."

"You'll do this with dispatch?"

"Try is all I can promise."

"Very well. Can Tillie go?"

"Why?" Aria asked.

"Then she won't throw me out."

Aria shook her head. *Dramatics, stupid dramatics.*

Chapter Forty

LeRoy dropped Aria's roller bag onto the centipede grass.

At the passenger door of his Buick, Aria ignored his deliberate, or accidental, bag handle slip. Her palms grew sweaty in Louisiana's brutal summer heat. Without drama, she'd survived the two-day ride from Chicago. Yesterday LeRoy relented and permitted her to drive as long as she avoided the rumble strips dug into the Interstate 35 shoulder.

"Why this cabin?" LeRoy asked. "There's no lake or other water body near Calhoon."

"It's all I need."

LeRoy clamped his fingers onto Aria's bag and carried both his and hers to the cabin's front porch. He waited, lips sealed, while Aria undid the double front door locks.

"After you," Aria said.

"Heavens."

Aria stepped into the front room. "Did you say heaven?"

Two travel bags thudded on the wood floor before LeRoy turned to face Aria. "Said 'heavens', because it's so hot it welcomes us to hell. Dante could've rented this cabin."

"Want to flip for the bedroom?"

LeRoy wiped perspiration from his forehead. "No. Spy a pullout couch." He flipped the seat cushions to expose a metal pull bar. He smiled. "Looks softer than the floor."

Aria let LeRoy's B&B reference dissipate without a retort. This tactic had worked when on two dates with him before she shipped off to the African Congo with Tillie.

"I'll be right back. Maybe thirty minutes."

Aria wiped her forehead. "Why?"

"Pizza. We gotta eat?"

Aria shrugged. Without a challenge to LeRoy's food choice, she fumbled with the single set of air conditioner controls while she waited. This one unit, wired into a living room window, meant she'd be required to leave her bedroom door ajar. *What a choice. Stuffy sauna or LeRoy's snores.*

When the front door knob creaked without a knock, Aria's skeletal muscles flexed. Her fists clenched before her controlled pivot.

"Half pepperoni, that okay?" LeRoy asked.

Aria exhaled; her reply half-facetious. "What else?" She tightened her facial muscles to ward off a lengthy chat while she searched drawers and cabinets for silverware and glasses.

Napkins sufficed for plates as the hiked analog television volume drowned out the requisite chitchat.

* * *

Aria counted three ice cubes in her sweet tea and watched them melt as she and LeRoy sat in Mr. Breaux's office. Twice LeRoy gawked at a shapely woman who emerged through the partition door to advise her boss detained on the telephone.

"At least it's cool, not like last night."

Aria clasped both hands to her face to hide her chuckle in celebration of her good fortune offering LeRoy the bedroom, even if the AC motor rumbled to blast recycled air all night long.

She lowered her hands in time to see Mr. Breaux enter.

"How good to see you. I'm just off the telephone with Aunt Maggie to calm her fear you're not delayed."

"And to get paid," LeRoy whispered into Aria's ear.

She elbowed LeRoy.

"The court evidence, you have it?" Aria asked.

"Definitely. Let's retreat to my office."

Aria's instincts urged her to grab the thick manila file centered on Mr. Breaux's mahogany desk. To do so required her to lunge forward, reverse course and try to avoid LeRoy who sat between her and the exit door. Even if successful she'd be easily captured outside since LeRoy drove and pocketed his keys.

"Since your attorney, Aria, didn't poll the jury, there's no good sense of what convinced them not to believe you."

LeRoy shifted his gaze from Mr. Breaux to her. "Did you cry on the witness stand?

"No. I held my chin high, spoke loud and strong."

"Then I see little hope."

Aria's shoulders slumped. *Tillie should have come.*

Mr. Breaux, hands on desktop, pushed himself half erect before he faltered and his descending weight creaked his chair springs. "Before second-guessing, let's focus on what I'd characterize as positive points to show reasonable doubt."

Whether reasonable, doubt paralyzed Aria's throat muscles. She coughed. What were her expectations to be? Would there be an immeasurable mind transformation should her review alter her innocent mindset? Brad, on their wedding night, ignited her mother's journey. Good-ol'-boy Louisiana won't shackle her dream. "And those are?"

"We'll get there. First, have you ever driven to the site where your husband died since that day five years ago?"

"Never." She interrupted Mr. Breaux's file reading. "So you know, I've rented what I'll call a cabin that's exactly like what Brad rented for our honeymoon."

He winked at LeRoy. "You two married?"

"Heavens, no." His stunned facial features relaxed during his neck twist toward Aria. "Well, not today anyway."

"LeRoy, tell the truth, no embellishment."

"Yes, dear." His smirk traveled from ear-to-ear.

"Understand." Mr. Breaux opened a notebook. "Did Brad drink alcohol? And did he have a favorite brand?"

"He preferred Scotch whisky. Glen something or other."

"Ever drink Tennessee brand whiskey?"

Aria shook her head. "Not when I knew him."

"Stop to buy a bottle on the drive to Louisiana?"

"Why is this important?"

Mr. Breaux rubbed his brow. "Prosecutor claimed you bought a Tennessee-branded whiskey from a convenience store. Criminal analyst bagged such a bottle at the scene, but Remy found no merchant record of your purchase."

Aria shivered. "Remy here?"

"He's off on a unique case. I suspect you and he don't get along. When the surveillance camera on the road leading to that bayou house showed excess time, I involved myself. While you have said nothing, my impression that day registered that you two meshed like a house afire."

Aria nodded. "Missing store receipt does not prove much."

"Correct. Not a key factor. Yet, it's the minor things that pile up and chip away at a guilty verdict and create reasonable doubt. That's why I had a lamp tested."

"Why? Brad stabbed."

"We'll get there. Scene report said neither Brad's nor your fingerprints on the lamp. Found that odd. There's no overhead light. I had the lamp retested on the odd chance 1, 8-Diazafluoren-9-one, DFO for short, wasn't used."

"Huh?"

"It's a chemical that reacts to amino acids, like those left by fingers. The fingerprints glow under blue-green light. Offers better ridge detail than other methods. When it confirmed no latent prints, I'm assuming someone, other than you, wiped it clean."

"Good assumption."

"Report says analysis found partial ridge impressions of your finger and thumb on the knife. That's problematic."

"I admitted I picked it up and tossed it away."

"My question is how you did that."

Aria bowed her head. "Don't remember."

"That's what the transcript says and memory less reliable than evidentiary facts. In this instance, this bedrock hypothesis swings decidedly to your benefit."

"How?"

"Again used DFO. The knife had your right forefinger and thumb print. Remember, it's a wooden knife handle. Wood is porous and well-used knives lose the shellac or oil originally applied by the manufacturer."

LeRoy squirmed in his seat.

Mr. Breaux paused for a deep breath. "Your fingerprints were on both sides of the knife handle's end. Says you carefully picked it up so as not to bloody your hand as you tossed it aside. If you'd stabbed someone, you'd have wrapped your hand around the handle. So, yes, you had prints on the knife, but no reasonable person can say that your grip plunged its blade into Brad's chest."

Aria gasped.

"My apology for being so blunt. But that's the truth."

LeRoy clapped. "Bravo."

Aria's elbow jabbed him a second time. "Then we have enough? Enough to erase my conviction?"

"Not quite."

Crestfallen, Aria forced her lungs to inhale. "Why not?"

"My DFO test confirmed no other fingerprints on either the knife's handle or its blade. Since smeared blood existed, the killer wore gloves, likely leather or latex. Your best argument would be if you're allergic to both materials."

"Can't say either. I wore latex gloves while working in Africa. No rash or other physical problem. Have worn leather dress gloves to fight off frostbite and snow during our winters."

"Expected that to be a loser."

"You're saying I've lost."

"No way. Sorry if I wasn't clear. Let me think a moment." Mr. Breaux gazed past Aria's left shoulder. "Fresh approach. It's summer in Louisiana. You'd not pack leather gloves. If I assume you didn't like wearing latex gloves in the heat of Africa, you'd not pack them for your honeymoon."

Aria stretched her facial muscles. "Exactly."

LeRoy, in a gesture of humility, raised his right hand. "Latex glove fingers, especially the thumb, can be used as an emergency condom."

"LeRoy, you're gross."

"Hold it, Aria. Don't lose sight of the fact you're on your honeymoon. Unless either of you were being treated for genital herpes the transportation of condoms unlikely."

LeRoy screwed up his face. "Don't tell me."

A bit uneasily, Aria murmured, "You'll never know."

"Okay," said Mr. Breaux, his voice raised a decibel. "I've saved our best argument for last."

Buoyed by Mr. Breaux's last assertion and willing to ignore LeRoy's third interruption, Aria breathlessly waited for the coup de grâce to justify her shelling out thousands of her mother's legacy to clutch her son to her breast.

"Are you listening?" Mr. Breaux asked.

Aria nodded.

"We're all but acknowledged today that it's hot in Louisiana in the summer. The prosecutor's best evidence was the letters 'A R I' scribbled in blood on the wall. We can't contest the blood was Brad's. But we can challenge when, and by who, the letters were written."

Confusion ruled in Aria's brain. "What are you saying?"

"Brad's blood was splattered on the wall beneath the letters. The splatter's origin being the knife's fatal thrust. Thus, the splatter hit the wall before the letters written."

"That's logical to my thinking," Aria murmured.

"Keep an open mind. The letter, when written, didn't smear the underlying splatter. Therefore, the splatter had dried before a person wrote the letters."

"You blamed the summer heat a moment ago."

"That I did, and it proves that you've been listening."

"What a minute," LeRoy interjected. "That's right, I've been listening, maybe not as attentive as a juror, but close enough. If there's this heat, which affects the written letters and what you say is blood splatter. How's this matter when Aria admits she came up to Brad lying on the floor?"

"I need to go back."

"Please," Aria said.

"I wasn't prepared to deliver a tactile blood explanation, but it should help you both achieve a greater understanding.

As an aside, Aria, I must give praise to Remy for his extra devotion to delve into this subject where my expertise hasn't been validated by advanced forensic certificates."

Aria prepped herself to utter a thank you, but then held back. If a saint had tried to attack her, and she believed Remy to be no saint, her disgust would be no less than what flared in her soul that recent day in the bayou.

"Okay. No comment. I'll continue. The cabin, as you call it, had painted walls in the kitchen. The cheap glossy paint doesn't absorb. That's to permit the owner to wipe the wall surface with a disinfectant and the wall looks good as new, well, at least for two or three years."

LeRoy squirmed. "Is all this necessary?"

"Yes. If the court requests Aria to testify again, she'll be prepared to explain these points."

"But I didn't testify about the wall paint."

"I know that. That's why when you do you'll be giving new testimony that doesn't contradict your prior testimony."

"Shouldn't my public defender have asked?"

"Absolutely. If we can't get the charges exonerated, we'll still have a grand point to argue for a new trial."

"Huh?"

"Inadequate representation. In other words, they appointed you an attorney who didn't do his job. That warrants you being given a new trial."

"From what I've heard, I'd vote her counsel a whack job."

"LeRoy, I appreciate your support, but I didn't hire you to drive to Louisiana so I'd stay here for a second trial."

Mr. Breaux's eyes widened. "Got it."

"I'm sorry. Tell me again why the letters and the blood splatter prove me innocent."

"In the simplest of explanations, the blood splatter hit the wall when Brad stabbed. The medical examiner wrote the blade severed an artery near the heart. The splatter confirms external blood spurts. Since the examiner noted a fatal wound consistent with a twisted blade, Brad survived no more than five minutes, maybe less. Regardless, his arms and hands would've had no strength to write even one letter, let alone three, after the splatter dried."

"So, hot was good?"

"Yes. Heat speeds up the drying process, while humidity slows it. It's not an exact science, but does not contradict my theory to prove your innocence."

"And that's what?"

"You were framed by an intruder, a third party killer. If Brad lacked the wherewithal to write the letters, then either you or the cabin invader did."

"Devil's advocate. What's to say she didn't wait and conjured up this scheme to point to another?"

Aria glared at LeRoy for his insinuation.

"Let's go back to heat and humidity," Mr. Breaux said. "We've receipt and witness proof as to time and date Aria picked up the pizza. We've timed the pizza parlor/cabin roundtrip. We have the recorded time you called emergency services."

Aria leaned forward. "Isn't that enough?"

"Tests tell us how long it took the splatter to dry. There's a crazy scenario that you stabbed Brad, went for pizza and then wrote the letters on your return."

Aria jumped up. "Never. Cross my heart and hope to die."

"I believe you," Mr. Breaux said.

Aria plopped into her chair and stared at her investigator.

"Science believes you, too. Again forensics. Red blood cells separate from the blood serum outside the artery. The letters were written with blood containing red blood cells. You were absent too long. No way does the splatter and/or written letter dryness coincide with your presence or the time of your absence."

"You now believe me?"

"Always did. And told your Aunt Maggie that too."

LeRoy's eyelids stretched heavenward. "Despise pizza, now do you?" He gazed at Aria; his lips a sly smile. "Well, bless my soul. It yanked your butt out of the fire, didn't it?"

Aria pressed her elbow to her side. LeRoy had a point, a very valid point. She shifted her gaze to Mr. Breaux closing his file.

"This sounds good, but I'm still a Yankee in a Southern court."

Chapter Forty-one

Aria heard the glass crunch beneath her right sole. A jagged hole above the latch in a front window pane spurred her to stop and shout, "LeRoy, LeRoy."

"Give me a minute. Rear tire's low."

"Forget the tire. We've been burgled."

He yelled, "Duck."

On her dive, Aria banged her right knee against a porch plank, her brain cells alert for the whistling bullet to sear her flesh. Both hands clasped her ears; her nose flattened a splinter.

"Relax, Aria." LeRoy's voice sounded close.

"Huh?"

"Stand up. I'm here."

Aria's heartbeat raced. "The intruder."

"Dust plume raced north; guess off-road pickup."

"Why'd you yell at me to duck?"

"Nervous. Find cover; save yourself too complex."

Upright, Aria punched the front door. Light streamed at her from between the door and its jamb. Hinged, the door banged against an unseen obstacle. She gazed at LeRoy. "Whatcha think?"

"Wait." LeRoy disappeared around the cabin's right corner.

Aria obeyed and, with her left arm outstretched, pushed the door inward. She encountered the sofa bed overturned and a Gideon Bible flipped out of an upside down drawer. Her suitcase contents strewn everywhere. "Go Home" written in red lipstick on a mirror. The shade from her toiletries.

When LeRoy rushed in, muggy humidity swamped the cabin. "No one outside. We're safe."

Aria continued to stare at the mirror. If LeRoy saw the ominous warning, his facial expression hidden. He advanced to her left side.

"Could you identify the driver?"

LeRoy shook his head. "Sure it was a late-model pickup, dark color, but dust disguises blue, black and gray."

"The driver heavy or lanky?"

"Damnit. Said I couldn't see."

"We should call Mr. Breaux." Aria plucked her cell phone from her front pocket. She dialed and listened.

"This is Remy."

Besides being surprised that Remy answered, the connection sounded outdoors rather than in an office.

"May I help?" Remy asked.

"This is Aria. Is Mr. Breaux there?"

"He's out. May I help?"

"Tell him my cabin's been vandalized. I'm going to call the sheriff or 9-1-1."

"I can be right there. Give Mr. Breaux a head start."

"As you wish." Aria pressed the END CALL button.

"What can the authorities do, we can't?" LeRoy asked.

"Not here. The hunting lodge."

"Whoa. You lost me."

"You said swirling dust hid a pickup. Brand the intruder a coward and a tricked up truck may be the key to a common denominator. Drive me to the hunting lodge."

"That's not a welcoming place."

"Don't sass, LeRoy. I'm playing the boss card and it's no cheap trick to ante up to a game invite not dealt."

"Yes, ma'am. Give me time to install the spare."

Aria's right hand hid her smile. She dropped her hand and said, "I can help."

While she did little more than hold LeRoy's lug nuts, she felt useful. LeRoy sweated with the task. She didn't. Both benefited from the car's air conditioning en route to the hunting lodge. Aria envisioned passing the Deputy Dog statue. LeRoy drove a different route as he acted unconcerned.

"There." Aria pointed. The white building known to her as the hunting lodge emerged yards beyond LeRoy's bumper.

"Don't see a dusty vehicle," LeRoy said.

"Could be in the rear."

"Yeah. I could drive around."

"Don't. That pickup. Would you say it's tricked out?"

"Definitely." LeRoy spun his gaze sideways. "Why?"

"Drips like it drove through a car wash."

LeRoy pumped his brakes. Aria contemplated her next move. She'd be fearful if the poker players present, but the empty parking lot advertised a lull time.

"Stay here, LeRoy. I might learn more if I'm not expected to have a witness."

LeRoy's complexion grayed. "FBI uses a wire."

"We're not them, nor am I James Bond or Superwoman."

"So what are we doing here?"

"Somebody doesn't want me to know my son was adopted, and like others, adopted for big bucks."

"And this southern Mafioso operates from this simple white building that claims to be a hunting lodge?"

"Looks can be deceiving."

"Aria, I don't wear a bulletproof vest."

"Neither do I."

"Your Aunt Maggie wouldn't approve."

"Have you abided by everything she says?"

"That's not fair. Have you?"

"Shove Aunt Maggie aside. Remember you're to stay here while I go inside."

"What's your code word?"

"Huh?"

"The word you utter that tells me to get help."

"I'm not wired, remember. No code word works."

A puzzled expression consumed LeRoy's face. "Okay, if you encounter trouble, light a fire. I'll take the flames as your call for help, consider it a Native American smoke signal."

"Did anyone ever say you're paranoid?"

"Aunt Maggie."

Aria shook her head. "Remember, stay here." She opened the passenger door, pushed it shut and gazed at the hunting lodge. Whatever existed behind the structure's outer walls she'd soon experience again or anew.

To bolster her courage, she cast no rearward glance.

An unlocked door offered her admittance.

"Well, well, you're still here."

Aria recognized the guard's voice, although his physical presence lurked unseen.

"You should've honored my advice to move on."

Aria strained her eyeballs to pinpoint the voice location. She failed. Did the static indicate a speaker? Was the speaker alongside the couch or beneath the poker table?

"You stole my flesh and blood."

"You cheated us."

Aria's hatred of her prison treatment flared within her. "Did not. Your guard buddies tied me down, again and again."

"Maybe so. After your mother's letter warned of a hereditary defect, we were on guard." He laughed, loud and sinister. The distorted sound waves convinced Aria she confronted a piped-in voice. *Where's the camera?*

Indecision raged deep within her. What was her choice? Freedom or fear; dread or liberation. Mother's letter never received. "You stole my letters?"

"We needed to protect ourselves. Condoms provided you fun and prevented needless abortion pain the last two years. The infirmary doctor advised your boy appeared healthy, no outward signs of family deficits. I counted the months and figured you didn't conceive during your marriage."

"Rubbish. I deserve to raise and love my son."

"A hundred thousand dollars will get you that."

"You'll blackmail me?"

A crackle preceded his response. "Let's not be nasty. Consider how much we've saved you. Five years food and shelter to equal a hundred thousand sounds fair to me."

"Oh, my God."

"Don't think he'll help. Not even Billy Graham."

"That kind of money is beyond me. It's crazy."

"Try a social media go-fund-me page. People are a sucker for mothers and children. I'll even forward you a picture."

Stymied, Aria tried an alternate approach. "I've discovered how you forge birth certificates. I'm sure the State of Louisiana will value my testimony."

"Remy told us he'd slipped up. We've recovered."

Aria congratulated herself on her intuition. Yet, did that revelation expand to include Mr. Breaux? He'd been so supportive on how Aria could overturn her conviction. Was it that simple? He'd pocket her mother's money, go through the motions and blame the adverse outcome on a tone-deaf judge or court. How could she prove she'd been scammed?

She tried guilt. "But families across the nation can't be forced to deny what you've done?"

"That's the beauty. They cherish what they have. Do you think they'll give up a child?"

Static disrupted word endings. Aria strained her ears.

"Never. They'll hug their child and deny any and all accusations they willingly participated in baby smuggling."

"But DNA?"

"Oh, hush. Non-family adopted babies never share adoptive parent DNA. Besides, there's always the papers mothers signed to give up offspring rights."

Aria gasped. Had she signed away her child? She'd signed papers while imprisoned. Had those medical consents to receive vaccinations really given away her rights?

No way. Justice begat justice and justice lived for her.

Aria scanned the premises for a speaker location. The ceiling her logical choice. Her gaze focused on a black recess where a haphazard light fixture repair patch existed.

She tested her skill. "I see where you're coming from."

"Nice bluff. You're wrong."

"Try to escape. It won't happen. You should've heeded my advice not to stay the day the board paroled you. Exit doors blocked and you've no entry onto the roof. Shouldn't have jabbered. Splendid news is Remy waits outside drooling to wrap his arms around you."

Aria tensed her leg muscles. "Watch me, if you can."

Explosive charges exploded behind the sofa. Caustic smoke billowed toward her. She dodged the secondary flashes with a strong leap left toward the entrance. Tear-gas quality smoke choked her throat. She bent forward to clasp her knees.

Forceful fingers squeezed her biceps, dragged her backwards. Her heels bumped against a threshold. Parking lot air cleared her nostrils. While her eyes stung, she could see.

Her voice sputtered. "Let me go. I was this close."

"This close to what?" LeRoy asked. "Dying?"

"No. Uncovering the prison's entire adoption scheme."

"So what?" He braced her against his Buick.

"Don't you get it? Not just me, others. Child-bearing age women imprisoned not because they broke the law but because they could titillate and enrich their captors."

"And in this fantasy of yours, who's the ringleader?"

"The prison guard who wanted me to go away."

"And where's your proof?"

"Don't have any. Only wish to hug and raise my child."

LeRoy's slow-roll expression imitated a theater horror film audience that expected gore and mayhem.

"Don't chastise my choice. Wait until you're a father."

Chapter Forty-two

Glances to the parking lot lessened Aria's jitters that the guard or Remy hunted her. Yet, she nagged LeRoy three times. "Can't we go faster?"

"Not courting danger."

"Doesn't follow."

"Front and rear not my concern. Side entrances are."

A black SUV blocked the road fifty yards ahead.

Jostled forward, Aria gasped as LeRoy's right foot slammed the brake pedal to the floorboard. A fishtail swayed her sideways. Her extended seatbelt snapped Aria's shoulder blades into the front seatback.

"You okay?" LeRoy asked.

"Will be if that's not Remy."

LeRoy leaned toward Aria and reached his right hand behind his right calf and under the driver's seat. His hand emerged; fingers wrapped around a tire iron. "This'll help."

Aria, aware the older gentleman exiting the black SUV wasn't Remy, still cautioned, "Hold on."

With the tire iron pressed against the steering wheel, LeRoy asked, "Why? If we wait, they could surround us."

"Sure that's Mr. Breaux."

"Positive? That quick step is coming this way."

A two-finger jab to unlatch her seatbelt, and a door push cleared her path to the front of LeRoy's car. She raised her right hand to return Mr. Breaux's wave when he backtracked to jump into his vehicle and drive toward her, his driver door ajar.

LeRoy, at her side, clutched his tire iron with two hands.

Mr. Breaux stopped his car and stood behind his car door. "You happen to run into Remy?"

Aria, uncertain it was worthwhile to restate the guard's assertion, clipped her answer to the barest truth. "No."

Under his breath, he muttered, "Can't trust him."

Stiff fingers shaded Aria's eyes as distant dust swirled. Although she hoped not, she alerted LeRoy, "Might be Remy."

Mr. Breaux twisted his upper body to garner a look-see. He returned his gaze to Aria. "Vehicle's left the road. Let me say what I came for and y'all can be on your way."

His tousled hair distracted her concentration. His stare reignited a loneliness within her soul. Her cemetery tombstone memory flash reincarnated the unresolved dread she'd absorbed from autobiographical tract scraps, purportedly written by an author too scared to disclose his or her name.

She bowed her head.

LeRoy coughed. "If no one minds, I'll stay."

"Please," Aria said. She lifted her gaze to Mr. Breaux.

"I'll be direct. While I believe in your innocence, Aria, my entreaties on your behalf have this morning met with an obstacle, a vocal few steeped in the status quo. Yet, you have my very best assurance your attorney will prevail as she marshals societal voices shouting into megaphones protesting violence against women. Public opinion today molds courts, even in this state, to abandon vile prejudices."

"How long until I know?"

"You must be patient. Three to six months."

"And then what?" LeRoy asked.

Aria's left hand fingertips touched LeRoy's shoulder. "I'll be one step closer to my chosen life."

Mr. Breaux warned, "Let's not celebrate just yet."

Chapter Forty-three

Express Mail delivery, especially repeated, frightened Aria, even with Aunt Maggie and Tillie sitting nearby in Tillie's front room for support.

"If it's a fifth attorney bill, I'll rip it up." Aunt Maggie gestured with her hands. "How much more can she charge?"

"It'll be worth it," Aria murmured. She blocked negative thoughts to nurse a frayed inner confidence.

Aria handed Tillie the third large envelope she'd received in the last six months. "If it's bad, I don't want to read it."

"I can't open it. Isn't there a law or something?"

Aria paced. "Be the god of victory. Just do it."

Tillie ripped the perforated tab. She pressed the envelope to her forehead. "And inside will be?" She reached in and extracted a smaller envelope. In a buoyant spirit with a smile on her lips, Tillie announced, "Another surprise."

"Oh, just open it," Aunt Maggie demanded.

Tillie gazed at Aria, now collapsed into a chair. Any willingness to fake the dramatic a punctured balloon.

"We have tickets," Tillie exclaimed. "No, wait. Says subpoena in English. The French "la assignation" sounds drastic. Guess that's not a ticket."

Aria bounced up. "Let's see."

Tillie extended both envelopes. "Take it all."

An explanatory letter from her attorney brought clarity. The subpoena issued for Aria's benefit to bypass any transportation hurdle to get to Baton Rouge.

The Louisiana appellate court required oral argument and Aria's presence on a Wednesday four weeks hence, two weeks after Christmas.

Since flying in ice and snow increased her jitters, Aria booked a Monday Spirit of New Orleans coach seat. Her plans allowed ample time to consult with her attorney.

LeRoy's offer to drive her to Union Station politely refused. Aunt Maggie whispered her approval.

While money bore no relationship to her desire to endure her ordeal, Aria had purchased a parka at the thrift store where she's purchased the retro skirt and jacket she packed for court. Jeans, an Aran sweater and boots fit the bill for train travel.

Aria's Wrigleyville hugs and good-byes swift and short. The El awaited. She promised to call upon her arrival.

She weathered two short Amtrak en route delays for track switching at three and eight hours without incapacitating anxiety. She longed for summer's varied scenery, now buried by snow, until terrain darkness and fog, darker than vintage coal-stoked steam engine smoke, blurred her gaze.

As she sat, her present neither rallied her against past agonies nor calmed an uncertain future. She expected an hour of straining to read judicial facial expressions.

Even her budget hotel mattress insufficient to mold her torso into a stationary sleeping form. On her fateful morning when a taxi dropped her at the courthouse, her pressed jacket and skirt blocked a gusty bayou wind that whirlpooled past city skyscrapers. Her attorney waved off the one encamped cameraman and a trailing reporter who stalked the sidewalk.

Once inside, Aria's gaze darted left and right. The space gigantic and more opulent than the photos she'd seen.

Halfway up the center aisle, a muscular man in a white fitted shirt and blue pants stepped in front of her. She gasped. *What was HE doing here?*

Caught unaware, Aria gasped aloud, her leg muscles paralyzed.

"Who do we have here?" A snigger in his voice.

Aria's attorney advised her. "Ignore him."

"She won't be able to when I reclaim my child."

Aria's jaw locked. Light-headedness invaded her brain.

"Move away, sir. Don't create a scene."

The guard's one sidestep followed by a deep chuckle. "Today won't be the last time we meet."

Urged forward by her attorney, Aria directed to a chair inside the railing by her attorney's hand motion. She asked, "Am I required to speak?"

"Don't expect you will. Two women imprisoned by state authorities last year have filed assault and paternity actions against three guards. Your encounter today is blatant intimidation. He may think you'll join the other women, but the court today considers only your conviction of five years ago."

Aria struggled to breathe. Lamaze training failed. She'd verified her pregnancy two months after Brad's death. Panic shivered her arms. Had she miscarried and been impregnated a second time? Did the guard's threat mean that? Her memory fuzzy.

A strong baritone voice called out, "All rise."

To her surprise she succeeded and then plunked her butt onto the previously chosen seat. She didn't understand the proceedings nor hear the words of her attorney and another when they stood in the well below the seated judges.

When her attorney half-turned to face her, she heard, "If the court pleases, the appellant is prepared to give testimony if questions remain not briefed."

"Not necessary," said the center judge. "We take judicial notice that Louisiana's summer air dries blood quickly and find no evidence to dispute the forensic affidavit that the writing of the three letters, in blood, occurred after the blood splatter dried. While we lament the fact that our competent sheriff has not apprehended the killer, we concur the record evidence sufficient to meet judicial standards that no reasonable jury could find the appellant guilty as charged. An order so stating shall be issued within seven days. Counsel are excused."

Aria didn't see the guard as she scrambled to get outside to call Aunt Maggie and Tillie.

Joyful tears dampened her cheeks as she hugged her attorney. When she released her arms, a familiar face stepped into her line of vision.

"Aria, congratulations," Mr. Breaux said. "Have you left your child at home?"

"I'm still searching." Her words pricked her aching heart.

"Have you read where nine members of a grand jury voted a true bill against authorities at the state women's prison? Abuse allegations and a baby ring."

"My client has no comment."

Aria stared at her attorney. What did she know that she hadn't told Aria?

"I'm not fishing for an answer. Aria's also been my client and I'll send her my report this month." He paused. "And, Aria, you should be glad to understand Remy no longer works for me. I found him in possession of years' old fake birth certificates. Very crude reproductions. I laughed when I saw the botched postal code for Louisiana, although an 'I' before the 'A' can easily be confused with an 'L'."

The attorney grasped Aria's elbow. "My car's here."

After a good-bye, Aria dislodged her gaze from Mr. Breaux.

At the hotel she telephoned Tillie's house. Aunt Maggie answered. "I've been guarding this phone since breakfast. Hold on while I summon Tillie. I promised her I would."

Constricted throat muscles stymied Aria's first two attempts to articulate words. She strained a third time.

"I'm free, really free."

Chapter Forty-four

LeRoy grinned ear-to-ear. Aria expected she pleased him with his driving rehire as he pranced his unique happy dance. Tillie and Aunt Maggie frowned, then gave in to applaud.

Tillie and Aria had the night before discussed the dread of driving west to Iowa in February. Neither disputed Aria deserved to be reunited with Caleb.

In what took a month, Aria provided a DNA swab to Mr. Breaux who had pulled strings to determine whether Aria's DNA matched that subpoenaed by the Louisiana Public Health Department. Disjointed information existed within Caleb's medical file. Those were the words Mr. Breaux used.

Caleb's adoptive parents asserted they did nothing wrong without challenging the health department in court. Aria preferred to describe her son's birth certificate as fake.

For the last four days, Aria's official, certified lab results remained locked away in Tillie's home safe.

"LeRoy." Tillie spoke to garner his attention. "You gonna fly your pizza delivery sign all the way to and from Iowa?"

"Don't make fun of my chauffeur," Aunt Maggie said. "He's working two jobs."

LeRoy's smirk accentuated by his raised chin. He dropped it to ask Aria "What time we leaving?"

She replied, "Five a.m."

His coat retrieved from the entry closet, LeRoy bid good night and Aunt Maggie led the three women to bed.

Only Aria awoke at four a.m., secured the DNA results in a briefcase and stood chilled to the bone next to a street light girdled in an orange sodium-vapor glow.

When LeRoy pulled up, Aria didn't ask where the pizza delivery sign went. She hopped in and asked the best question she could. "You eat breakfast yet?"

The expected "no" materialized and Aria flashed the fast food coupons Tillie had saved. "I'll be ready for Rockford."

At a rest area across the Illinois/Iowa border, Aria didn't offer to drive, nor complain LeRoy drove too slow.

"I'll guess you're excited?"

Aria relayed LeRoy's ecstatic full-face grin.

A gray dawn's dull reflection in LeRoy's rear window hitchhiked with them for two hours into Calhoon, Iowa.

"Place hasn't changed." LeRoy's droll tone announced his want to retrace their route as quick as possible.

Aria hadn't bothered to make a B&B reservation, although she telephoned Little Miss Muffat, aka, Madeleine Swanson, as a courtesy gesture. The Louisiana Public Health office copied Aria on their update letter to the daycare and Caleb's adoptive parents.

If trouble loomed, Aria convinced herself it wasn't because of her actions. She planned for LeRoy to go with her into the daycare to pick up her son. The covered sandbox and idle rope swing didn't set off alarm bells as they cruised to the end of the block and turned around to park.

Before them, the black SUV with Louisiana plates did.

"Someone hijacked our preferred spot."

Aria didn't chuckle. Black sedans in Louisiana forecasted perils and pitfalls. "See any marking or a magnetic sign?"

"Someone from adoption services?"

"Letter sent me said no health officer travels this far."

Aria exited and stretched her frame to its fullest height. No small truth pebbles littered the ground nor did bread crumbs divine their shoveled path to the front door.

LeRoy caught up with her. "One window decal authorizes DOC lot parking. Doesn't do much for me."

"Anything on the seats?"

"Highway maps. That's all."

"Forget that. I want to hug my son."

"And, get out of here?"

Aria nodded and her right finger pressed the doorbell.

No answer.

She knocked. Two quick raps.

No answer.

LeRoy stepped forward to pound his fist twice.

No answer.

"We ain't leaving without my son." Kicking snow, Aria trudged to the nearest window. Behind the partially frosted window pane, Little Miss Muffat sat bound to a chair. No child visible.

"Anything interesting?"

"Childcare owner appears tied to a chair. Could be an innocent game of hide and seek."

"Let me see." LeRoy adjusted his stride to the snow depressions Aria created. He peered into the window and they returned to the front door.

"Look away."

Aria peeked as LeRoy jammed and probed a credit card into the door's lock.

"Lookie here. Someone left the door unlocked,"

They both froze in place as a pickup truck zoomed past.

As LeRoy inched the heavy wood door outward, its hinges squeaked. "We're in luck. Hear those chair legs bang on the floor? Gives us cover."

"But there are no kid noises. Wasn't this quiet before?"

"Nap time is my guess."

"Don't be silly. Not with that chair rocking."

LeRoy paused. He turned to Aria. "Here's the deal. On my count of three, I'll yank this door wide open. We'll rush in, me first." He held up one finger, then two, then three.

They rushed to the first doorway on the right.

Madeleine Swanson shouted, "He's taken my kids."

"Where?" Aria asked.

"Basement."

LeRoy hustled to untie Madeleine. He asked in a soft voice, "There a police officer in Calhoon?"

246

"No. Sheriff in the county seat."

"What about men at the hardware store or saloon?"

"Hardware store, maybe. Too early for the Tipsy Hog."

Aria gathered the loose rope and said to Madeleine, "You get help. We'll find my son, save the others. First, does this house have a fire extinguisher, knives?"

LeRoy's jaw drop joined his raised brows.

Madeleine replied, "No knives, too dangerous. Fire extinguisher mounted on the kitchen wall near the rear door."

"Thanks," LeRoy said. "Your kids will be fine. Now go."

LeRoy assumed command and unlatched the fire extinguisher before they both tiptoed to the basement door.

"We won't surprise anyone."

LeRoy frowned in disbelief.

"Anyone in the basement can hear first floor footfalls in a house this old."

"So," LeRoy asked.

"We'll announce our trip downstairs so that whoever is there won't hide and strike out. We need but buy time for the sheriff to arrive. That hardware store has guns. We don't."

"Nice thinking. I'll lead."

"No. If I go first, the fire extinguisher will be partially hidden. Whatever minor surprise we muster bodes well."

Aria jerked the basement door. "Whoever's there, be ready. I'm coming to see my son."

A baritone replied, "No tricks."

In an instant the SUV's Louisiana plates completed the six-piece puzzle. Except for one point. Did the prison guard who threatened her in the Baton Rouge court bring friends?

"You won't get away with this. I know who you are."

"This boy can grow to manhood without living with a whore for a mother."

Rage consumed Aria. The past blurred the shapes she discerned. Four children, each mouth sealed with gray duct tape, sat with their backs to each other with wrists and ankles taped to wooden chairs crafted for their size. Aria couldn't see Caleb's face unless she walked to the circle's far side.

"You won't get away with this. The boy you think is yours, isn't and DNA proves that."

"Even if you're telling the truth, I offered you the chance to pay me what I'm owed," the guard shouted.

Aria tried to find human shapes in the shadows. She couldn't see behind the large oil furnace and the space large enough to hide two men, if they squeezed together. While the guard wore a white shirt and blue pants, only one parka lay across a chair seat. Aria saw no weapon except the baton in the guard's left hand. She strained to remember if that was his dominant hand. She hungered for whatever advantage she could garner.

"You two will step off the stairs and I'll carry this boy to my vehicle. No tricks and three kids stay alive with but a slight taste of trauma. It'll be less than what grade school bullies will dispense in a year or two."

Keep talking. You're the bully.

"You should thank me this boy still lives."

"Don't understand what you're saying. You're talking crazy stuff." Aria gulped. She didn't need to goad him nor unnecessarily insult him into acting crazy. "What I mean is, he appears healthy."

"His grandmother didn't think so."

Aria steadied herself with a bannister grip. She remembered his earlier claim. "You stole my letters."

"Darn right. Others, who spotted Downs babies, voted to have this child suffer the same fate. I said no. Persons wanting to adopt would count the ten fingers and ten toes and see the rosy cheeks and wire the money to the offshore account, no questions asked."

The indistinct noise above her head caused Aria to speak louder. "You've got your money. Leave him with me."

One child behind the guard rocked his toddler chair. The guard stared, then jerked his gaze toward Aria. "That's the problem."

Aria lowered her voice as the noise she heard wasn't repeated and the guard seemed not to notice. "What's the problem?"

"Earl messed up. He failed to collect on three children. Only four months ago did Remy tell me birth certificates misspelled the state abbreviation for Louisiana. That's why my chasing across Louisiana for years futile, waste of good high-octane gasoline."

Aria thought this Earl person the same as the one married to Edmee, but her better self cautioned her to stay mum. "You can't disrupt the lives of these children?"

"Who says I can't. They're still in demand and I'll recoup my expenses and I'll not have to share with Earl or anyone."

"You won't get away with it."

"Just wait and see."

Aria dared not rotate toward the kitchen door lest she expose LeRoy and the fire extinguished he carried.

The guard snarled, "Told you once. Get off those stairs. Want to listen to a nice little girl scream?"

The guard shuffled backward, set Caleb's chair on the basement floor and positioned himself behind the girl Miss Moffat had called Cindy when Aria first visited.

If Aria rushed the guard, she'd stumbled over Caleb before she reached him. If she tried to snatch Caleb, he'd leap Cindy and grab her. *Can't win. Must be a better plan. How does LeRoy help?*

The guard knelt behind Cindy and placed his thumbs on her throat. He sneered at Aria and LeRoy as he wiggled his thumbs.

Aria tempered her voice. "Hurting this little girl will only madden a jury and lengthen your prison term."

His hearty belly laugh echoed throughout the basement. The guard then coughed. "You should be on stage with Seinfeld."

Aria edged down two steps, four more to go. No sound behind her meant LeRoy stayed put.

"How you feeling, Cindy? Nod your head to tell this lady not to encourage me to bruise your larynx." He must have exerted thumb pressure as Cindy cried. "That's right."

"Don't you hurt her? I'm following your instruction." Aria hung on to the bannister and finished the last four-step distance with two bounding leaps.

"Not enough," the guard said. "Hey, pimp. Join your whore."

LeRoy flinched. His left hand slid across the bannister as he positioned his right behind his hip to hide the extinguisher.

The guard left Cindy and pointed his baton at Aria.

"Slide left you two." Aria and LeRoy sluggishly complied. "I've gotta blow this joint. That is, after I tie you two and see if my thousand buck daycare owner bribe is rewarded with interest."

The pit of Aria's stomach gurgled. She wanted to calculate the distance necessary for LeRoy to swing the fire extinguisher. Then the guard foiled her plan when he holstered his baton and lifted Caleb, still tied to a chair, and balanced both on his left hip.

Caleb shielded the guard from LeRoy's swing.

When a voice at the top of the stairs yelled, "Who's down there?" Aria dove beneath Caleb's chair legs with an aim for the guard's left knee. She heard a crunch and pain stabbed her left shoulder.

The guard screamed, his arms flew high as he staggered backward, able to maintain the semblance of a man still able to keep his feel under him.

Caleb and his chair struck the concrete basement floor.

LeRoy stepped to Caleb's right and swung the fire extinguisher at the guard's head. Missed.

John from the hardware store jumped off the last two stair steps. He and LeRoy pinned the guard to the floor.

Aria untied Caleb's wrists and ankles.

"Here LeRoy, use this." She tossed him four rope segments. They weren't the best restraints, but LeRoy stood guard with a baton while John's arms cradled the fire extinguisher.

The guard snarled at John. "You! Earl said his letters to you for four years kept being returned. You'll never be free of me. You understand that."

"Not afraid of you. I left my fear in Calhoon, Louisiana."

LeRoy tugged a knot on the guard's hands tighter and smiled when a female voice shouted into the basement: "The Sheriff called to say he'll be here in forty minutes."

Aria allowed the information to float away, unanswered. She hugged Caleb and whispered, "My son, my beautiful son. Now this might hurt, but mommy needs to pull off this duct tape." She kissed his forehead, not once but twice, as she jerked the tape free with her right hand.

Her left shoulder ached. She didn't care.

LeRoy twirled the guard's baton. "Wish I had a camera?"

Aria continued to cuddle Caleb. "Why?"

"Hallmark pays big for card art."

Aria released her loneliness into a mother's eternal love.

LeRoy's question grounded her. "We driving to Chicago tonight, or not?"

Aria hesitated. LeRoy's legitimate question deserved her response, and she didn't wish to turn a tender moment into a squabble. She faced a drag-out fight with Aunt Maggie if she broke free to set up her own life.

"Did you hear me?" LeRoy asked.

"Yeah, it'd be nice not to be quizzed by the sheriff." Aria gazed at her bound tormentor. *He deserves to be poked, pricked and caned worse than I was.*

"What about this guy?" John pointed the fire extinguisher at their captive. "He's got a mean reputation."

"We need to wait for the sheriff." Aria said.

Madeleine clomped down the stairs. "Can anyone help me carry the kids upstairs?"

Aria nodded and began with Caleb. After she set him on a bean bag chair in the upstairs room, she carried the little girl wet with tears and red indentations on her slender throat.

"You're safe now, Cindy. That mean man won't hurt you. Can you play with Caleb?"

Cindy's nodded in rhythm with her body shakes.

When all the children, their duct tape removed, sat upstairs in a circle, Madeleine distracted them with oatmeal cookies and milk. Madeleine asked Aria what her plans were and offered a piece of advice. "You shouldn't drive tonight."

"Why?"

"It's freezing cold and blowing snow's unpredictable."

"We have no reservations."

"Stay here. I've stored cots and the furnace works."

Flashing red and blue lights that infiltrated the front window followed by a knock on the door announced the sheriff's arrival. Aria stood aside as they marched the guard through the house and outside to a waiting sheriff vehicle.

LeRoy, the baton in his left hand, approached Aria.

"You promoted to a beat cop?" Aria teased.

"Saving evidence." He turned to John, who set the fire extinguished on the floor, "Pleased to meet you."

"Night Madeleine, all," John said. He whispered to Aria. "Wasn't Christian of me to lie to you. My daughter's so precious, I'd do anything to protect her."

Aria nodded as John departed the childcare center.

LeRoy whispered to Aria. "He grooves on his hardware store. Know what he said to me?"

"Don't have the slightest."

"We nailed the guy, didn't we?"

Aria's pent up emotion burst. Not the gentleness of a spring bubbling up, but the water's roar from behind a dam that had weathered storms for centuries. Tears streamed across her cheeks; round droplets crashed to the floor. She half-heartedly swiped at the onslaught washing her chin.

Madeleine, who carried blankets and pillowcases, handed a rose-embroidered white pillowcase to Aria. "Here use this."

"Thank you."

LeRoy leaned in Aria's direction. "It'll be great to have you living in Chicago."

"Don't think so."

"What?"

Aria formulated her tentative plans on the spot. LeRoy would always be her friend, along with Tillie. She'd convince Aunt Maggie to return to Harmony Square, at least until the heat drives Chicago residents to summer homes.

Caleb deserved not to lose his childcare buddies, nor be torn away from his adoptive parents until Aria was employed to support them both. After a week in Chicago, they'd return to Iowa by bus to establish a residence for her driver's test.

"Marie at the B&B is seeking help," Madeleine said.

The words struck Aria as the final puzzle piece.

She hugged Caleb before she released her arms to clasp his youthful hands in hers. No finger appeared elongated. Aria internalized no fear for Caleb's health. The medical heredity predictions cast no shadow on her love.

Brad's love flourished in their child. He'd fathered Caleb for her to cherish and had funded Social Security survivor benefits to ease their financial burden.

Society no longer imprisoned her or Caleb.

Her loneliness evaporated.

Sanity ruled.

To contact Author Donan Berg,
see the next page.

Albert's Deadly Fate

Publisher's Note: Author Donan Berg loves to hear from readers. Write to him at

DOTDON Books
514 17th Street
PO Box 1302
Moline IL 61266-1302

Fiction works By Donan Berg

Novels

A Body To Bones
First Skeleton Series Mystery

The Bones Dance Foxtrot
Second Skeleton Series Mystery

Baby Bones
Third Skeleton Series Mystery

Adolph's Gold

Abbey Burning Love

One Paper Heart

Alexa's Gold

Into the Dark

Short Stories

Bubbling Conflict and
Other Stories

Amanda

E-mail him at: bergdonan@gmail.com
Search "Donan Berg" at www.authorsden.com,
www.smashwords.com or www.goodreads.com.

If you've enjoyed *Aria's Bayou Child* or any of his previous novels, he encourages every reader to express their reading experience via a published review.

Experience the gift of Donan Berg's unique writing with a sneak peek at his forthcoming novel entitled *Albert's Deadly Fate*. It begins on the next page. Enjoy.

One

The silver dollar coin dropped into Albert's outstretched right hand. His four trembling fingers grasped the oversized metal disk lest it bounce wildly or skid willy-nilly on the pink Tennessee marble floor. Fast-moving, home-bound evening commuters jostled inside Chicago's Union Station. Any kick, intentional or inadvertent, and the coin could be forever lost.

He'd followed directions to spot the brown corduroy sports coat being worn by the bearded man in a baseball cap and Ray-Ban sunglasses. Albert cozied up close behind, ready when the man stretched his closed, veined and hairless hand to the center of his back. Without a sound, but a shake of his fist, the man's fingers released the coin.

Before Albert refocused his gaze, the man disappeared toward the Jackson Street exit. A flaring brown hair fringe visible beneath the ringed black and gold black baseball cap. Albert surmised the cap sported a Pittsburgh Pirates script P logo above the bill he'd never seen.

He had entered the Great Hall from Clinton Street and waited near one of the eighteen Corinthian columns. Beneath the soaring atrium, the historical Beaux Arts rail hall with its terracotta walls had always made him feel insignificant.

Per received instructions, a male figure cut in front of him and slowed. He tapped the left sport coat shoulder twice from the rear. So far so good. He clenched his hand and didn't act upon his macho instinct to chase the coin carrier. *Most like a stooge delivery person, not the mastermind who played games with his emotions.*

Albert could neither stare at the coin or at anyone in the blur of humanity around him. A sensation radiated from his palm up his right arm. It started first upon bare finger pads and then centered on a sweating palm. He trusted the coin to be the unique one-of-a-kind coin he'd painstakingly sought for near on three years.

He swallowed a circular Bach's red-striped peppermint, savoring the lingering taste of a crunched fragment. The transfer had been planned and timed to be undetectable. A uniformed police officer with his bulging abdomen hanging over a wide black belt with a holstered weapon tapped his chest-high open palm with a nightstick. His unblinking eyes gazed at the north concourse commuter track doors that swallowed the maddening crowd. Within sixty minutes, Albert knew he'd be conspicuous if he lingered.

Albert rotated his torso right, away from the officer's vision field, to slip his right hand into the outer pocket of his blue suit.

He lifted his now unburdened hand out of the previously empty pocket as quickly as he had slipped it in. With a delayed upturned glance, he failed a second time to locate the brown sports coat as men and women's heel clicks on the marble floor escalated another beat into the overlapping din.

Albert pivoted on his right heel. His sudden, awkward and against-the-grain movement resulted in a collision with a head-down, charging woman equal in height to his five-foot-ten. Her shoulder-strapped leather briefcase swung a glancing blow to Albert's groin. He winced. Separated pursed lips muttered a one-word apology to the fast-fleeing woman.

On higher alert, he squared his shoulders and angled to the crowd's perimeter. He struggled against the commuters headed for the train platform, all the while clamping his right hand against the pocketed coin. Five minutes later he squeezed through the exterior door exit to Jackson Street to hail a cab with the expectation he'd soon be home himself.

Before the 9/11 terrorist attacks, now approaching a ten-year anniversary, he could've easily proceeded to the next step inside Union Station by approaching a public storage locker. Homeland Security had decreed the lockers a potential public bomb location and Union Station janitors and security personnel had carted away all lockers.

Last month he'd spent half of July scouting for a perfect location. While at first promising, the Chicago main post office had also removed public lockers. Nevertheless, he proposed the post office's general delivery, but the anonymous telephone voice he had dialed directed him to a Northside Loop Speedy Boxes packaging service that offered delivery boxes for rent.

Upon arrival, he entered to the left of a scrolling neon message board where his eyes gazed at the three corridor aisles extending in three compass directions. He froze, unable to decide which way to go ahead. He'd been directed to use the package service counter as a starting point. The erected plywood panels he determined now hid the referenced counter. His mental coin flip said go left. After two tentative strides, he figured out the box numbers trended lower. At a metal box front numbered 435 in black half-inch numerals, luck prevailed. An inserted key protruded from its lock.

Albert's thumb and forefinger twisted the key left, then right. The door sprung open.

The box's entire contents, one letter, stood vertical, tilted against the box's interior. Albert glanced in all directions. The gray-haired old lady he passed inside the entrance door with the tubular wheeled bag carrier who refused his offer to hold the door didn't threaten or distract him. The woman allowed the automatic door to work and wobbled through the opening onto the sidewalk outside.

Fast approaching footsteps, the clatter amplified by the tiled floor, halted his raised left arm a foot from the box's interior. A sigh of relief deflated his lungs as two teenagers, one in flip-flops, raced past and disappeared at the aisle's end.

Stomach-knotting panic for the weekend had roiled

Albert's every waking moment after he had deposited ten C-notes, sealed into a business-sized envelope, into box 435. He dreamed his money would be ripped off after he followed instructions to leave the box's key inserted. Relieved, it hadn't happened, his hand reached into his right suit coat pocket.

Tilting his head forward, both blue eyes beheld the silver coin with the word "Munich" cupped in his right hand and supported by the left. Thirty-nine years ago, they had scheduled the 1972 Olympics in Munich, Germany. The murderous attack on Israeli athletes then dominated the world news.

The controversy about the official Olympic host coin lost in the turmoil. In the years preceding, each issued coin bore the name of the host country. This 1972 coin departed tradition to feature the host city. The oversight promptly rectified, but not before thousands of Munich stamped coins had been sold into circulation. Recall inducements proved unsuccessful.

Albert the earlier month linked to and downloaded an Internet advertisement for rare Olympic coins. In 1983 he'd inherited his Dad's 1968 Mexico Summer Games Olympic coin originally obtained from a cousin in repayment of a loan. In later years, Albert purchased other official Olympic coins. With reasonable ease and expenditure, he purchased the 1972 Olympic coins imprinted with "Germany."

In the 1990s, a coin dealer acquaintance explained to Albert that for his collection to be complete he needed the four coin set struck with the "Munich" die. The dealer emphasized the coins, if obtainable, would command a high premium above both the face value and the silver metal content. However, if added to Albert's other coins, the four coins promised to quadruple his collection's resale value.

Albert slipped the coin he'd collected at Union Station four days earlier into his right inside suit coat pocket and reached for the envelope inside the rental box. The envelope's flap seal intact with one of its ends slit neatly.

Albert paid an extra thousand dollars by stuffing ten C-notes into the envelope and removed a lined paper sheet folded in half, twice.

He unfolded the paper.

The words were few: "Albert, I'm safe. I'm told Rebecca is too. Please do as you're told."

(To be continued in Donan Berg's upcoming novel, *Albert's Deadly Fate,* expected to be released in 2021.)